Praise for *Echo Valley*

"I thoroughly enjoyed this story! It is a wonderful tale of mystery, romance, faith and adventure. Join Marie as she confronts her issues of religious self sufficiency and the intersection of faith and life's sorrows. You will be glad you did. I heartily commend this story to readers of all ages!"

BILL TAYLOR
Executive Director,
Evangelical Free Church of Canada

"There's nothing quite like a well-told yarn to entertain and—before we even know it—instruct us too. With intrigue, warmth and realism, Martha addresses the big questions we all voice when life turns out to be more than we can handle."

PHIL CALLAWAY
Speaker and Author of *Laughing Matters* and
Making Life Rich Without Any Money

"Although I don't often read Christian romances, Martha Anderson's latest novel *Echo Valley*, gripped me from the start with its sense of mystery on multiple levels. Complex characters cope with the consequences of past actions. Some are suffering deep personal loss, some labour under profound misunderstandings, some are driven by greed. From warm friendship and romance, to tension and conflict, I experienced a wide range of human emotions. I particularly appreciated how God's message of love and restoration was woven throughout the story: a right relationship with Him makes it possible to find a fulfilling purpose in life, and—maybe—a person to share it with."

JACK POPJES
Author, Former CEO of Wycliffe Canada
Linguist/educator/Bible Translator Canela people, Brazil
President, Inscribe Christian Writers Fellowship

"I have known Martha for many years, and heard her tell several stories. In *Echo Valley*, she tells a wonderful love story that keeps you reading to find out how it ends. It has mystery, intrigue, romance and, most importantly, the Gospel of Christ woven into its pages."

DEBORAH GREY
Author and Speaker

ECHO VALLEY

Adventures in the Foothills

Martha Toews Anderson

ECHO VALLEY: ADVENTURES IN THE FOOTHILLS

Copyright © 2011 by Martha Toews Anderson

Scripture taken from the New King James Version. Copyright © 1982 by Thomas Nelson, Inc. Used by permission. All rights reserved.

ISBN: 978-1-77069-259-6

Printed in Canada

Word Alive Press
131 Cordite Road, Winnipeg, MB R3W 1S1
www.wordalivepress.ca

Just Write!

MIX
Paper from
responsible sources
FSC® C016245

Library and Archives Canada Cataloguing in Publication

Anderson, Martha Toews
    Echo Valley / Martha Toews Anderson.

ISBN 978-1-77069-259-6

    I. Title.

PS8601.N4445E35 2011   C813'.6   C2011-901690-7

Dedication

No one shares more keenly my anticipation of seeing this book in print than my husband. Despite his battle with Multiple Myeloma, he has prodded me on these past weeks because he is convinced this story will leave an imprint for eternity on the hearts and minds of the readers.

So to you, Eilif, I dedicate this novel in appreciation for your love and support. Thank you for your show of confidence in standing with me in prayer that this book will be a blessing and challenge to many readers and so bring glory to God. I love you, Eilif.

Martha

Table of Contents

Acknowledgements

When it comes to acknowledgements it is hard to know where to begin. To all the friends who have given encouragement along the way, thank you. For Inscribe Christian Writers Fellowship members, a strong support group willing to share information and encouragement with fellow writers, I am grateful.

To our wonderful family: children, grand children, and great grandchildren, who have given encouragement and support in practical ways, I owe a great deal. Thank you for your confidence in my writing efforts.

Special mention goes to daughter Bonnie for producing the wrap-around cover for *Echo Valley*, and grandsons, Erik and Marc, on whom I rely heavily for technical support. Thank you to all of you.

For any good that will result through the reading of this book, all credit goes to God, the originator of everything good.

1

OPERATION INVESTIGATION

Marie Stumbur sat beside her brother and sister in the back seat of the Ford sedan, oblivious to the passing harvest scene. Cattle lolled in the shade of scattered trees, while in the fields combines gathered up the golden grain. Ordinarily Marie would have been thrilled at the beauty of the rural landscape in autumn. Now she noticed none of this. She sat in quiet thought, her emotions torn between anticipation and apprehension. She was determined to learn firsthand what had happened to Marc, yet shrinking from what she might discover.

Friends had cautioned Marie against taking a teaching position in Echo Valley. Even her parents, Arnold and Julie Stumbur, had questioned the wisdom of their daughter's decision. They had pointed out that moving to the community where Marc had spent his last months might only sharpen her sense of loss.

"This is something I have to do," Marie had countered without further explanation. To diverge her fears, she felt, would have been disloyal to the man she still loved. When they recognized her determination, her parents had said no more.

Accepting this teaching position was the right thing to do, Marie told herself again and again as the family car sped along the highway that linked Alberta's two major cities. Once they turned west off the main road her emotional conflict increased with each passing mile. Marie wiped her clammy hands with a tissue. *I want to know what really happened,* she cried inwardly. *I want to be sure.* With a sigh she leaned back in her seat and closed her eyes, continuing her mental debate. *I'm bound to find out the truth. There must be a logical explanation. Even if I never find the answer, I'll still be glad I tried.* She weighed her thoughts carefully to make sure she meant what she was telling herself. *Even if I find out that he wasn't faithful...*She shuddered and dismissed the subject.

As her gaze fell on her father's reflection in the rear-view mirror she studied briefly the ruddy face framed by a stock of red hair. Pained by Marie's grief, he winked at her in the rear-view mirror. Her only response was a weak smile.

"We should be there soon," he said. "Didn't you say sixty miles from our turnoff, Marie? We're almost that far now."

"That's it!" Marie gasped as she caught sight of a cluster of cabins nestled beneath the trees along the shore of a quiet lake. "That's Crystal Lake. It's got to be." Her heartbeat quickened. She leaned closer to the window as they neared the buildings. "Now to locate the house."

"That should be no problem in such a tiny place," Arnold said. He drove past the community's only store.

Marie recalled Mr. Wilson's instructions. "A two-story house with cedar siding," she said.

"This must be it," her mother said as she spotted the house. "An attractive place, too." She watched Marie's reaction. "I hope the people will be nice."

"I expect they will be. The superintendent said the teachers boarded with them last year were happy with the arrangement."

As Marie approached the house the front door swung open. A beaming Anna Charter stepped onto the stoop. A pleasant looking woman, she smiled her welcome.

"Glad to see you, Marie." She greeted her new boarder with a generous handshake. "Come in. Come in. Bring them all in." She beckoned to the family with a wide sweep of her arm.

Stewart Charter came around the corner of the house with quick, decisive step, a smile breaking out on his weathered features. He greeted the family warmly.

After Marie's luggage was carried upstairs to her new room, Mrs. Charter served refreshments. When the family rose to leave, Marie walked to the car with them.

"Just think, you'll be living in all this beauty while the rest of us stagnate in the city," her sister, Ruth, groaned.

"I'm glad you have congenial people to board with," Julie said, kissing Marie good-bye. "I agree with Ruth. This valley is beautiful. I hope you'll be happy here."

"Hey, Dad, you think Echo Valley might need a fire chief?" Oscar, her kid brother, joked.

"Maybe Marie can find out," Arnold Stumbur laughed. "In the meantime I'd better get back to my job in Edmonton."

Tears glistened in Marie's eyes as she hugged each one. As the family car pulled away and disappeared behind the trees, Marie suddenly felt very much alone. She wiped her eyes before walking slowly into the house and up the stairs to her room. Here she busied herself with unpacking her bags and arranging her books and pictures. By the time Mrs. Charter gave the call for supper the spacious bedroom had taken on a homey appearance.

Over supper that evening Marie made the acquaintance of Burton Greenfield. He was the assistant manager of the Bank of Montreal in Hillside, about 20 miles away. He was a short man in his late twenties with plain features and mouse-coloured hair. He wore a red, plaid sports jacket crisscrossed by yellow lines. She smiled at the contrast he was to her stereotyped image of a banker, a sombre, middle-aged, overweight man in a dark business suit. *He must think the flashy jacket adds lustre to his appearance*, Marie thought.

She wondered why he chose to live in Echo Valley instead of near his place of employment. Noticing that he was very much at home with the elderly couple, she concluded that they were long-time friends. Although he occupied a self-contained basement suite she guessed that he was a frequent guest at the landlord's table.

"That's a long drive to work every day, but I suppose the view is worth it after dealing with something as boring as money all day," Marie said casually.

"Boring?" Burton laughed heartily. "Money has a beauty all its own."

"Well, I guess if that's your job, but it's not my line. Balancing my check book is enough for me. But this valley has a special kind of beauty. I love it already," she said, being careful not to reveal any prior knowledge of the area.

As the conversation continued, Marie found herself growing more and more restless. Even the scenic surroundings and excitement of beginning her career could not keep disturbing thoughts from cropping up in her mind. Everything about Echo Valley intensified the pain hidden behind her smiling face. As soon as she could conveniently excuse herself from the table, she put on a sweater and went out for a walk.

The winding trail to the wharf was flanked by a natural growth of trees in autumn colour. Beyond the sparsely-spaced cottages the evergreens stretched up the mountain side like a deep-green blanket, broken only by an occasional rip where vividly coloured foliage outlined cascading streams.

Marie walked fast toward no particular destination. Once she reached the lake she followed its sandy beach for a distance before striking out into the woods. She had always found a walk through trees relaxing. She hoped it would have a soothing effect on her now. As hard as she tried, she could not rid herself of the nagging questions tumbling around in her head. Her restraint at last gave way.

"I want to know," she sobbed aloud to the trees and the sky. "I want an answer." Half-blinded by tears she stumbled on. When at length she broke out of the darkening woods she found herself on a narrow, winding road. A car suddenly rounded a blind curve in front of her. Slowly, as if awaking from an unpleasant dream, Marie became aware of screeching tires. Sudden panic seized her as a man leaped from the driver's door.

"Are you hurt?" he asked.

"N-no, no," Marie stammered, embarrassed by her dishevelled appearance.

"I'm sorry I scared you."

"You didn't. I-I was in your way." Weeping had left her voice husky.

"If you're lost, maybe I can help. I live in the area." The man introduced himself. Marie did not catch his name and did not care.

"I'm Marie Stumbur," she answered with forced politeness. She did not notice the stranger draw in a quick breath at the mention of her name. Leaning forward he studied her tear-streaked face.

"You are Marie Stumbur," he repeated slowly, understanding dawning in his dark eyes. Marie pushed back her long, blonde hair, conscious only of his intense gaze. She wished he would leave. She moved to walk past him, but he laid a restraining hand on her arm.

"I'll give you a ride if you tell me where you want to go."

"Charter's. But I'll walk…"

5

"Charter's. You came to teach school then." It was a statement rather than a question. "Get in. I'll drive you there."

Marie eyed the man sceptically for a moment. "No, I was just out for a walk," she said, trying to sound casual. "I'll just go on walking." With that, she turned and headed through the trees to her new home.

2

A NEW CAREER

The sun was shining brightly through Marie's window when she awoke the next morning. She had slept soundly and felt rested despite her experience of the previous evening. Mrs. Charter was pouring coffee when Marie entered the dining room.

"Good Morning," she greeted her boarder cheerily. "Sit down." She indicated a chair. "Just you and me. Stewart had to go to Calgary on business this morning."

As they ate, the landlady chatted on. By the time Marie had cleared away her eggs and toast she had learned that Matilda Grimm, principal of Echo Valley Elementary School for many years, owned a cottage beside the lake. Marie wondered secretly whether her boss would be anything like her name indicated. She would have to wait until Monday to find out. Another teacher, Olivia Barr, would also board with the Charters.

Olivia arrived before noon. *I think I'll like her,* was Marie's first thought as she watched her prospective co-worker bound up the front steps of the house, her long, loose skirt billowing in the breeze. Over lunch, Marie learned that, although Olivia had several years of teaching experience behind her, she was also new to Echo Valley. She had driven up from her home in Southern Alberta a week before to settle into her boarding place and the principal had given her a tour of the school premises at that time. As soon as lunch was out of the way, she offered to show Marie around.

Two hours later they were browsing through the post cards in the general store when a stranger approached and greeted them. Marie and Olivia returned her greeting. "We have just moved in at the Charter house," Olivia added after they had introduced themselves.

"Yes, I heard. News gets around in a little place like this." The woman gave a cheery little laugh. "I'm Beryl Carpenter. I hope you will enjoy our community."

"We already do," Olivia assured her.

In the few moments that they talked with Beryl she invited them to the church services. "The church is close to the school. You probably noticed it already." A tall man wearing a tan Stetson entered the store. Marie gasped as she recognized him as the stranger she had encountered the evening before.

"Oh, Bill's here for me." Beryl turned to leave. "Be seeing you."

"Good bye," Olivia called after her.

Marie watched the man follow Beryl out of the store. Slowly she turned to her companion. "She said her name was Carpenter, didn't she?"

"Yes, Beryl Carpenter," Olivia answered.

"She called him Bill." Marie said. "Bill Carpenter." Reviewing names of Marc's friends mentally, she could not recall Marc mentioning that name. Marie felt ill at ease to realize that Beryl had heard of her from the man who had found her crying in grief and confusion. She said nothing about it to Olivia.

"Do you think we should go?" Olivia asked.

"Home?"

"No, to church. Like she asked us to. That would be a good way to meet the locals."

"Yes, let's," Marie agreed. After all, if she wanted to find out anything, that would be a good place to start.

The newcomers arrived at the church the next morning just as Beryl drove up. She waved as she stepped from the car. Much to Marie's relief, Bill was not with her. Beryl explained that the men had been detained because of a sick cow. She quickly introduced the girls to other parishioners including some prospective pupils and their parents. Marie recognized an occasional name Marc had mentioned in his letters, but no sign of the Cardinals. Several people indicated that they would extend an invitation to them shortly. She found the atmosphere genuinely friendly, like Marc had said, but her own haunting memories of Marc's description of Echo Valley made her uncomfortable. She was glad when it was over.

All afternoon they prepared for the opening day of school, and Marie plied Olivia with questions. The deeper questions that she could not divulge continued to haunt her through the night. They were still with her when she walked into the school on Monday morning. Matilda Grimm called a teachers meeting for nine o'clock.

"Well, you're about to meet the Grimm One," Olivia said under her breath as she and Marie approached the staff room together. A petite woman in her mid-fifties stepped briskly forward as they entered.

"Good Morning, Mrs. Grimm," Olivia greeted her. She introduced Marie.

"Good Morning, Marie," the principal spoke, her dark, penetrating eyes doing a quick appraisal. She smiled as she extended her hand, apparently satisfied with what she saw. "Welcome to our staff." She motioned for the girls to be seated.

As Marie pulled out her chair she became aware of a fourth party in the room. Across the table from her sat a man whom Mrs. Grimm introduced as Nikolaus Nicole. He nodded his thin head in acknowledgment, his sombre expression unchanged. He was the only other teacher in the four-roomed school.

Mrs. Grimm sat down, opened her notebook, and began to outline precisely what she expected of her staff. Although she was small in stature her presence permeated the room. Marie braced herself for the challenging job ahead, making careful notes as she listened. Nikolaus, meanwhile, was staring absently out of the window. Apparently he had heard it all before.

"Apart from the few right in the village, the pupils come mostly from the ranches and a few from the Rocky Mountain Forest Reserve," she said. "Being small does not mean being inferior. I won't have it said of the pupils coming from Echo Valley Elementary School that they can't read." She emphasized every word. "I expect you to see to it that the children in your classrooms learn the fundamentals. Do you have any questions?"

At exactly nine-thirty by the clock on the wall Mrs. Grimm snapped shut her book and rose to go. Registration was scheduled for ten o'clock. Already the early arrivals were coming through the front doors and heading to their respective rooms. Marie guided the newcomers to her room, helping them find appropriate desks. Across the room those returning for the second year eagerly chose their places with an air of superiority. Eighteen expectant faces looked up at Marie as she moved to the front of the room. She smiled at them warmly. The children responded with broad grins.

"Good Morning. The first thing we are going to do today is to get to know each other. My name is Miss Stumbur." She printed her name on the blackboard. "I am your teacher. First I will tell you something about myself." She told of growing up in Edmonton with her family.

"Now I want you to tell me something about yourselves." Marie sat down and opened the register. "When I read your name, stand up. Mitchell Bruce."

Heads turned as a husky boy in the back row clattered noisily to his feet.

"Mitchell, I understand you are new here. Tell us where you are from and how you happened to come here."

"From Montana," the boy answered haughtily. "My dad's a rodeo rider. He works on a ranch here, but he worked on a bigger one in Montana. Far bigger."

"That's interesting, Mitchell," Marie said. "You'll be able to tell us all about rodeos."

"Everything, ma'am," Mitchell responded as he slunk back into his seat. Marie continued down the list of names, asking questions and making a comment as each child rose.

"Now the Grade One Class. Peter Cardinal." A youngster in the front row stood up, a shy smile showed two teeth missing. "Peter, what do you like to do for fun?"

"Ride my Shetland pony."

"A Shetland pony!" Mitchell snickered. "Call that fun?"

"I think that would be fun," Marie smiled at the darkly-tanned boy.

When the roll call was finished, Marie picked up a book. She had chosen the story to read on this first morning particularly as a means to capture their attention. She hoped to fire them with a desire to learn.

"Would you like to read that story by yourself?" she asked when she laid down the book. "When you have learned to read you'll be able to read any books you want."

The day was a success for Marie, but she was tired when it was over. She retired early. As she lay on her pillow, her eyes tracing the moonbeams on the ceiling, she reviewed again her reasons for coming to this area.

She had been scanning the job openings for a teaching position when the words Echo Valley jumped out at her. Excitedly she read the advertisement:

> Echo Valley Elementary School requires teacher for grades one and two, duties to begin Sept. 1. Contact board chairman Harley Wilson.

The words set her head spinning. Life had lost its appeal for Marie after Marc's death, but the thought of moving to Echo Valley had awakened a new interest. In Echo Valley she might find answer to the questions bothering her. A new enthusiasm had begun to creep back into her being. A tiny light had begun to flicker at the far end of the long, dark tunnel through which she viewed the future. Excitedly she jotted down the phone number.

The reply had not been long in coming. The board chairman would be in Edmonton in a few days' time and would contact her then. The ensuing meeting went well and Marie had signed the contract.

Now that she was in Echo Valley she wondered how to find the answer to the doubts she harboured deep inside. She searched her mind for ideas, but drew only blanks. *I'll just have to wait. Sooner or later I might unearth a clue unexpectedly,* she concluded. *After all, I have ten months to spend here.* Consoling herself with that thought, Marie drifted off to sleep.

3

STRIKING UP FRIENDSHIPS

In the days that followed, Marie adjusted well from being a student to a teacher with eighteen youngsters in her care. She learned to appreciate their individuality and they responded well to her. She soon gained their respect. By week's end she felt at home not only with the pupils, but with a number of parents as well. She and Olivia even accepted an invitation to join the community ball game.

"Good," Mrs. Charter beamed when her boarders spoke of the upcoming game at the supper table. "Burton is playing as well."

The following evening, Marie and Olivia approached the ball diamond where a small group had already gathered. Marie was pleased to recognize some faces in the crowd. "Look, Olivia, there's Beryl." Marie liked this charming woman. Already Marie felt a friendship developing between them. Nonetheless underneath was the disturbing thought that eventually she would have to meet Beryl's husband. Would he embarrass her by saying, "Oh yes, I know her. I found her stumbling along the road."

Seeing the girls approach, Beryl turned to greet them, her short, jet-black hair curling softly around her well-tanned face. She introduced them to the players they had not yet met. "Bill and John have gone to pick up the equipment," she said.

"They're late," Burton spoke irritably. At that moment two men drove up in a blue Mazda truck. As they walked toward the group, carrying bats and balls, Marie recognized the taller of the two as Bill. If he recognized her he gave no indication. Beryl introduced the other man as John. The game was soon underway and Marie suddenly realized that she was having fun.

When the game was over Burton got up from the grass where he was sitting and stretched. "I'm tired tonight. I'm going to turn in early."

As Beryl headed toward the truck, John threw his arm across her shoulders and fell into step with her. He opened the passenger door and they both got in. William slid in behind the wheel.

"Who was the other man with Beryl and her husband tonight?" Marie asked Burton on the way home.

"That's her brother. They're a religious bunch."

"Do you have any other entertainment in Echo Valley?"

"Fishing and swimming in summer, of course," Burton replied. "Nothing goes on at the beach once September comes."

As soon as they reached the house Olivia bounded up the steps two at a time. *Eager to write another letter to Grant,* Marie guessed. Then she remembered the many letters and telephone calls she and Marc had exchanged, and a new wake of loneliness engulfed her. Sudden weariness crept over her as she slowly followed her companion up the stairs. She entered her room, jerked off her jacket, and flung it onto a chair. It slithered to the floor.

Marie glanced at the papers on her desk, but decided she was not in the mood for work. Instead she opened the dresser drawer that contained the part of her life she was trying to hide and gently lifted out a framed photograph of a young man. She studied it long and lovingly. Like a tender caress she ran her fingers over it.

"Oh, Marc," she whispered softly, "I love you so much." Kneeling on the rug in front of the open drawer she continued to study the face in the picture… the thick growth of dark brown hair that curled ever so slightly at the ends… the nose that could have been described as large, but that she had thought looked just right for him… the pleasant mouth showing white, even teeth. *And those eyes*, Marie recalled. *Bright eyes.* It was not their colour that was outstanding. It was the way they sparkled, the way they smiled even before his lips responded. Tears of grief, of uncertainty and pent-up tensions, flowed unheeded down her checks.

If only I had someone who could understand. But I could never tell anyone my thoughts. If Marc is innocent I would never want anyone know I even entertained any suspicions about him. She felt shame at admitting these fears even to herself. Marie did not know how long she sat there when a light rap on her door brought her to her feet in a flash. She dropped the photo back into the drawer just as Olivia poked her head around the door.

"If you care to…" Seeing the room in semidarkness the caller was about to retreat, but at that instant she caught sight of Marie leaning against the dresser. "Marie, what happened?" she blurted. "Why are you standing there in the dark?" She turned on the light. "I mean…" She left her question dangling.

"I'm okay." Marie swung around to look at herself in the mirror. Puffy eyes looked back at her out of a smudged face, damp with tears and perspiration. Her hair was dishevelled from repeatedly running her restless fingers through it. "I guess there's no use telling you I'm okay." She gave a nervous laugh.

"You're upset," Olivia said. She waited while Marie fumbled with her hairbrush. "Throw on a jacket and let's go for a walk," she said finally.

Marie resorted to the bathroom to splash cold water on her face. Then retrieving her jacket from the floor she followed Olivia down the stairs. Anna looked up from her knitting as they passed. She was alone.

"It's a beautiful evening for a walk," Olivia volunteered.

"Enjoy," Anna nodded in agreement, "It's a beautiful evening."

Olivia chatted casually as they walked, Marie making brief responses. They had reached the wharf before Olivia opened the subject.

"I know you are troubled about something, Marie. I thought so even before tonight. Do you want to talk about it?" Marie bit her lip and shook her head without comment. "That's fine," Olivia continued, "But if sometime you want to talk I'm here for you."

"Thank you." Marie squeezed her hand in appreciation. They did not talk again as they stood looking over the moonlit lake. No sound reached their ears except the steady dip, dip, dip of a paddle in the distance. As they turned to retrace their steps, however, they were startled by footsteps coming along the path. The man almost bumped into them before he became aware of their presence.

"Pardon me," he stammered, stepping aside to let them pass.

"Burton!" Marie blurted when she had found her voice. "Going for a swim?"

"Why not? It's the best time for a swim," his voice came back as he moved past into the darkness. An owl hooted in reply.

4

SHATTERED DREAMS

Indian summer continued till the end of October. Marie decided to make the most of the warm weather by taking her pupils on a field trip into the woods. They were scampering around picking out the prettiest leaves to take back to their classroom. Peter ran up with some yellow leaves clutched in his fist and dropped them into the bag.

"I'm glad you took us on a hike," he said. "My mommy used to go with me to gather pretty things in the woods." Then he wiped away an unexpected tear, checked whatever he had started to say next, and ran off.

After they returned to the school and everyone else had gone home, Marie wandered to the window and stood looking out at the mountains. Peter Cardinal came to mind again. What had brought about the sudden change in him in the woods, jubilant one minute, wiping tears the next? *Is it because his name is Cardinal that I feel such empathy for him?* Marie wondered. Marc had written often about William and Deedee Cardinal and about the time he had spent with them at the Drummond Smith Ranch. *He can't be the boy Marc often referred to as Bill's youngster because Peter comes from the Double C Ranch.*

Since losing Marc, Marie often turned to reminiscence and introspection. As she gazed at the changing shadows on the mountains, her mind traced the events of her life. She had a strong home training, she realized. Her parents believed in discipline, family loyalty, and honesty. They ingrained in her the importance of keeping herself for the man she would one day marry. These values influenced her relationship with young men. She had many friends, but her determination to make the most of her life kept her from entanglements.

Marie had met Marc during her second year of university. She had sat down in the only empty table in the lunch area in the cafeteria when someone approached her with a request to share her table. Marie had smiled her consent as the personable young man pulled up a chair. "I haven't seen you around. I'm Marc."

Marie introduced herself.

"How do you do, Marie," he had said as he added some cream to his tea. "I just heard a good lecture on the condition of Canada's native people."

Now that's a unique way to start on a conversation, Marie had thought, but she warmed to the subject. "I think that is where I should have been," she had answered. "For my English paper I'm writing on the status of Indians in Canada."

"Really? Have you done much work on it?"

"No. I only started this morning. I spent the last two hours in the library getting some background material," she had explained, "But I expect to interview people to get firsthand information."

"Excellent idea," Marc had encouraged her. "You might like to talk to Professor MacKay. He was the guest lecturer this morning."

"Do you think there is a chance?"

Marc had smiled at her enthusiasm. "He lectures again at eleven tomorrow. I've met him. Maybe I can arrange a meeting for you." They become so involved in their discussion that one o'clock had rolled around before they realized it. They had rushed to their separate classes, but not before they had exchanged telephone numbers.

Marc had called as soon as Marie got home that afternoon.

"I talked to Professor MacKay an hour ago," he said. "He agreed to see you over Marie liked the sound of the clear voice coming over the telephone.

"How'll I find him?"

"That's the good part. I'll introduce you," he had said, obviously pleased with the idea. "We'll eat at the table where we had lunch."

When Marie had entered the cafeteria, students were making their way to tables with food trays in their hands. She had felt a flutter of excitement as he came through the crowd toward her. She had reminded herself that this meeting was purely academic. His unorthodox opener at noon, however, and his continued interest in wanting to help her pursue information about Canada's native people did more to capture her attention than the flattery or flirtatious comments of other men. After that, they had worked together to collect information.

Now standing at her classroom window, her eyes focussed on the distant mountains, Marie's thoughts continued to travel down paths she had traversed with Marc for a year after that initial meeting: Paths that had been all sunshine and roses at the time, the memory of which now evoked only a dull emptiness within. She felt a pang of bitterness as she recalled how their casual acquaintance had blossomed into friendship, which in turn had resulted in steady dating. They had become engaged the next Christmas. Her chest ached as she recalled the happy experience of planning and preparing for a summer wedding that was not to be.

Marc had completed his studies in January and headed south to Echo Valley for a temporary ranch job. Marie then threw herself into her studies, hoping that by filling her time with work she could keep from undue loneliness during Marc's absence. Frequent letters supplemented by telephone calls and visits kept them in close touch. They had agreed to correspond often, believing that to express their thoughts to each other in writing would strengthen their relationship. Marc's writing was so warm, so natural, so much a part of himself that Marie felt his closeness as she read and reread his letters. Often she shared an amusing anecdote with her family.

Marc made a trip to Edmonton in February, to deliver her valentine, he said. In March they shared two more weekends together, full of fun and promise. He showed up again for the long weekend at Easter. The farewell after that was imprinted on her memory.

"I love you, Marie. I am looking forward to making you my wife." He paused, looking long into her blue eyes. "I'm glad you insisted that we wait till we're married. Doing it right will only make it that much better."

He pulled her close and kissed away the tears that glistened in her eyes at the thought of parting. "I'll see you again in two weeks, I promise." He planted one more lingering kiss on her lips and was off. Marie stood in the doorway of her home watching his Monte Carlo glide along the Whitemud freeway until it was swallowed up in the flow of traffic. She did not know that was the last time she would see her fiancé.

Now she shook her head and turned from her classroom window where she had stood reminiscing. *Marie Stumbur, pull yourself together.* She deliberately turned her thoughts to the weekend stretching before her. *I'm glad I've no activities planned,* she told herself, revelling in the freedom of having time to do whatever she felt like doing. Marie considered what she would like to do. *I'd like to meet someone who knew Marc,* she answered herself. Yes, she wanted to meet Bill and Deedee Cardinal. She'd been here for two months with no sign of them.

She thought of finding a number and telephoning the Cardinals, but dismissed the idea. *Pardon me, Mrs. Cardinal. Did Marc Forest work on your ranch?* she imagined herself asking. *I want to meet you because Marc was my fiancé.*

Her mind toyed with the possible answers. *Would this woman called Deedee say, "Oh, yes, Marc spoke often of you," Or would she explode in disbelief, "You can't be talking about the same person. Marc was in love with Elizabeth."* No, she would just have to wait. She turned back to the window, her eyes drinking in the changing patterns painted by the setting sun. *These mountains emit an aura of serenity,* she mused. *They have a quieting effect. No wonder Marc was enthralled with this country.*

Her eyes grew misty. It had changed him. It had happened after that final visit in April. In the next letter he told of meeting with his friends for Bible study. Oh, he'd mentioned before that the Cardinals were Christians, that he was attending church with them, things like that. Not until he explained this new biblical understanding did Marie realize he was not talking about religion as she understood it. No, it wasn't the mountains that changed him. It was religion. Slowly her memory replayed his words, *I want you to experience this, too.*

The sudden slamming of the front door of the school jarred Marie from her reverie. She glanced at the clock. Startled to realize how long she had been daydreaming, she snatched her jumbo sweater from the coat rack and hurried from the room.

As she started down the hall she heard sounds coming from inside Room Three. She paused outside the door, about to knock; then checked her action and walked on. If Mr. Nicole came back for something why should she check up on him? On her short walk to the Charter house she wondered about the oddities of her fellow teacher. She'd been on staff with him for two months and knew nothing about the man. When she greeted him in the hall he'd nod and walks on like a windup toy.

Later that evening, Marie was writing a letter when the ring of the telephone sounded through the house. No one else was in so Marie laid down her pen and went downstairs to answer. Beryl was calling to say she was in town and would like to come over while her husband was attending a meeting.

Marie welcomed the company. The two were sitting at the kitchen table, chatting over tea and oatmeal cookies when the Carpenter's car pulled into the driveway.

"Oh, here's John," Beryl said, carrying her cup to the sink. Marie looked out the window to see the man she thought was Beryl's brother stepping from the vehicle. She opened the door for him, at the same time trying to decipher this new puzzle.

If John is Beryl's husband, then William must be her bachelor brother, she deducted as she poured him a cup of tea. The Charters arrived home just as Beryl and John were driving away. Marie was washing and drying the cups when they entered the kitchen, their arms loaded with packages.

"How was your day in town?" Marie asked.

"Good, good," replied Stewart.

"I made tea for my company," she added, "I hope that's okay."

"You're welcome to have friends over any time," he assured her.

"Thank you," said Marie, smiling in thanks. She noticed at the same time that her landlady's usually talkative mouth remained tightly sealed, her expression stern. Marie assumed she must be exhausted after a day of shopping. She said good night and retired to her room.

5

RAMBLING

What a perfect day, Marie breathed as she surveyed the morning through her open window. Airy breezes were blowing down from the lofty mountain slopes where fresh snow had fallen during the night. The air was clear and crisp. The day was hers to enjoy. She savoured the feeling of freedom that the thought evoked. By the time she had showered and dressed she'd made up her mind. She would hike through the countryside and shoot autumn scenes for her slide collection.

"I'd like to pack a lunch," she informed her landlady over breakfast. "I intend to spend the day exploring the woods."

"You intend to stay out all day?" Anna asked. "It's cold out. You better dress warmly," she advised.

Marie set out in better spirits than she had experienced in months. The morning sun shone brightly, casting long shadows across her path. Like a cotton ball stuck on a blue background, one cumulus cloud hung in the sky. Not a leaf stirred in the calmness that had settled over the woods. The air became warmer as the hours wore on. Marie pealed off her jacket and stowed it in her knapsack.

She was breaking her way through dense undergrowth when she stopped short. Her breath caught in her throat at the magnificent scene not fifty feet in front of where she stood, still partially hidden by the brush. A courtly buck, holding high a magnificent rack of antlers, poised elegantly in the centre of the small clearing, two doe close by. The trio stood motionless on their long, slender legs, their heads erect, their nostrils twitching, like animal ballerinas balancing on tiptoe. She moved her camera up to eye level very slowly lest any sudden movement frighten them away. Carefully she focussed and pressed the button. Her subjects remained motionless. Then as if by a given signal they leaped gracefully into the air and vanished into the forest.

Marc's words came to mind again. "Since I have come to know God and recognize that everything is a gift from Him I appreciate nature even more," he had written.

It's because I'm constantly thinking of Marc that thoughts of God keep coming into my mind, she concluded.

Marie suddenly realized that she no longer knew how far she had roamed or what direction her feet were taking her. She kept walking till at length she stepped out of the forest. Shading her eyes from the noonday sun she scanned the hay field that stretched across the valley to the horizon beyond. In the distance cattle grazed on the late fall growth.

With this vast expanse of land and sky spread out before her, Marie sank down at the forest edge to relax and enjoy her sack lunch. Her appetite was keen. As she tucked away the roast beef sandwiches and carrot sticks she was glad Mrs. Charter had insisted that she pack plenty. She stuffed a handful of cookies into her pockets for munching along the way.

The warm sun made her feel drowsy. She leaned back against the rough bark of a fir tree and closed her eyes. Before long she dozed. When the lowing of the cattle woke her the sun was hanging low in the sky. For a moment she looked around, startled by the nearness of the animals. She clambered to her feet, at the same time scanning the countryside to determine her whereabouts. As long as the sun was riding high she was unconcerned about finding her way home. Now a hint of uncertainty crept into her mind.

As she cast about for a familiar landmark she saw a man on the top of a huge rock far in the distance. Stepping close to the trees to keep away from the cattle, she watched his profile against the sky. She wondered what he was doing. Then her eyes detected what she took to be a pair of binoculars in his hand. Upset to think that this stranger might have been observing her while she slept, she instinctively backed into the shelter of the trees. Anger, sparked by fear, welled up from deep inside. Had he been following her all day? The more she allowed her mind to mull over the man's possible intentions the more frightened she became. She turned and bolted deep into the woods.

Sure she was out of his view she paused to check the time and formulate a course of action. Almost five o'clock! She must hurry home before darkness descended. Marie was completely disorientated. Well, she would be systematic about finding her way out. Unstrapping her sack again, she took out her jacket and jack knife. She pulled on her jacket to ward off the falling temperature. As she resumed her walk she cut notches in the bark of trees in true woodsman fashion. When she did not come across any of her markings, she assumed she was walking more or less in a straight line. Occasionally she paused to listen, but heard no sound that would indicate that she was being followed.

She soon relaxed, concluding that whatever the man was after probably had nothing to do with her. She assured herself that she would surely find her way out of the forest before the last light of day vanished from the sky. When at length she broke out of the density of the trees she gazed in wonder at the domestic scene before her. She was standing on the edge of a cliff that formed a backdrop for the corrals in front of her. Beyond the whitewashed corral fences stretched an expanse of lawn, bordered on one side by a row of fruit trees, stripped now of both leaves and fruit. Two ranch houses flanked the garden patch that lay behind the lawn. Further afield, she saw a body of water shimmering in the lingering light and to one side of it a cluster of buildings. Her heart leaped.

"Echo Valley," she murmured in relief.

She watched a man on horseback wind his way along a trail to a spot directly across the corral from where she stood. Around his neck hung a set of binoculars. At this close range the girl recognized the rider at once. She shrank back into the darkening shadows. Too late.

William waved a friendly greeting. "Come on down," he shouted above the noise of the cattle. He gave directions she could not hear, but his gestures indicated she should follow the path to her right. Throwing his reins around a post the rancher walked along the trail to meet her. As he drew near, he held out his hand to help her down a steep decline. Marie felt somehow conned into this unexpected meeting with the man she had been trying to avoid. As she walked beside him along the narrow trail her embarrassment returned.

"Why were you out there with binoculars?" she demanded.

"I was checking the cattle," he said, "The pasture has dried up so we turned the cattle onto the hay field to graze on the growth that has come up since the last cutting. The field is unfenced so we keep an eye on them. Besides," he added, "We suspect someone is stealing cattle."

Marie hardly heard him. Remembering her first meeting with William she blushed to think what his impression must be of a girl that was repeatedly getting herself lost.

"How do I get back to town?" she asked abruptly.

"I'll give you a ride."

"I'm hiking," she stated flatly. "I meant which direction."

"You've walked enough for one day." William was being patient. "Besides," he said, pointing at the sun just slipping over the rim of the earth, "The sun is down now."

The thought of walking back home along an unfamiliar road after dark stirred a feeling of uneasiness. Marie, however, attempted to sound unconcerned as she refused his offer. William looked at the slight girl beside him, not understanding her attitude.

"Have a cup of tea with Beryl while I finish chores and clean up." He escorted her to the newer of the two dwellings. Beryl was outside when they approached.

"What a pleasant surprise!" she sang out.

Marie was still searching for words to explain her unexpected presence on the ranch when William spoke up casually, "I'll be driving Marie to town later on, but you can have the privilege of a visit while I finish chores."

Despite her predicament Marie was impressed with the ability of this man to accept these situations. He treated her with as much courtesy as if she were royalty instead of a bedraggled woman stumbling in like a vagabond. *Judging by the way he handles my dilemmas you'd think finding women standing dumbfounded in the middle of the road or stranded behind his corrals were a daily occurrence,* she thought.

"Come on in," Beryl invited as she swung open the door. "It's a treat to have company." She offered Marie a chair. "You'll stay for supper, won't you? I've got the soup kettle on."

"I'm not dressed for socializing." She looked down at her crumpled jacket and grass-stained jeans. "I've been hiking all day."

"You've had a fun day then. You can use the washroom to freshen up." Marie relaxed somewhat at the realization that her hostess did not think her rambling strange. She liked this woman.

"I hope you feel free to pop in often," John greeted Marie when he came in.

"Thank you," Marie smiled in appreciation. She was beginning to feel at ease.

"This would be a good evening for sitting in front of the fireplace," John suggested after the meal. He went out for logs. When he came back with the load his brother-in-law was with him. As they chatted Marie forgot her earlier discomfort in William's presence. Always eager to learn something new, she asked many questions about ranching and found the subject exciting.

"Would you like to have a tour of the ranch, Marie? I could show you around on Saturday," William offered.

"Oh no, no," she replied quickly. Too quickly to be polite, she realized. "I mean, I don't want to make a nuisance of myself." She did not want him to think she was angling for another chance to be with him.

"No problem. I will be glad to show you around any time," the tall rancher repeated his offer. "Just let me know when you're ready."

6

FORGOTTEN RESOLUTIONS

Although Marie was tired after the long walk, sleep did not come easily. For a long time she lay thinking. *Beryl and John have the same religion that Marc found in Echo Valley*, she decided. *Bill, too.* During the evening there had been occasional reference to God, she recalled, but not in the usual, careless manner. And hospitality for them did not mean serving alcoholic drinks, she had noticed. Marc had said that about his friends, too.

Marie thought back to the time she and Olivia had first met Beryl in the general store. In the few minutes they had talked with her that day, she had invited them to attend church. Marie had gone with Olivia then, not only to meet the locals as Olivia had suggested, but because she wanted to find out what it had meant to Marc.

Lying in her bed, she recalled that service. Negative thoughts tumbling around in her mind had made it difficult to concentrate on the preacher's words. What she had heard had been reminiscent of Marc, only making her more keenly aware of her loss. She had not gone back again after that. Marie wished now that she had.

Before Marc wrote about his conversion Marie had considered herself a Christian. After all, she believed in the existence of God. As much as possible she had lived by the Golden Rule and adhered to high moral standards, even when it was not popular to do so. In her estimation Marc had been a good Christian, too. In fact, it had been his high ideals that had aroused her admiration for him when she had learned to know him. That was why she could not follow his reasoning when he had written about his spiritual need and subsequent conversion. How could a man like Marc have had any lack in his life?

"Last night Bill and I had a long talk about many things, especially about religion," he had written once. That was the first time he broached the subject. The letters and phone calls followed fast on each other after that telling of studying the Bible with his friends. He had elaborated on the discussions with great excitement. Then came the letter telling of his turning point.

"I realized that if Jesus died for my salvation and I want His forgiveness then He has a right to my life. Bill showed this to me in the Bible and it made sense, Marie. I acknowledged it in my heart and last night I made my decision. The pastor asked people to come up and receive Christ. I decided this was the way to acknowledge publicly what I was saying in my heart: 'Okay, God, here I am. I'm yours.' Well, that's what I did."

Marc's excitement had flowed through the letter. Marie was glad for him, glad he was finding fulfilment. At the same time uneasiness gripped her innards with the realization that she had no part in this new experience. How would Marc's new interest in God affect their relationship? She did not have long to wonder. Marc wrote the next day expressing his concern that their marriage must be based on the same commitment to God.

"I still love you, Marie," he assured her. "In fact, I love you more than ever. Try to understand, Sweetheart, that as a follower of Jesus Christ I want to put Him before all else." In the rest of the letter he had urged her to investigate the validity of Christ's death and resurrection. "And when you see the overwhelming evidence you'll come to the same conclusion."

He said he was praying for her. He was not cancelling their wedding plans, he explained. "I am willing to wait if you need more time to consider the matter."

She had read the closely-written lines again and again, trying to understand, willing herself to understand. *Does Marc love me as he would have me believe? Did he really have some spiritual experience that made him a different person?* "A child of God," he had called it. How could he say he still loved her, and then terminate their engagement? Well, he did not say that, not exactly. He referred to postponement if need be, of merely waiting till she accepted God's salvation. Confused and hurt, Marie had battled within herself until at last she fell into a troubled sleep.

Even in her sleep her subconscious mind had wrestled with tangled thoughts. In a dream she had seen Marc riding away on the back of a chestnut stallion, galloping into the sunset. She had cried, "Marc, Marc, come back, come back." Her own cries had awakened her. For a long while she lay thinking over the contents of his letter. Finally she had dozed only to dream of him again. She saw Marc on his knees, praying, and knew instinctively that he was praying for her.

By morning she had made up her mind. If Marc had hit on something vital she would share it with him. If God made us and sent His Son to die for us, then we belong to Him like Marc had said. She would find what Marc found. If she was going to share his life as his wife she would also share his faith. She would write him about her resolve at once.

With a zest she did not know she could muster after her restless night, Marie had dressed for breakfast. Studying her face in the mirror Marie felt satisfied that the ache within was not obvious on her face. The weeping of the night had added a new brilliance to her eyes. With a new day came a new hope and a new determination. No point in letting her family know what she planned to do. Marc would be up on his next day off. That would be time enough to break the news.

The whistle of the train as it rolled into Echo Valley jolted Marie back to the present. She rolled over and glanced at the clock on her bedside stand. *I better get to sleep now because I'm going to church in the morning*, she promised herself.

7

SHOCKING DISCOVERY

Classes were dismissed early at Echo Valley Elementary School on Monday in favour of the scheduled parent-teacher interviews. Marie busied herself straightening up her desk, arranging the displays of coloured leaves the children had made that morning and doing what she could to improve the appearance of her classroom. She was arranging chairs for easy conversation when a large, stern-faced woman marched briskly up the aisle.

"Hello, Mrs. Bruce," Marie smiled weakly. The woman glowered at Marie, momentarily touching Marie's extended hand before lowering herself onto a chair. Marie took a deep breath.

"I have been looking forward to meeting Mitchell's mother," she said sincerely. "How are you enjoying Alberta? Mitchell says you're from Montana."

"Yeah, but we didn't know when we came here we'd have to work for Indians." Mrs. Bruce spat out the last word.

"That's interesting," Marie said, amused. "I didn't know any of the ranches were owned by Indians, but then I don't know many of the people in the area. I'm new here myself."

"I know. Mitchell said so."

Marie walked over to Mitchell's desk and picked up the books he had laid out for his mother's inspection. As she flipped the pages she explained to Mrs. Bruce the work Mitchell had done. Mrs. Bruce's mind seemed to be on something else.

Marie wished she could tell Mitchell's mother something positive about him. She wanted to say how well he applied himself or how well he played with the other children, but none of that was true. Then she thought of something.

"Mitchell is a good actor," she said.

"A what?" Mrs. Bruce was incredulous.

"Actor," Marie repeated, "You see, sometimes after we have read a story and answered the questions, I give the pupils a chance to act out the story. They think that great fun."

"I send Mitchell to school to learn, not to clown," Mrs. Bruce exploded.

"Oh, dramatizing the story takes only a few minutes," Marie explained, "and it makes learning more interesting."

Marie got the impression that Mrs. Bruce would have objected to her teaching method no matter what it had been. She wondered why the woman was so defensive. Mrs. Bruce let out her breath with a slow hissing sound like air escaping from a balloon. Her chest fell accordingly.

"I'd think you'd do better spendin' your time finding out who done the stealin."

"Stealing!"

"Yeah, stealin." Mrs. Bruce placed her fleshy hand alongside her broad mouth as if she were about to confide a secret. "Mitchell says it's that Peter Cardinal that done it."

"Peter! Why Peter?" Marie blurted. "It can't be Peter." She was sure of that. Not innocent-looking little Peter!

"Cause it's in their blood, 'tis." Mrs. Bruce rose to go. With a promise to do what she could to get to the bottom of any theft, Marie saw the disgruntled woman to the door.

The next name on her list of parents to interview was Cardinal. She felt excitement building up at the prospect of meeting someone by that name. Surely she would find out from them the whereabouts of the couple that had been so close to Marc. Instead, William came through the door. He made his way toward her, his mouth curving into a smile as she greeted him.

Marie's quick response showed her pleasure at this unexpected interlude. She settled back in her chair as she watched him casually drape his frame over the student's desk directly in front of her.

"If you're free Saturday, Marie, I'd like to give you that tour of the ranch I promised you," he offered.

"I'll be delighted," she said. Then, afraid that she may have appeared too anxious, she quickly added in the most casual tone she could muster, "I'm always glad to learn something new."

William, on the other hand, made the invitation more personal. "I would like to have the honour of cooking dinner for you, so bring a good appetite."

I'll tell him about Marc, Marie decided as she accepted the invitation. *Yes, I can trust this man.* They talked for a few minutes more before Marie reminded her caller of the parent-teacher interviews that were scheduled.

"I know," he said simply, "That's why I came." There was a brief pause. "I was to see you at 2:45, I believe. About Peter."

"You," she gasped, "You are Bill Cardinal!"

"I am Bill Cardinal," he repeated slowly after her as he rose to his feet, not understanding her sudden bafflement. "You wanted to see me?" Marie's mind was racing madly. She felt totally confused and could think of nothing to say as William stood looking down at her.

"Can I do anything, Marie?" Bill asked, noticing her disposure. "Maybe a drink would help." He hurried from the room and soon returned with a cup of coffee from the urn set up in the hall for the visiting parents. Pulling a chair close to hers, he sat down and held out the cup to her.

Marie's hand shook as she reached for it. The drink helped her regain her composure. "I'm sorry," she said weakly.

"No need for that," he reassured her. "I apologize for startling you."

"I didn't know you were Peter's father," Marie explained.

Understanding dawned in the man's eyes, although Marie was sure he could not know why his identity mattered to her. She could not tell him that, not now. Out of all the unanswered questions tumbling about in her mind one thought was taking shape: *If he is Bill Cardinal, he's a married man.*

"About next Saturday," she said bluntly, "Forget it." Marie was too distraught to notice the man beside her stiffen. He said nothing as he slowly rose to his feet and moved around the room. When he returned to face her he spoke gently.

"I think I better leave now and give you time to collect yourself before the next interview. I'll talk to you about Peter's school work some other time." He reached for her hand, but she drew back. William walked to the door, then turned around. "About next Saturday," he said, "We'll talk about that later, too."

As soon as he had gone, Marie rushed to the washroom to splash water on her pallid face and apply fresh makeup. When she walked back into the classroom to meet the couple now waiting for her, she was composed, outwardly at least. The remainder of the interviews went well. Finally the last name on her list was checked off. Her day's work was done. Relieved, she slumped into her armchair, kicked off her shoes, and stretched her legs. She slid down lower in her chair and closed her eyes, allowing herself to relax.

There came a brisk rap at her door. The next moment high heels tapped out a rapid crescendo as Mrs. Grimm marched up the aisle. Marie sat up and pulled her skirt straight. She felt around with her feet for her discarded shoes. Marie knew her undignified posture had not escaped the quick eyes of her boss.

"Marie, I am calling a staff meeting for the noon hour tomorrow. We will discuss any matters that have arisen from the interviews."

"Alright, Mrs. Grimm," Marie agreed, wiggling her left foot into her shoe. She stood up and took a step forward to retrieve the other shoe.

"Furthermore, an urgent matter has come up," the principal continued, a momentary flash of uncertainty in her eyes. "A matter the police want to investigate. See you then." Matilda Grimm turned on her heel and marched from the room.

Marie's mind whirred. That urgent matter that has come up must be the theft Mrs. Bruce told of. If police are investigating it must be more serious than some child picking up pencils and erasers. But what did it have to do with her? Did it happen in her classroom? Marie's self-pity was mounting as she put on her coat and walked home.

8

THE GOLD WATCH MYSTERY

Several youngsters were clustered around Peter when Marie walked into the classroom the next morning. She saw nothing unusual about that until she came abreast the little group. Lying in the palm of Peter's outstretched hand was a gold watch.

Into Marie's mind flashed Mrs. Bruce's words: *It's that Peter Cardinal that done it.*

No, no, not Peter, Marie shouted inwardly. Outwardly she retained her composure as she reached for the pocket watch of yesteryear and slowly turned it over in her hand.

"Isn't it beautiful, Miss Stumbur?" one of the boys exclaimed. "Isn't Peter lucky?"

"Yes, yes, it's beautiful," Marie agreed absently. "Where did you get it, Peter?"

Peter said nothing. Marie asked again. When she still received no answer Marie knew she faced a problem.

"Peter, this is an expensive watch. Would you like me to keep it for you so it won't get broken or lost?" Peter was reluctant to give up his new treasure, but he nodded in the affirmative. Marie felt sick inside as she slipped the watch into her pocket. All morning the incident weighed like a rock on her mind.

Marie strolled down the aisle to observe the work being done by her pupils. She made a suggestion here, answered a question there. Peter was the last one to bring up his book. He laid it down hurriedly and turned to join his classmates at the project table.

"Just a minute, Peter," Marie halted him. "I want to talk to you." She lowered her voice so the other children would not hear.

"Peter, will you tell me the secret of how you got that watch?"

Peter shuffled his feet and looked at the floor. This wasn't like Peter. She asked him what he intended to do with it. Peter leaned toward her, a smile breaking out on his face.

"It's a birthday present for my daddy," he whispered.

"How nice of you," Marie encouraged him to go on. "Did your Mommy help you buy this present, Peter?" Peter looked blank for a moment before he answered.

"My mommy's in heaven."

"Oh," she gasped. "I-I didn't know that. I'm sorry, Peter. You may go now."

She watched him make his way to the project table. As he passed Mitchell's desk, the bigger boy gripped Peter's arm and muttered threateningly to him. Peter winced and pulled away.

Noticing his teacher's eyes on him Mitchell slunk down in his seat and hid his face behind the book in his hands. Marie walked up to him and turned the book around.

"I think you will find it easier to read if you hold your book right-side-up." Mitchell's face turned red as several children tried in vain to smother their snickers behind their hands.

When Marie entered the staff room at noon Nikolaus Nicole was sitting motionless at the window looking more withdrawn than ever. His eyes fixed on some faraway object, he seemed not to notice the other teachers coming in for the scheduled meeting.

When the Royal Canadian Mounted Police officer joined the little group, however, he suddenly emerged from his passiveness. Pulling his chair up to the table he turned to face the law-enforcement man with a look of expectancy.

Mrs. Grimm introduced the policeman to Marie and Olivia as Constable Todd Richards. Richards came straight to the point. "Sometime between four and six o'clock on Friday a brown cardboard box was lifted from Mr. Nicole's desk drawer," he said. "There is no indication of a forced entry. We're considering two possibilities: The door left unlocked or the thief hid in the building until everyone left and then took the package and walked out." Richards looked directly at Olivia and Marie sitting across the table from him. "Did either of you notice anything unusual Friday afternoon?"

"No, nothing. I left right after class for Calgary," Olivia answered simply. "I did not come back to Echo Valley until Sunday night."

"Mrs. Grimm has already confirmed that she was out of town as well." The officer turned to Marie. "What about you?"

"Friday. Let's see. I stayed after school on Friday," she answered, "I was here by myself."

"Doing what?"

"I had taken my pupils on a field trip. I was looking after the flowers and leaves they had collected."

"How long did you stay?"

"I left at five o'clock. I know it was five because..." Marie stopped short and looked at Nicole. "Because...I heard someone come into the school and I looked at the clock," she admitted slowly, "I noticed it was five o'clock. I left immediately."

Her listeners moved forward simultaneously. The constable's voice was seasoned with incredibility as he asked, "You did not keep the doors locked, Miss Stumbur?" He paused. "And you did not find out who came in?"

Marie cringed under the officer's piercing gaze and intense questioning.

"I can't say that I thought about whether the door was locked," she admitted. "I was going to find out who came in. Then I heard sounds coming from Mr. Nicole's room. Normal movements. Noisy, in fact. Not like anyone sneaking around, I mean. I assumed Mr. Nicole had come back for something. I decided not to interrupt him."

"It wasn't me!" Nikolaus exploded. "I didn't come back until six o'clock."

"And what did you do then?" the investigating officer continued questioning Marie.

"I went home. I thought no more about it."

"Did you lock the door when you left?"

"Yes. Yes, I know I did. It seems to me the lock had been turned by whoever came in. Yes, I remember now. That was another reason I was sure the person who had come in was Nikolaus. A kid coming in would not likely have had a key or even thought of locking the door after himself."

"You don't know if the door was locked before someone entered?" he asked. Marie shook her head.

"Constable, I am sure I was the last to leave the school, apart from Miss Stumbur," the principal spoke up. "I locked the door when I left."

"Then we can assume that the thief had a key. Mrs. Grimm, who are the people with keys to this building?"

"Not many. Everyone on the staff. The janitor. That is all."

"Do you have any spare keys?"

"Yes, one. I keep it as a safety measure, but that is locked up in my safety deposit box in my bank." The officer wrote in his book, then turned to Nikolaus.

"Did anyone else know you took your valuables to school?"

"No. The jewellery was in a plain box. Nothing suspicious-looking about it. No one was in the classroom when I set it into the bottom drawer. I piled some papers on top. It was still there at the end of the class period."

"Why didn't you take it home with you then?"

"I didn't go home." Nicole moved closer to the edge of his chair, talking excitedly. "I brought it to school with me because I intended to leave for Calgary right after class, but before I could get away one of the boys came back into the classroom to tell me I had a flat. I can't understand that. I had good tires. Well, anyway, after I had changed it and had it repaired, well, it was close to six o'clock." He threw up his hands in desperation. "When I got back to the school the drawer was empty. That's when I called the police."

"Did anyone know you took the contents of your safety deposit box to school with you?"

"No. I told no one."

"Nikolaus has listed the contents of the box," the officer said. Mr. Nicole leaned forward as he watched the officer unfold a sheet of paper.

"If he makes one more move forward he'll be sprawled on the floor," Olivia whispered through her teeth, trying to suppress a giggle. Marie did not seem to notice. She drew in a deep breath and held it as the officer began listing the items.

"A set of matched wedding bands, gold brooch with a cluster of emeralds, gold pocket watch with chain..." Marie heard no more. Her hand tightened impulsively around the offensive object in her pocket.

"And that's it," the officer finished. "If you see any jewellery that fits this description let me know at once." He rose to his feet.

"Just a minute." Marie's voice came out in a squeak as she slowly withdrew her fist from her pocket. "When I came into my room this morning the children were admiring this." She heard a swift intake of air around her as she handed the watch across the table. It clung to her sweaty palm.

"It's mine!" Nicole was on his feet. "That's it. My grandfather's watch!"

"Not so fast." Todd Richards held up his hand. "This may well be part of the loot, but I'll have to take it back to the station with me." His gaze returned to Marie.

"I want to talk to you, Miss Stumbur. The rest of you may go now. Thank you for your co-operation."

Olivia patted Marie's shoulder as she rose to leave. "Good luck, Chum," she whispered. "You might be onto something."

"You say you were in the building at the time the robbery could have taken place. You say someone came into the building, but you did nothing to check it out. Now you come up with this watch. Why did you not produce it earlier, Miss Stumbur?"

Marie shook her head. "I didn't know what to do when I saw it. I-I couldn't believe it. I knew you were going to be here so I waited for the right time." She hesitated.

"Can you give me more particulars, Miss Stumbur?"

"About Friday," Marie began, "There is really nothing else to tell. Even when I heard about the robbery I never connected that with someone coming into the school on Friday until you questioned me about it. Like I said, I thought it was Mr. Nicole."

"You heard about the jewellery theft before I questioned you?"

"I didn't know what was stolen, but..." Marie related Mrs. Bruce's accusation. "Then this morning I walked into the classroom to find a first grader displaying this...this watch. But he didn't act guilty or anything." Marie was careful not to divulge the youngster's name as she spoke of the incident. "Oh, another, there was this bigger boy. It was his mother that talked of the stealing. He seemed to be threatening the younger boy after I had questioned him about the watch."

"Better send in the boy that had the watch first," the officer said as he recorded Marie's words.

"But if he stole the jewellery, wouldn't he try to hide it?" Marie made herself ask.

"Most likely, yes. Just the same, I need to talk to him. He may tell me where he got it."

Mitchell was telling some of the other pupils about the glories of Montana when Marie came into the class room. He fell silent as Marie walked to Peter's desk where the small boy sat looking at a picture book.

"Peter, will you come with me?" she asked softly.

As Peter followed her from the room unsuspectingly, she heard Mitchell's loud whisper, "Boy, is he in trouble for stealin!"

"There is someone here to see you," Marie smiled reassuringly, leading Peter into the staff room. At sight of the uniformed man Peter froze, his eyes big with terror. For the first time Marie's confidence in her pupil's innocence wavered. The officer momentarily stared back at Peter, shock registered in his eyes. Then he drew himself together.

"Peter," he said sharply. "I didn't expect it to be you." Peter did not reply as he reached up to grip his teacher's hand. The officer pulled a chair up close to his own. "Here, sit down, Peter. I want to ask you a few questions. Alone," he added, looking at Marie. "Thank you, Miss Stumbur."

9

Evasive Peter

During the days that followed the watch episode, Marie tried repeatedly to contact William by telephone. Finally she called Beryl to ask for him.

"The men are hauling cattle to market every day now so they're in the corrals or on the road," Beryl explained, "So Will's not been in the house much."

"Then where's Peter?" Marie asked.

"Peter? He's gone to the pasture with the men. They are bringing in the last of the critters right now, but I expect them back before long."

"I need to talk to William."

Beryl was suddenly concerned. "Can I help?"

"Yes, thank you. Maybe you can give him the message. I must talk to him regarding an incident at school that involves Peter."

"I'll tell you what!" Beryl spoke, striking on an idea. "Why don't you and Oli come on out for a visit? Then you can see

Will when he gets back." A minute later Marie knocked on Olivia's bedroom door.

"How would you like to drive out to the ranch tonight?" she asked as soon as the door opened. "I just got us an invite from Beryl."

"From Beryl?" Olivia teased as she laid aside the book she was reading. "I would have thought it might have been from that handsome brother of hers." Marie ignored the comment.

"I need to talk to Peter about the watch incident and I don't want to talk about it in school. I don't want the kids to think he's a thief. Besides, maybe his father can help me."

"I detected a mysterious ring in your voice." Olivia paused to check her face in the mirror. "I thought maybe we were going to help round up cattle rustlers, or something like that. But it's clues about the robbery of Nikolaus' treasures we are after. In either case, I'm game."

Olivia continued her light-hearted chatter as they put on their jackets and went down the stairs. "You know, when I was a kid, my friend and I used to read a lot of Nancy Drew books. Whenever something happened in our community, a robbery or anything criminal, we would go sneaking around, looking for clues. I used to wonder what it would be like to really crack a case. I never found out."

"Oh, isn't this beautiful?" Marie exclaimed at the sight of the soft snowflakes lazily floating downward as the girls stepped out of the front door into the first snowfall of the season.

"It is beautiful. Really good for tracking," Olivia replied. She gave a word of acknowledgment to Burton who was coming up the walk, then continued. "If there are any thieves or cattle rustlers out tonight, tracking them should be easy with this fresh snow on the ground."

The banker stopped short. He swung around and stood watching the girls drive away in Olivia's Mazda. As they turned the corner at the end of the street Olivia saw him in her rear-view mirror, still standing in the snow. She cast a sidelong glance at Marie.

"You know, I think that guy has his sights set on you."

"Oh Oli, just because we find out he is Beryl's brother instead of her husband..."

"No, no, I'm talking about Burton."

"Burton? Oh no. Except that Anna keeps implying what a wonderful husband he would be. She must think it her duty to find him a wife - any wife."

"You're wrong there. Not any wife for Burton," Olivia corrected. "Anna never directs those comments at me. And another thing. I noticed that when I'm not going to be home for supper she asks Burton up to eat with you, but when you're away, she doesn't find it necessary to bring in anyone else to eat your share."

"That's because she knows you are spoken for," Marie laughed. "Besides, what I eat would not be enough to satisfy Burton."

"What I eat is, I admit," Olivia countered. "But that is not Anna's concern."

"Well, if matchmaking is what she has in mind, she is wasting her time," Marie replied.

The snow had stopped falling by the time the girls drove into the ranch yard. Several men stood clustered beside the corral fence, two small figures among them. The smallest of the boys broke from the group and sprinted across the yard toward the teachers. The second youngster disappeared behind a truck parked nearby. Marie knew he was Mitchell by his exaggerated casualness.

"Miss Stumbur," Peter's excited voice rang out through the clear evening air. "We were looking for the missing cattle and you know what, somebody stole them, Daddy thinks. Why would they do that?"

"I don't know, Peter," Marie answered, not sure what to say. "Some people take whatever they get their hands on no matter whose it is."

"Not talking like a thief, is he?" Olivia said to Marie in a half-whisper as she turned to go into the house, leaving Marie alone with her pupil.

Marie hesitated a moment before plunging into the subject she had come to discuss. "Peter, do you know that the watch you're planning to give to your dad was also stolen?"

"I know. The policeman told me." He looked anxiously into her face. "You don't think I stole it, do you, Miss Stumbur?"

"No. I don't think you stole it, Peter," Marie reassured him. "What I want to know is how you got it. Did someone give it to you?" The slight nod of Peter's head was barely perceptible.

"Who, Peter? Who gave it to you?" No answer. Marie tried another approach. "Mitchell Bruce was with you when we arrived. Does he often come to play with you?"

"Mitchell sometimes is along with his dad when he comes to work," Peter explained, "But he doesn't much want to play with me."

"Mitchell's dad works for Bill—For your dad, I mean?"

"Yeah."

"Peter, did Mitchell give you that watch?" Marie hoped the direct question would spark an uncensored response. Peter's reply, however, was not what she expected.

"No, Mitchell doesn't much like me."

Marie heard the Bruce truck start up and turned to wave. Mitchell saw her gesture and slunk down low in his seat as the vehicle drove away.

"I was wondering when I'd get a chance to talk to Peter's teacher," William said pleasantly as he and John joined Marie and her pupil. Marie blushed, remembering her confusion on the day of the interviews.

"No need to worry about Peter," she said, trying to mask her embarrassment. "He is doing just fine." Peter beamed up at her from under his cowboy hat.

"I am glad to hear that about you, Son," his father said, pulling Peter close.

"Why don't you come in?" John invited. "No need to stand out here."

"Thanks, but Peter and I better head on home. It's past Peter's bedtime," William answered. "But why don't you all come over to my house after a while? I'll make coffee." He reached down to take his son's hand.

"Good night, Miss Stumbur. Good night, Uncle John," Peter said, reluctantly turning toward home. Under the eerie gleam of the vapour light overhead, Marie watched the two walk toward the big, dark house, their cowboy boots leaving imprints in the fresh snow. Then she became aware of John waiting for her at the door and turned her steps toward the house.

10

GUESSWORK

William had tucked Peter into bed and was putting on the coffee when he saw the women coming along the walk, Beryl with them. He met them at the door.

"John had some work to do," Beryl said, shrugging off her coat. She went through to the kitchen with an offer to pour the coffee. Olivia followed.

"I take it you want to talk to me about the watch," William said as soon as Marie was seated on the couch. He settled himself in an armchair close by.

"Oh, you know about that," Marie said, relief in her voice. "Did Peter tell you?"

"No. Todd Richards did. It's strange."

"You don't think Peter stole it, do you, Bill?

"No." William shook his head. "But telling the police that Peter found it is not a very convincing argument."

"Found it? I thought it was given to him."

"Is that what he told you?"

"Yes. Well, not exactly. I asked him if it was given to him and he nodded. At least, I thought he did. Maybe that was not what he meant," she ended weakly.

"It's strange," the rancher sighed. "I can't understand why he is so secretive about it. That's not like Peter."

"I don't know who stole the jewellery," Marie said, "But I have some suspicions." She told William of Mrs. Bruce's accusations and of Mitchell's behaviour. "Peter was displaying the watch with obvious pride," she pointed out. "If he had stolen it he wouldn't flash it around school."

"You think it was Mitchell then?"

"No. Taking that package from Nicole's drawer is hardly a kid's prank. It was more likely an adult. Someone who knew its value."

William absently took the cup of coffee Olivia was holding out to him. "You have a point there, Marie," he said.

"What would be the first thing a thief would try to do?" Olivia broke in as she joined Marie on the couch. "He'd want to throw suspicion off his trail." She was warming up to her old game of sleuthing. "By giving the watch to Peter he has made Peter the suspect."

Marie gave a brief laugh. "I wondered how long it would be till you'd come up with some wisdom gained from your years of sleuthing," she teased. "But that's a valid thought, Olivia. Now do you have a file of ideas on the kind of person that would do this?"

"I've been thinking over Mr. Nicole's story and the whole thing doesn't make sense," the amateur detective answered seriously. "Going back to the day he took his keepsakes out of the deposit box at the bank and left them, of all places, in an unlocked drawer in the classroom, well, wasn't that a strange thing to do?"

"But then, Mr. Nicole is rather an unusual person," Marie reminded her.

"Even so, why would a man, even an unusual personage like Nikolaus Nicole, for no good reason take his treasures out of a safe place and put them into a desk drawer at school and then go off and leave them there?"

"Oli, what are you getting at?" Marie came to the defence of their fellow teacher. "Nikolaus may have had his reasons, even if we don't know what they are. Why should he have to explain to us why he withdrew his valuables from the bank?"

"If we have no evidence, Marie, we have to consider all possibilities. We have no witnesses that saw the box of goodies. Maybe it was never there."

"Why would he make that claim then?"

"Insurance, that's why."

"But someone did come into the school on Friday," Marie said with a twinge of guilt. "I heard him."

"Even if the package was in his desk, couldn't Nicole have come back for it himself? After all, who else knew it was there? Couldn't he have picked it up to deposit some place else before he reported it stolen? Maybe that was why he got so excited when you said you heard him come in." Olivia looked around at her audience. "I'm not saying that's what he did, mind you. I'm saying this is a possibility. Even a probability."

"It's a possibility," Marie conceded, "A slight one." She toyed with the thought for a moment. "Of course I don't know Nikolaus," she added. "I don't know him at all. But I never thought of him as a criminal. More like an uncommunicative individual who tends to his own business and leaves everyone else to theirs."

"Uncommunicative describes Nikolaus Nicole precisely, but who's to say the thoughts behind that mask are always innocent? We don't need to mention my suspicions to anyone else, but I think we can't dismiss the possibility till...till we come up with a satisfactory answer somewhere else."

"He is talking more now than he did before," Marie observed.

"Exactly," Olivia exclaimed. "Now why would losing his valuables make him happier? This morning he actually smiled when I greeted him. I could hardly believe what I was seeing. Then he stopped to comment about the weather. Not a very exciting subject generally, but coming from him, wow, that was something!"

"Nikolaus was not always like that," William said softly. "Oh, I suppose he was always a quiet person. We had them in our home a number of times. He was pleasant enough."

"Them?" Olivia leaned forward. "Is he married?"

"He was," Beryl said. "His wife was an Easterner and never got over raving about Montreal. She missed the city."

William took up the story again. "Everything here scared her, the cattle, the wide open spaces, the mountains, the loneliness." He shook his head. "But Nikolaus loved her."

"What happened?" Marie asked almost in a whisper.

"Who knows? They were here for one term. Then they went East for the summer. When he returned in the fall, he came alone." William sighed. "He was never the same after that. I try to engage him in conversation when we meet. We invited him to visit. No dice. Women especially seem to scare him." A new idea hit William. "Maybe he would consider an invitation now, seeing I am alone, too."

In the silence that followed, Marie sat thinking about Nikolaus. For the first time she thought of the disappointment and loneliness that must be his lot, causing him to retreat into a shell. William sat his cup on the coffee table and leaned back.

"Have you any other possibilities?" he asked Olivia.

"Well, there are always the Bruces. I've not written them off. They could have been accomplices." The rancher looked at Marie.

"Didn't you say that Peter denied getting the watch from Mitchell?"

"Yeah, but in this I'm inclined to agree with Oli. I think Mitchell knows something. I can think of no other explanation for his actions. Or Mrs. Bruce's."

"You don't mean...?" William looked from one to the other. He ran his long fingers through his raven black hair as he studied the insinuation. "No, I have no reason to believe Joe Bruce is a thief," he said at length. "Oh, he's prejudiced against Indians. Considered it a letdown to discover his boss is part-Indian, but burglary? No. Now would anyone like more coffee?"

"No, thanks," Olivia answered, checking her watch. "Time to call it a night." She carried the cups to the kitchen.

William turned to Marie. "I'll talk with Peter tomorrow. I've not pressed the issue. He has always been open with me before so I expected if he had anything to tell he would come out with it before long." The rancher's face was grave. "Besides, the watch was only one of a long list of stolen items. I expected the police would soon pick up the scent, but..." He looked around the group, his face breaking into a grin, "Apparently, they don't have as many ideas as Oli here." Beryl laughed her cheery laugh. It seemed to Marie she was always laughing.

"Remember, we have no evidence," William said as he handed the girls their jackets. "Only suspicions and wild guesses."

"I guess you're right, Bill," she conceded, smiling sheepishly. "We're so anxious to free Peter from suspicion that we are apt to clutch at straws."

"Right. If we unleash our imaginations every coincidence can look like evidence and everyone around can become a suspect," Bill agreed.

"How many coincidences do you allow a man?" Olivia asked, her eyes sparkling. "I say we keep looking for proof."

"Right," William said again, "And until we have something concrete, we best let it ride." He shook his head. "It is a serious matter to accuse an employee. I hope our leads are taking us in the wrong direction."

Olivia pulled her ski jacket around her and skipped out to start the car. William walked out with Marie.

"About next Saturday," he asked, "Is the tour on?"

"Yes, if you haven't withdrawn the offer," Marie said. "I apologize for my foolish refusal. Maybe I can explain."

"No need for that," William assured her. "Your acceptance is enough. I will call for you at 8:30 then. Okay?"

As Olivia turned the car around and headed toward home, Marie kept her eyes riveted on the ranch yard until it was out of sight.

11

QUESTIONS

Saturday dawned sunny and mild. Marie dressed excitedly and hurried through her breakfast. "I am in a rush. Bill said he'd be here for me at 8:30." She excused herself and rose from the table. Anna Charter's face took on a look of surprise and disappointment. "You're not going with Cardinal, are you?" she asked.

"Yes, I'm going to tour the ranch," Marie replied, smiling as she headed toward the stairs.

"Why does she go with him?" Anna demanded of Olivia as soon as Marie was out of earshot.

"Why not?" Olivia answered offhandedly. "Bill's a great guy. Besides," she added, "They're not dating. She's just going to see the ranch."

"Burton says you can't trust them," the blonde lady spoke with indignation. "They're Indians, you know." The young school teacher fought to keep her temper in check. She sipped her coffee slowly, trying to think of something to say.

"By the way, Anna, what is your secret recipe for good coffee?" she asked after what seemed a long time to her, "It's always the same. Perfect." The face before her brightened.

A short time later, Olivia knocked on Marie's door. "Someone here for you," Olivia sang out.

Minutes later, as William turned the car in the direction of the ranch, Marie began questioning him about the ranch she was about to see.

"How did you happen to go into ranching?"

"You could say I was roped into it," the rancher replied. "My Grandfather Drummond came from England as a young bachelor. He dreamed of finding a stretch of land he could call his own. He perused that dream and the spread we have today grew out of that dream."

"The ranch has been in your family for three generations then?"

"More or less," William answered. "My grandfather married about a year after he bought the land. He was drafted the next year. That was World War One. He never came back. My grandmother, her name was Canary, waited for him to return. Even after she heard that he had been killed in action she hoped that there had been a mistake, that someday her Albert would show up. She carried on the best she could alone, even when the baby came, but the ranch was too much for her to handle."

"What happened?"

"The Smiths owned the neighbouring ranch. They helped her out with the work and when the war ended and Grandma Canary accepted the fact that Grandpa was not coming back they soon amalgamated the two properties."

"Did your grandmother ever remarry?"

"Yes, several years later. To a man called Joseph Cardinal. He worked for the Smiths at the time. He adopted my father legally."

"And that's how you got the name," Marie finished for him.

"That's correct. He was Cree like Grandma so my father was generally regarded as Indian, even though he was Métis. Joseph Cardinal was a real father to him and a Grandpa to me."

"You knew your grandparents then?"

"Oh yes, I remember them well. My grandmother was a beautiful woman. My father often told me what a beauty she had been. Even as she grew older she retained a striking appearance and bearing. She also had a beautiful character, as striking as her appearance."

William related some anecdotes from the lives of his grandparents. "I enjoy researching my family history," he told Marie as he brought the car to a halt in front of his house. "I hope I've not bored you with it."

"Bored?" Marie tossed her head. "Of course not. The opening up of the west is a subject that fascinates me."

"In that case how would you like to meander down that hill over there? That log house at the bottom is the honeymoon cottage Grandpa Drummond built for his Canary when he first settled here."

"Would I?" Marie was enthusiastic. "I would like that very much." As Marie stepped from the car she remembered her reaction the first time she laid eyes on this site. The day she had come upon it unexpectedly on her hike through the trees, her overwhelming thought had been, *What a wonderful place this would be to live.* Now as her eyes swept over the view she took a deep breath and let it out slowly.

"It's as beautiful blanketed in snow as it was in the garb of autumn," she muttered half to herself. Then she added, but only in her thoughts, *And it must have been as enchanting when Marc saw it bursting out in the greenery of spring.*

"Perhaps a hot drink would be a good idea before we start our walk around," her host was saying. "How about a cup of tea?" He glanced around to see Peter leading his pony from the barn. "I see Peter intends to go riding. Will you excuse me while I help him saddle up?" He opened the door for Marie. "Go on in," he said.

Marie stopped in the roomy back porch to remove her boots and parka. As she passed into the large dining area she suddenly froze. There on a shelf directly in front of her stood a large framed photograph identical to the one hidden in her dresser drawer. The familiar blue eyes held her immobile as they looked laughingly into hers.

Marie's mind whirled. This unexpected encounter with Marc's picture sharpened the pang of loss, escalating the feelings of uncertainty and bitterness that lay smothering within in her. Unanswered questions bombarding her mind now increased in intensity.

Ironically, on the shelf beside Marc's picture poised that of a young woman. *Elizabeth Cardinal*, Marie guessed.

Marie's confidence in Marc had never wavered, even while they had been separated. Not until that scanty newspaper account of the accident had come to her attention had she harboured any doubts. The clipping now crumpled and smudged by tears lay in the drawer with other mementoes. She could see it in her mind's eye now.

> "A two-vehicle accident on a public road one km east of Echo Valley claimed the lives of two Echo Valley residents. Marc Forest, 24, driver of the Eastbound Monte Carlo, and his only passenger, Elizabeth Cardinal, were killed instantly when a three-ton truck struck the Forest car head on. The driver of the truck, Stanton Link of no fixed address, escaped injury. He was charged with impaired driving."

Why had Marc never mentioned Elizabeth Cardinal? Why was she with Marc that night? Was she someone special to him? Was she Bill's sister... or was she Bill's wife?

"No, no! Horrors, no!" The denial escaped Marie's pale lips. No, she couldn't believe Marc was disloyal to her, let alone take another man's wife. His best friend's wife. No, Marc was a man of principle. And he loved her. She knew he did. Besides, William was married to Deedee. If this is the Bill Cardinal that Marc had worked for. He must be the same man. Why else would his picture be here?

The picture blurred before her. Marie fumbled in her jean pocket for a tissue and blotted at her tear-filled eyes. Uncertainly she reached for the picture and caressed the face with a shaky hand.

"Oh Marc, Marc, what really happened?" she cried.

The door opened behind her. Marie hurried to replace the picture. In her haste she knocked over the smiling face beside it. A gasp escaped her lips as the woman's picture cluttered to the floor.

Someone behind her bent down to pick it up. A hand reached past her to set it back in its place. Then Marie felt the hand on her shoulder gently turning her around. Her attempt at diverting her eyes was fouled as the man placed a finger under her chin and lifted her face to meet his gaze. Taking a table napkin from the island counter nearby, he blotted away her tears.

"It is hard to lose the one you love, isn't it?" he said gently.

Marie's eyes widened. "You know?" she gasped. "You know about Marc and me?" His arm tightened around her.

"Yes, I know, Marie. You see, I lost the one I loved that same day."

Marie's head shot up. "You mean...Oh Bill, tell me all about it. I want to know...Please."

12

ANSWERS

William led the distraught woman into the living room. She sat down gingerly on the edge of the chesterfield, her body erect, every nerve tense.

"What do you want to know?" William asked gently, lowering himself onto the cushion beside her.

"Everything. What you know about Marc, what happened that day." She paused. "The newspaper said his passenger was Elizabeth Cardinal. That was your wife?"

"You didn't know that!" William was incredulous. "Yes, Deedee's given name was Elizabeth Deidre. Her family always used her second name. When she learned to talk she called herself Deedee. So Deedee became her nickname. It stuck with her."

Marie voiced the question that was simmering within. "Bill, how come she was with Marc?" William had guessed by now that Marie was wrestling with more than grief. Now understanding was beginning to break through.

"Marie," he said evenly, "it was not what you are thinking. Deedee loved me. Marc loved you. I didn't know Marc long before I knew about you. Marc was here for only four months, as you know. During that time we became close friends." William told Marie of the talks he had shared with Marc.

Marie nodded. "He told me about all that."

"The night he made his stand for Christ he was so happy. The only shadow on his newfound joy: the fact that you where not there to share in that decision with him. He had just come back from his Easter holidays with you."

"He told me that, too," Marie agreed.

"The next day I sensed that Marc was fighting a fierce battle," the rancher continued. "He said nothing about it until he had written you about postponing your wedding. But that was only to give you time to make your decision. He never doubted that you would make the same commitment once you understood."

"That's what he said." Marie's voice was barely audible. "I decided to study the Bible and learn what it was all about. I wanted what Marc had." She paused. "I wrote and told him that. I don't know if he ever got that..."

"He did," Bill broke in. "I knew when he came dashing up the walk that he had heard from you. 'It's Marie,' he burst out even before he came through the screen door. 'She's going to search it out for herself and when she does that she'll come to the same conclusion. God's answering my prayers.'" William bent his head closer in his eagerness for Marie to understand. "I wish you could have been here with him those last two weeks."

"I guess...Well, I never carried through on that resolution," Marie confessed self-consciously. "But finish your story."

"Well, the day Marc came with that exciting news was also a special day for Deedee and me. Our eighth wedding anniversary. We had invited some guests for a barbecue that evening. Marc was helping with the cleaning around the yard. He was leaving to see you the next morning.

"I had a surprise for Deedee. New office furniture. Computer, everything. It was stored in the shop, under a canopy on the back of the truck waiting to surprise Deedee. I wondered how to get it into the house without her noticing. Well, Marc and I were setting up the barbecue when she came out to say she was making a quick trip to the store. That was my chance. I was expecting some tractor parts on the bus so I suggested that Marc go along to pick them up. Thought he could detain her a bit to give me time to get things moved into the house. Marc took the cue and offered to take his car." The young widower was fighting to control his emotions. Marie realized he was reliving the tragedy of that fateful day and did not interrupt him.

"As soon as the car had disappeared behind the trees, Peter rushed out to call John and Beryl." William coughed, drew a deep breath, and continued his monologue in short, choppy phrases. "Peter was stationed at the window. Hopping up and down. Just couldn't contain his excitement. He loves surprises." William's mouth twitched, but after a few moments he went on. "I was beginning to feel uneasy. Wondered what was taking so long. When Peter announced the police car a charge went through me." William gave his head a sudden shake, as if trying to clear his mind.

"There was nothing Marc could have done," he said, rising to his feet. Slowly he walked to the window and stood looking out. Marie watched his shoulders sag, his knuckles turn white as he clenched his hands at his side and she realized his loss was as great as hers, maybe greater.

"Bill, I'm sorry." Her voice came out in a whisper. "I should not have put you through this." He swung around to face her then.

"You had a right to know," he spoke in a raspy voice. "I should have told you long ago. I didn't realize..."

Sinking into an armchair, he dropped his head into his hands. In the silence that followed, they sat lost in their individual memories. When the monstrous clock in the corner announced one o'clock with a resounding boom, William rose quickly.

"Dinner time," he said, holding out his hand to his guest. "It would do us both good to have something to eat." He led her to the kitchen.

The aroma of roast chicken pervaded the room as he opened the oven door. He pulled out the small roaster, eyeing the browned fowl and potatoes critically.

"Apart from being overdone, it looks alright," he concluded.

"Oh, it looks delicious!" Marie spoke truthfully, although she wondered whether she would be able to eat any of it. When Marie noticed him setting only two plates on the table, she suddenly remembered Peter.

"Peter? I arranged for him to go over to Beryl's house after his ride. We were going to tour the ranch this morning, remember?"

"I guess I blew that plan."

"Not at all," William assured her. "I can still show you around the place." He put the last of the food on the table and pulled out a chair for Marie.

"Let's pray," he said simply. He bowed his head and talked to God as naturally as one talks to an intimate friend. Marie had expected he would pray before they ate. The words he said, however, were not what she had expected. He gave thanks for the happiness he had shared with Deedee, for Marie's engagement to Marc, and for their memories of good times. He thanked God for His comfort and ended his brief prayer with thanks for the food.

Marie's thoughts lingered on his first items of thanksgiving. To thank God for a promising relationship that had come to a sudden, gory end seemed unreal. *How can he be thankful for dreams that have gone up in smoke? I'd be better off never to have known love than to have loved and then to have lost the one I loved.*

13

DECISION

"Did you know that I invited you over here so we could talk about what happened?" William asked when the meal was under way. Marie put down her fork and looked at him.

"No, I didn't," she said finally.

"I did not know just what was bothering you, Marie, but I knew you needed to open up about Marc, to share what was on your mind. That was another reason I sent Peter to Beryl's house. He does not know about your relationship with Marc. I thought it best not to tell him yet. He was very fond of Marc. And now you are very special to him." Marie felt a wave of gratitude for William's consideration of her. She was glad her pupil had not been around to witness her display of emotion.

"Why did you come to Echo Valley?" William's candid question caught Marie by surprise. She toyed with the food on her plate, diverting her eyes.

"Let's see, why did I come to Echo Valley?" She asked the question of herself. "It seems a long time ago now," she began slowly. "My objectives have changed since I came here. At least in order of importance. I'm beginning to see that now." She paused, weighing her reasons.

"Why did you come?" her host asked again after a considerable wait.

"Well, I needed a teaching position. I was reading the ads in the Edmonton Journal when the one about Echo Valley caught my attention. It appealed to me because of Marc. He loved it, the scenic countryside, his job on the ranch, the friends he made here, the church. He made it all seem so wonderful. I thought by coming here I might be able to capture some of that pleasure. To feel alive again. That was one reason."

Marie wet her lips. "I wanted to see the place Marc loved so much. To meet the people he enjoyed. I thought it would make me feel so close to him. I wanted especially to learn more about his final weeks," Marie ended weakly, "and about the accident."

"Those are the reasons why I thought you would have come," William picked up the conversation again. "That is why I thought you would want to talk to me...about Marc. I don't understand why you tried to avoid me. Or why you skirted the subject whenever we met. You see, Marie, I told you who I was the first time we met."

"I did not catch your name that night we met on the road," Marie said, "Also, Marc never called your place the Double C."

"I never thought of that." William was apologetic. "We were in the process of forming our company when Marc was here, so the shingle still carried the old name."

"The Drummond-Smith Estate?"

"That's right. Marc did tell you about that?"

"He often used that name. He seemed to be so much at home here. I understand the name now that you told me about your grandparents."

"You would have had no way of knowing before."

"Another thing. You are in a company with John and Beryl now, but Marc never mentioned them. Where they not involved before?"

"Oh yes, but Marc hardly knew them," William explained. "They took a few months off last winter to assist with the evangelistic work in Russia. They had arrived back just two weeks before the accident."

"It's all making sense now that you explain it."

"It is regrettable that I was not sensitive to your dilemma before."

William ate in silence for a few minutes. Then looking at Marie keenly, he asked, "Do you want to tell me more about your reasons for coming here? You implied another motive."

Suddenly Marie found herself telling William about the kinship and love she and Marc had shared. She told him of the telephone call from Marc's mother informing her of his fatal accident, of driving to Bonneville with her family for the funeral. She had half expected his friends from the ranch to be there. She now realized why they had not come. William had that day lain to rest his own sweetheart.

"Especially, Bill, I wanted to find what Marc found." She looked into his eyes and saw there a look of understanding and compassion. "I wanted God to be real to me like He was to Marc. I wanted to know God and enjoy Him like Marc did. I guess that was the underlying reason. The weighty one. I felt I owed that to Marc."

She fell quiet, recalling the deep feeling that Marc's letters had stirred in her. A lump stuck in her throat that she could not swallow. She took a drink of water but it did nothing to relieve the pressure.

"When Marc...died, well, I resolved more than ever to do what he would want me to do. But I guess it takes more than resolve...or maybe my resolve was too weak...Whatever it was, my determination sort of faded."

"Marie, you mentioned a change of priorities. What became more important?"

"I hate what I was thinking," Marie confessed. For a moment Marie rebelled against this scrutiny. She fought to gain control of her emotions. *Come on, Marie, he's trying to help, isn't he?* she reasoned with herself.

The widower sensed her emotional struggle and spoke encouragingly. "Marie, you'll feel better if you continue. Shaping your motives and feelings into words will help you see them more objectively. Can you put your finger on what has become your priority?"

Marie determined to lay everything on the line. "A few days after the funeral I received a letter from Marc's mother," she began. "It was very kind of her to think of my loss when she was also suffering. She had lost a son. She sent me a newspaper clipping. It was that accident report that roused my first doubts about Marc. I guess I was so upset that I was not being reasonable. That was my other reason for coming."

She folded her hands on the table and continued. "I wanted reassurance that Marc's love for me had been real, that his religious experience was not just a way out of our engagement, that Eliza..." She faltered.

"That he had not fallen in love with someone called Elizabeth Cardinal," William finished for her.

"It seems so foolish now. Downright wicked to even have thought that. At first, when the fear gripped me I believed underneath that Marc was not like that, that he would not be untrue to me. I expected to find proof that he was true to me to the end. But I learned nothing. I did not find this Bill and Deedee Cardinal he talked about so much. Not even the Smith-Drummond Estate Ranch. My fears grew. To find out who Elizabeth Cardinal was became an obsession. I began to think all sorts of things about her." She looked at her host. "I never guessed that your name was Cardinal."

William pushed aside his plate. "Oh, if only I had been aware of your feelings." He leaned closer to Marie. Reaching across the table he folded his hand over hers and felt them tremble.

"Marie, do you still have questions about Marc and Deedee?"

"No, no," Marie shook her head. "Oh William, it was so wrong of me!"

"You didn't know," William said. He got up to make a hot drink. "What will you have, tea or coffee, or that cup of hot chocolate I promised you earlier?"

"It doesn't matter," Marie answered. She dropped her head into her hands.

They did not speak again till William set the tea cups on the table. "You've not eaten much, Marie. At least have a hot drink." They sipped their tea in silence.

"Deedee was a great woman," William said at last. Memory of her brought a hint of a smile to his lips. With a distant look in his dark eyes he spoke of the one he had loved. "Perhaps her most unique characteristic, her underlying quality, was her insight into Scripture. That, and her prayer life."

The bereaved man was warming to his subject now, eager to share with someone the memories most precious to him.

"You know, before I met Deedee, I had a deep desire to know God better and to better understand the Bible. There's a verse in the Bible that says, 'As the deer pants for the water brooks, so my soul pants after You, O God.' Well, that was how I felt. God answered that desire by giving me a woman that saw truths in the Bible I had never seen or heard."

His smile widened. "To live for God was her whole life. She looked at everything through the Bible. It was the window through which she saw life from God's prospective. And she helped me become a man of the Bible."

Marie was not sure what he had meant by everything he said. He was talking about a dimension of living foreign to her. The desire to know it stirred in her heart again.

The voice continued. "And she was always ready to talk to God about anything that came up. We prayed together about everything. That's what I miss so much."

"And I painted Elizabeth so wicked in my imagination."

"You couldn't have known."

"But how could I have suspected Marc?" she sobbed. "I accused him of being untrue. Not aloud, mind you. I was torn by grief. Confused. When that clipping came into my hands and I read about Marc's only passenger, well, the most awful thought hit me."

Marie was unmindful of the tears coursing down her cheeks now. "I didn't realize to what extent that thought was taking hold. But now I think by this time I was suffering less from the grief of losing Marc than I was from the bitterness that was building up. Now, when I should be relieved, knowing my fears were ungrounded, I feel guilty. Dirty. Like I was the one to betray Marc."

She sprang to her feet and began to pace back and forth. "And I was," she cried, her voice rising in crescendo. "I betrayed his trust by my suspicions of him."

At length she sank back in her chair. "Before Marc started writing about being a Christian I was satisfied with my religion. Proud." She was speaking more calmly now. "But it did nothing to help me see the situation in the right prospective. It really didn't do anything for me when I needed it."

"Marie, Marc came to that realization, too. The Bible tells us how to live, but we need a personal relationship with the Author to make it real."

"But how?"

"Because of sin we come short of what God intended for us. Do you believe that?"

"Yes, I know I do. I see that now."

"God knows we cannot change ourselves. Oh, we can improve our conduct, learn tact and manners, but what we need is a change on the inside, in the secret recesses of our heart."

"Like the imagination that runs wild."

"Exactly. We can't do that ourselves. Knowing about Jesus is not enough. You said earlier that you had resolved to find what Marc found for his sake. We are not talking about a resolution, but about a relationship between Jesus and yourself. It was not your resolve that was too weak. It was your objective. We must personally acknowledge that we need a Saviour. Jesus Christ is that One. He loves you personally, Marie."

Marie looked puzzled. "Jesus loved the whole world. How can that be so personal?"

"How many pupils do you have, Marie?"

"Eighteen."

"Do you teach one group or eighteen individuals?"

"Oh, they're individuals alright. I try to recognize their individuality."

"Do you think God would do less?"

"But I only have eighteen pupils. He has a whole world full of people."

"And you are only a finite being. God is infinite. His power, knowledge, and wisdom are without bounds. Marie, if you were the only person in the world, Christ's salvation plan would have been for you no more and no less personal than it is now." He gave her time to contemplate that, then continued. "Christ's death on your behalf cannot benefit you unless you accept it. He is offering you a new life, but you have to receive it. Are you ready to do that?" Marie hesitated.

"There are still so many things I don't understand about God."

William walked to the cupboard and picked up a Bible. Moving his chair alongside of hers so that she could look on he flipped the pages quickly.

"Marie, take a look at this." Indicating the place with his index finger he read clearly: For as the heavens are higher than the earth, So are My ways higher than your ways, And my thoughts than your thoughts."

"Does that mean I never can understand God?" Marie asked.

"The natural mind cannot comprehend Him. Remember, I said before, that God is infinite. How can our finite minds grasp infinity?"

"But you have a grasp of God. Marc did. And you said Deedee did."

"When Jesus told His disciples He was going back to the Father in heaven, He promised to send the Holy Spirit." William pointed to the words of Jesus and read slowly, "'But the Helper, the Holy Spirit, whom the Father will send in My name, He will teach you all things, and bring to your remembrance all things that I said to you.' When we accept God's gift He comes to live in us by His Spirit. He is the One that interprets the Bible for us. He helps us understand." Marie's forehead crinkled as she thought about that.

"So when you accepted God's gift like you said, then you understood?"

"Not all at once, Marie, but little by little. Just like a newborn baby does not know everything at birth, but daily he grows and learns. The same thing is true when we are born from above. It is a new life. It is a spiritual life. The Holy Spirit is with us to teach and lead us. And He often uses other Christians to help us learn."

Marie recalled Marc's letter full of excitement over new discoveries in the Bible. She thought of how he had learned from Bill and Deedee and how he had tried to pass on to her what he had learned. *But I didn't understand because I'd not accepted Christ, just like Bill explained it.*

William rose silently to clear away the neglected dinner, giving his inquirer time to think about what he had said. At length Marie turned to him.

"Marc went forward at a church meeting. Do I have to wait until I'm in church?"

"No, Marie," William answered, depositing the package of leftover chicken in the refrigerator. "Many people reach their point of decision at a public meeting, but not necessarily." He sat down again. "A public meeting can also be a good place to acknowledge a decision that has already been made. It is one way of letting others know that you have joined God's family. But you can make that decision any place."

"I want to do that," Marie said suddenly.

"Let's kneel down and talk to God."

Marie needed no more coaxing. Sinking down beside her chair, she spoke earnestly to God. "Dear God, I need Your forgiveness. I want to accept Jesus as my Saviour. I want to be a new person. I am sorry for my sins. Amen."

14

A New Prospective

Marie returned to her room that evening with a new sense of excitement. Her hands shook slightly as she opened the drawer that housed her mementoes of Marc. She took out Marc's framed picture and looked at it long and lovingly before setting it on her dresser. Then she settled herself cross-legged on the rug to peruse the packets of letters and pictures that they had exchanged between them.

Many of the people and places mentioned in Marc's letters were now familiar to her. For the first time since his death Marie found herself smiling at the numerous amusing incidents he related so well. She suddenly recognized under the pain of loss, a pleasure in remembering.

I did have good memories, she acknowledged. *All the in-depth discussions we had, all the planning for our future. And the fun times like the waterslides and the picnics in the park.* Bill had been right, she conceded. She was glad to have experienced this relationship with Marc. That was what led to her decision today. Right then she bowed her head and offered a prayer of thanks to God for the many good memories tucked away in her mind.

Finally Marie turned to the letters Marc wrote during his last week. It was then she discovered the deepest change within herself. For the first time she could identify with him when he wrote of his need to give his life to God. She could appreciate his commitment to Christ, even at the expense of postponing their wedding date. If only she had grasped the truth sooner! A longing, deep and strong, came over her to be able to tell Marc she now understood. She wanted him to know that now, if he were here, nothing would stand in the way of them getting married.

"Oh, Marc, I wish I could talk to you now!" she whispered. "If only I could tell you that your prayers are answered. I'm a believer now. Oh, how happy we could be together if only..." Then into her mind flashed the words William had said to her while driving her home just two hours before. We cannot wish our loved ones back, Marie. Being with Jesus outranks any pleasure on earth.

Marie thought this over. *For me to have Marc here would be wonderful. For Marc this would be a letdown compared to Heaven.* Marie resolved to do what Jesus would want her to do, even if it meant living alone the rest of her life. What was that verse William showed her, a promise that God would never leave her? Marie wondered if she could find it for herself. Dropping the letters back into the open drawer, she picked up her Bible.

When Olivia bounded up the stairs a few minutes later, Marie was seated on top of her bedspread with her Bible on her knees. Finding Marie's door partly open, her friend stuck her head in to inquire how her day had gone. Marie laughed. "I didn't see the ranch."

"No tour?" Olivia strolled into the room. "You were so excited about it, I can't imagine what could have been more important." She held up her hand as Marie was about to speak. "No, don't tell me. Let me guess. Oh, I know! You have been doing some sleuthing. Did you catch the cattle rustlers or find Nikolaus' treasures?"

"Strange, I didn't think of either one today," Marie mused as she watched her friend's curiosity grow. At that instant Olivia caught sight of the photograph on the dresser.

"Oh, oh, this must be the reason," she joked, studying the face in the frame. "Now what am I to make of this," she kept on inquisitively, "You left the house this morning with that handsome rancher and you come back with the mug shot of someone else." She looked at Marie for an explanation. "Did you find him among the cattle or what?"

"Nothing like that. The man in that picture belongs to my past, but he is very closely connected with what happened to me today," Marie said seriously. She felt a nervous sensation in the pit of her stomach as she continued. "You asked me once what was troubling me. Well, sit down, Oli, and I'll tell you all about it."

Olivia settled herself on the foot of the bed and leaned her back against the wall. As the November night settled over the foothills, she listened quietly as Marie told of her romance with Marc and how his tragic death led to her coming to Echo Valley. She ended her narrative by relating the momentous decision she had made a few hours ago.

The next morning, Marie's alarm sounded half an hour earlier than was usual for Sunday. When she had showered and dressed she knelt down beside her bed with her Bible in her hand. William had stressed the importance of beginning each day with Bible reading and prayer and Marie was eager to start out right. Bible reading, she determined, would be part of her daily agenda from now on.

It was not that she had never read the Bible before. The Book had lain on a shelf in the family living room as long as she could remember. Occasionally her mother would read a story from the large volume to the family at bedtime. Sometimes Marie had picked it up herself and flipped the pages, reading a bit here and there.

She remembered the day two men from the Gideon organization had visited her grade five classroom to present a copy of the New Testament to each pupil. They had said it was a letter from God. She had thought of that as she had read from its pages in the months that followed.

On her twelfth birthday her father had given her a complete Bible. He had made a tradition of presenting family members with suitable books on their birthdays. Being an avid reader Marie looked forward to each new selection. Before the day was through she was curled up with the new book in her hands. The day she received the Bible was no exception. Thrilled to get a complete copy of this letter from God she started at once to read it through. The account of the six-day creation and the adventures of Adam and Eve had been an exciting beginning. Stories of Noah's ark, of Joseph and his jealous brothers, of baby Moses in the basket, of the plagues in Egypt and the crossing of the Red Sea on dry ground, followed by a catalogue of miracles in the desert, all captivated her imagination.

Much, however, was beyond her comprehension. When she got into the ceremonial laws in Leviticus her enthusiasm waned. Gradually she gave it up. Now and then she would flip its pages and read a few verses here and there. During her university years she had read it occasionally as a guide to moral living.

Now Marie turned to the words penned on the flyleaf in her father's bold handwriting. *Happy Birthday, Marie. This is the most important gift I can ever give you. I hope you will read it and make it your guide for life. With love from your dad.*

Marie wondered what had prompted her father to give her a Bible and to write those words. She wondered what God's letter meant to him. At the time she had taken his inscription to mean that he wanted her to follow the teachings of Jesus in principle; to live by the Golden Rule. She had tried to do that, as well as she knew how.

Now as she pondered his words she wondered if he was implying something deeper. Arnold Stumbur had seldom talked religion, but he had emphasized right living. Did he know that doing unto others as you wanted them to do to you was not enough? Did he know that a personal relationship with Jesus was necessary? Was that what he wished for her?

"I found it," she whispered to God. "I've found what this Book is all about. Jesus, You are my Saviour. Thank you. Thank you for showing me that I could never make it on my own. Thank you for coming into my heart. Help me to explain it to my mom and dad."

Overcome with a desire for her physical family to be part of God's family, she prayed earnestly for their salvation. She resolved to write to them that afternoon. Mentally she coined the letter as she prepared to go down for breakfast.

> *Dear Mom and Dad,*
>
> *I am going to tell you about the most wonderful thing that ever happened to me. I have found in Echo Valley what Marc found here. I don't know if I ever told you that Marc wrote of having made a decision to follow Jesus Christ.*

She stopped suddenly, realizing that this would be the first time since Marc's death that she mentioned him in her letters. Somehow it seemed an appropriate way to introduce the subject she wanted to share with them. *After all, my search for God began with Marc's commitment. I knew Marc would not embrace a theory without researching it,* she reflected. *I knew if Marc accepted this wholeheartedly, it was worth my investigation. I'll tell them that.*

15

THE LETTER

Arnold Stumbur lingered over breakfast on his day off from work. The buzz of the doorbell announced the arrival of the mail and Julie Stumbur stepped out on the stoop to retrieve the letters from the mail box. She shivered as she retreated to the warmth of her cosy kitchen.

"I feel sorry for anyone who has to work outdoors on a day like this. I'm glad you don't have to fight fires today."

"Let's hope the boys don't have any bad ones," her husband replied from behind the sports section of the Edmonton Journal. "This must be one of the weatherman's Siberian highs."

"You can't fault the weatherman when the weather comes," Julie laughed good-naturedly. "He was right in his predictions last night. Oh, here's a letter from Marie, a nice, fat one."

She slit the envelope with a knife and drew out the contents. Her face grew grave as she began to read. Without taking her eyes off the page she felt for her chair and lowered herself onto it. Her husband watched her for a few moments.

"Well, what does she say?" he asked, a tinge of impatience in his voice. Julie continued reading without comment until she had turned the final page.

"I love you more than ever. Your happy daughter, Marie." The letter ended. Julie's hand shook as she handed the sheaths of paper to her husband.

"Read that," she said uncertainly, "and see what you make of it."

Slowly and thoughtfully Arnold perused his daughter's neatly-penned communiqué. Then he laid the pages on the table and turned his face to the window. For a long time he sat gazing out at the swirling snow and pallid skies.

Julie cleared away the breakfast and turned to her typewriter. She rolled in a clean sheet of paper and pecked at the keys. Halfway down the page she paused, reread what she had written, and scrapped it. The second page followed the first one into the wastebasket. After a third attempt the anxious mother went into the basement to tackle the family wash. She was sorting the clothes when her husband came down the stairs.

"I'm going to start on the bookshelves I promised Ruth," he said as he turned into his workroom. Soon the shrill whine of the table saw sounded from behind the closed door, blending with the hum of the washing machine and the splish-splash of the clothes in the tub.

Conversation over soup and sandwiches at noon was sparse and inconsequential. Julie pushed aside her bowl and poured tea, accidentally spilling on the table cloth. She muttered under her breath and handed the cup to her husband.

"What do you think of Marie's letter, Arnold?" she asked abruptly. She studied his face for his reaction. He returned her gaze.

"Her letter really upset you, didn't it?"

"Oh, I don't know what to think." Julie patted a wisp of hair into place. She took a sip of tea and cleared her throat.

"I keep wondering..." She paused, running her index finger along the lip of her cup. "This new religion, could it be some sort of cult Marie has got herself involved with?"

"Oh no, Marie knows what she's doing. As she said, it makes sense." He pushed away his half-full cup.

"More tea?"

"No, thanks. I must get going. I have to get some more brackets from the lumber yard." He rose from the table. "Good thing the wind has died down. Any errands you would like me to do while I'm out?" Julie shook her head absently. Arnold put his hands on her shoulders.

"Like I said, don't fret about Marie. She knows what she's doing. It's a good thing, in fact. A real good thing." He planted a kiss on her brow and left the room.

Marie stood looking out of her bedroom window before retiring that night, thinking of her family. *Mom and Dad probably got my letter today,* she thought. Earnestly she prayed, "Oh God, help them to understand about You."

She pressed her face against the pane to get a wider view of the dark sky. The twinkle of the stars was subdued by the street light, but still they were there. *Like little pinpricks in the black canopy stretched over the world for the night,* Marie imagined, *with God's light shining through from the other side.* Bill had said that the Bible is studded with God's promises just like the stars in the sky. Each promise lets a little of God's light shine through, but we can only see that light with the eyes of our souls.

16

Touring the Ranch

The following Saturday Marie looked out on a world of dazzling white. The air was calm. The temperature, though dropping, was only two degrees below freezing. Fresh snow lay where it had fallen during the night, clothing the houses and trees in thick robes of picturesque beauty.

It's a good thing Oli left yesterday to spend the weekend with friends before this fresh snow came down, Marie thought. She wondered now if the snow would cause a cancellation of her own plans to return to the ranch. She was relieved therefore to see the truck pull up to the curb at the scheduled time.

At the ranch Marie accompanied William to the corrals to watch the execution of the regular chores. Peter's excitement knew no bounds as he explained to his teacher the activities taking place. When the feeding was finished the Cardinals guided Marie through the barn, tack room, and other outbuildings.

"If you are not afraid of the deep snow," William said, "I will show you the old house...that is, if you are still interested."

"No worry," Marie said, "I'm ready for the snow." They headed toward the old, log house nestled between a steep slope on one side and a clump of jack pine on the other. Marie tried to visualize life in the settlers' cabin about seventy-five years ago.

"When your grandpa built this honeymoon cabin he made it a real hideaway, didn't he?" she observed.

"My guess is that it was not a hideaway that Grandpa had in mind as much as shelter from the winds," her guide explained. Two ancient pine trees, standing like sentinels in front of the cabin, half hid the door from view. Gingerly making his way through the narrow space between their spreading boughs William pushed open the door behind, dislodging the snow on the roof as he did so. Marie did not hide her amusement as she watched it cascade down on top of him.

Hearing her laughter William scooped up a handful of snow and threw it at her. She dodged the soft snow and in so doing backed into the snow-laden pine behind her. Her laughter changed to a startled shriek as the loose snow on the branches descended, turning the joke on her.

The interior of the cabin seemed dark after the glittering brightness of the snow and sun. "Housewives had to contend with very little light in those days," Marie mused as she looked at the tiny, dingy windows.

"Yes. About the only part of the structure that didn't come off the land was the glass for the windows, so they used it sparingly. Besides, the idea was to keep the cold out as much as possible. Not only did the single sheets of glass let through the cold, but it was difficult to seal them in. The wind would find its way through the cracks around the frame."

"What did the settlers use to seal the cracks?" Marie asked. She examined the plaster that showed signs of once having been whitewashed, but now was cracked and grimy. In some areas it had fallen to the floor in a dirty pile.

"Mud," William answered. "Clay with some straw added for strength. This was mixed with water so it could be spread on the wall like icing. It was worked in between the logs both inside and out to make it as windproof as possible." He pointed out the bed frame built against the wall. "The mattress that went on top of this wooden structure was stuffed with straw. Later they raised chickens and Grandma made feather ticks, one to lay on top of the mattress and another one to cover with." He paused, allowing his eyes to rove around the interior of the ruins.

"One of our projects for next spring is to clear out all the old buildings on the property. I have left this old relic standing till now because it is a reminder to me of my heritage. It makes me feel grateful for this property, for the perseverance and courage of the pioneers, and for my Christian background."

"Both your parents and grandparents were Christians?"

"Yes. Whether Grandpa was a Christian before coming to Canada, I don't know. I am under the impression that he was. Do you remember me mentioning Rob and Marsha Smith?"

"The Smiths of the Drummond-Smith Estate?"

"Yes. They came west from Ontario about the same time Grandpa did and they were friends from the start. Grandpa was active in their Bible studies and church services."

"You mean this Smith was both preacher and rancher?"

"That's right. They owned the land along the lake. They came west, not so much to ranch as to establish a church and school for the homesteaders and ranchers. The land was their source of livelihood while they carried on their mission. Once the schoolhouse had been built and a teacher and preacher found to carry on regular services and classes the Smiths moved to a new area further north."

"That was a wonderful thing to do!" Marie exclaimed.

"It was. Many areas that opened up to settlers much earlier did not have a church or school till years later."

They were climbing the hill again when William remembered that he had not told Marie about his talk with Peter. "Peter explained the watch episode after I convinced him how important it was," he told Marie, "But it's weird, really weird."

Marie stopped. "What did happen?"

"According to Peter, he was riding in the pasture at dusk when he saw something dark in the distance. He took it for a stray steer that had been missed when we brought the cattle in for the winter. But when he got closer he saw it was a man. When the stranger saw Peter riding up he headed into the trees. As he ran Peter saw him drop something shiny."

"The watch?"

William nodded. "Peter called after the man, but whoever he was just called back that he could keep it if he promised not to tell where he got it. Apparently he threatened that something would happen to me if he told."

"Didn't Peter recognize the man?"

"No. Never saw him before. Of course, he didn't get a good look at him. The man made sure of that by staying under the trees."

"Do the police have no idea who it might have been?"

"No. I called them right away and they took Peter out to the pasture to show them the spot where he had picked up the watch but they found no further clues."

"Daddy, Miss Stumbur, dinner's ready," Peter called across the yard. At the sound of his voice the two turned their footsteps quickly toward the Charter house.

"So you took Marie to see your grandpa's old cabin," John said from his place at the head of the dinner table.

"Yes, I did. Not that there was much left to see. Since Marie is keenly interested in Canadian history I thought..."

"Reminds me of the time three years ago when I came here for a visit," John cut in, "and Beryl took me to see the old house my grandparents built."

"Were you not from this area?" Marie asked.

"No, my grandparents moved from here when my mother was eighteen. While I was attending university in Edmonton I decided to drive to Echo Valley one long weekend to see the place where my mother grew up."

"I was away from the Peace River area for the first time and missed my family and familiar surroundings more than a young fellow likes to admit. Listening to my classmates at the University of Alberta, many of them products of broken homes, I began to see how fortunate I was to have had a solid home life. I came to appreciate my family more. Not only my immediate family. My extended family, too. I became interested in Grandpa Smith's ministry. That was when I decided to visit the old homestead and the church he established here."

"You mean…" Marie started to say. William answered the question she left hanging.

"The Smiths I told you about were John's grandparents."

"Did that make you one of the owners of the ranch?"

"Not really. My mother was, but at that time the Drummond heirs were negotiating to buy out the Smiths. Bill's father had been managing the place, and done a good job, too. But he had other plans. He wanted to settle up the estate before moving on. I had no intentions of getting involved."

"When you came to see the place was that when you decided to come here to live?"

"It was meeting Beryl that brought him to that decision," William teased.

"Visiting the old ranch site was a turning point in my life alright," John spoke earnestly. "I understand my grandparents had a comfortable living out East. They gave it up to come west because they were concerned that children growing up on the new frontier should have a chance for a general education and Bible training. When I saw what had been the ranch home and church and heard stories related by some old-timers who remembered my grandparents I began to appreciate their dedication." John continued his reminiscing. "To think that they came with such high motives. When I attended the church in town which is the outgrowth of their work I resolved that I, too, wanted my life to count. So in that way it affected my future, but I still had no thought of leaving the Peace."

"Then how did you end up here?" Marie wondered.

"Will was right," John answered with a smile. "I was more interested in the girl that showed me around than in ranching. Interest in the ranch came after, sort of an added blessing." Beryl gave a cheery laugh as she laid her hand on John's large one.

"I'm glad you don't think of it the other way around, that you became interested in the ranch and got me thrown in on the deal."

Turning to Marie she explained. "You see, Dad was phasing out of the job, handing more and more of the responsibility of management over to Will. Will needed help."

"I couldn't let John take away the only help I had," her brother put in.

Beryl laughed again. "I'm glad you considered me worth hanging on to. In the process you got more help by taking John in." She poured the tea.

"I was just thinking I never went back to that spot since you showed me around the first time I was here," John recalled.

"Didn't you say the Smith buildings were right on the lake?" Marie asked. "Don't you swim down there?"

"We prefer a sheltered spot east of the buildings. There is a little bay there ideal for swimming."

"You know, I think we should go take a look at the buildings."

"Just for the sentiment of recalling the first time you showed me around?" John asked, shaking his head. "No, my Love, those buildings are ready to collapse."

"Next spring we'll give them a boost in that direction," Will agreed. "When Peter and I were looking for cattle along the lake I noticed the church roof already caved in on one corner."

"Can't we walk out there anyway, Daddy?" Peter coaxed.

"The snow is too deep, Son."

"I have an idea!" Beryl's eyes sparkled. "Why don't we all don skis and go for an outing down to the lake?" Her face sobered. "Actually, I'm not being sentimental. I have a different motive. Maybe we will pick up a clue to the cattle rustling."

"Let's Daddy! Let's go skiing," Peter pleaded. William looked at Marie for her opinion.

"I have not had skies on my feet in years," she confessed, "And I have no skis."

"I am sure we have an old pair around here that you could use," Beryl volunteered. "It won't take you long to get back into it."

"Peter knows who to turn to for support when he wants to go skiing," John laughed. "Beryl is as enthusiastic about skiing as Peter is."

"If the snow is too sticky we can always turn back," Beryl argued.

"Okay," John nodded, "But as for clues, if we didn't notice anything earlier, we are not likely to find any clues under a foot of snow."

Once the decision was made to cross-country ski John brought out the skiing equipment.

Don't bother looking for any old ones," William told him. "I have a pair at my house Marie can use."

He turned to Marie. "Let's head over there right now. Then you can have a little time to try out the skis before we take off across the pasture."

Marie sat down on the bench in the Charter's roomy back porch while her host brought out the skis. As he crouched down to strap them to her boots she wondered at his willingness to loan her the skiing equipment that had obviously belonged to his wife.

"But are you sure you don't mind?" she asked hesitantly, "I mean, me using these?"

"I don't if you don't," was all he said on the subject. Will went on to explain the techniques of cross-country skiing. She was glad William was there, she realized. Somehow his presence no longer made her feel ill at ease. Marie tried out her new feet, cautiously at first, but with William's gentle encouragement she soon pushed ahead with long confident strokes.

Peter soon showed up for his skis and the three started on their way toward the lake. As they passed the Charter house William whistled to let Beryl and John know they were heading out.

"No need to wait for them," he explained to Marie. "They will soon outstrip us."

The temperature had fallen, making the snow ideal for skiing. As William had predicted, his sister and her husband soon left them far behind. Peter kept between his father and his teacher, looking with pleasure from one face to the other as the conversation flowed between them. He threw in his own comments from time to time.

"Look, Dad, they're going past the buildings," he said now.

"They probably plan to circle the lake," his father commented as he watched the two experienced skiers skirt the old yard site and continue along the shoreline. "There is nothing left to explore anyway."

As they neared the buildings William indicated to Marie to stop. Waving his ski pole toward the decaying shells he said, "Next spring all this will give way to a new dream."

"What do you mean, Bill?"

"We are starting a new project, Beryl and John and I and my mom and dad are going to help, too. This is something we have mentioned to very few people." He went on to explain.

"For years various people and organizations approached my dad about developing this beach. Some offered to buy it. Others hoped it would be turned into public property. The nicest stretch of sandy shore anywhere on this lake is on our property. But Dad had reservations about allowing this spot to be turned into a commercial recreation spot."

"But you have definite plans for developing it now?"

"For developing this spot, yes. For a commercial recreational centre, no." His eyes scanned the snow-covered landscape. "I thought this place should be something special. Something more than a watering hole for our cattle, but nothing definite came to mind. Then Deedee came up with the perfect answer." In reply to the question in Marie's eyes, he continued. "I told you of the woman Deedee was. Always concerned about people with problems, she visualized a place where troubled individuals could come for help. Whether someone wanted a place to be alone, maybe to study or write, or just to relax. Whether couples were looking for a Christian environment for a family holiday or just wanted to get away by themselves to work out their problems. This will be a place to make new friends or hold reunions. There will be sports, crafts, singing, different events for those who want them. We are thinking of special seminars and workshops, sessions in photography or painting or whatever the interest is. But it should always be a place where people can meet God."

"Like your place already was for Marc and for me," Marie said softly. "Oh, Bill, this is a marvellous idea!" Encouraged by Marie's enthusiasm William continued to reveal what was on his heart.

"One day when Deedee rode out to check on the cattle, she stopped her horse right here and suddenly she realized something of the potential for this place. The herd faded from her thoughts, as in her mind's eye she saw hordes of hurting and lonesome men and women coming from all across the land to find here the healing, the relief, the victory for which they longed. When she shared her vision with me I recognized it at once as the answer to what to do with this beach." Cardinal paused, a faraway look in his eyes.

"The idea seemed so vast it scared me at first. As we discussed the plan, however, it seemed to crystallize in our minds. We have stood at this spot many times and prayed for God to guide us."

"A place where troubled people can find someone who will lend an understanding ear, someone who will pray with them and council them," Marie spoke in awe. "Oh Bill, this is wonderful."

William raised his arm and pointed out the buildings as if they were already there. "A family-style dining room and chapel. That building will also house a recreation room, fireside room with a piano, prayer rooms, counselling rooms with qualified counsellors on hand." He made a wide sweep with his arm. "Cabins under the trees and a trailer court." William paused. When he spoke again it was with deep feeling in his voice. "When Deedee went to be with the Lord, well, I determined not to let our dream die. We're going ahead on the first stage of the project as we had planned. Although..." His voice faded. "Although without Deedee I don't know how we'll manage," he finished weakly. As Cardinal unfolded the dream to Marie she listened quietly, carried along with his deep rooted conviction and enthusiasm.

"What a plan," she said at last. "What a potential. It seems so appropriate, so right, that the land where the first church in the community was established should become the site for an extended ministry for helping people. I can see it now." Her eyes scanned the snow-clad beach.

"There are so many hurting people: pregnant girls needing sound advice or just a chance to make up their own minds about the baby, couples on the verge of breaking up, women who are rejected and abused. Or just busy people wanting to get away to a quiet place." She turned to face the man beside her. "What are you going to call it?"

William smiled. "I am thinking of *Rest Awhile Resort*. I got that idea from Jesus' words to His disciples, 'Come ye yourselves apart and rest awhile.' I plan to put those words on a large sign." With his index finger he traced the letters on the imaginary billboard as he spoke, underlining the last two words.

They stood in silence after that, envisioning the future of this site.

"Would it be alright," Marie began self-consciously, "I mean, could we pray about it now? I want to learn to pray with others like you told me to last week."

"Marie, there's a good suggestion." Together they bowed their heads and said a brief prayer for God to bless this project.

17

SLAUGHTER IN CHURCH

"Daddy!"

While William had been revealing his plans to his interested companion Peter had wondered off to explore on his own. He was standing now at the door of what was once the church.

"Daddy," he shouted again. "I can't get this door open."

"The snow is piled against it," William called back, "But we don't want to go inside anyway."

"I can push away the snow," Peter said, "It's this lariat." Even before William heard his son's words he saw the nylon rope tied to the makeshift latch. He skied quickly to Peter's side. Deftly he unknotted the short end of rope and examined it.

"This is new rope," he said. "Why would anyone tie shut a crumbling old building."

Cautiously he stepped over the decaying threshold with Peter and Marie close behind. The sun was sinking toward the west, allowing little light to filter through the small openings that had once been windows.

"What's that?" Peter asked, pointing to the floor at her feet. Marie looked down and gasped.

"It looks like blood," she said uncertainly. She bent lower. "Yes, it's blood. Old blood mingled with dirt and frozen to the floor. Maybe some wild animal..."

She looked around for an explanation, but saw nothing else except the pile of rotten logs and dirt in the corner where the roof had caved in. Turning to her host who was examining a scrap of brown paper he had picked up inside the door, she asked, "Bill, what happened here?"

The rancher tucked the bit of paper carefully into an inside pocket before joining Marie and Peter at the support post in the centre of the building. A low whistle escaped through his teeth at sight of the gory mess.

"Yoo-hoo!" Beryl's voice rang out through the clear air. William stepped outside to see the pair coming quickly along the shoreline.

"In here," he called to them, beckoning with his arm, "We thought you two were heading around the lake."

"We went to see what was sticking out of the snow back there," John explained as they drew closer. "Looks like someone built a makeshift wharf just behind those trees. Better come take a look, Will, and see if you can figure out what it's all about."

"I think we have the answer right here," his partner replied. "Come see this and you'll know what I mean." The rickety old door groaned on its leather hinges as William forced it back further to allow more light. He indicated for the couple to walk through.

Beryl stepped through the opening and bent down to look closely at the area of floor Peter eagerly pointed out, muttering as she did so, "Of all things! Who would have thought it, right here on our own property." John crouched down beside her, silently taking in the scene. Then raising himself he reached up to test the strength of the crossbeam above his head by pulling the rope that dangled from it.

"This is new rope," he observed.

"And that's a new two-by-four nailed to the rafters to hold the weight," William added. The two men stood facing each other, their looks of surprised shock hardly distinguishable in the deepening shadows. Peter had been quietly watching the adult's reaction to his discovery, waiting for some clarification. When he could no longer contain his curiosity he made his way to his father's side.

"Daddy, what happened?" he asked in a mystified tone of voice. He tugged at William's sleeve. "Where did all the blood come from, Daddy?"

"Someone has been using this place for a butcher shop. Now we know why we did not notice the rustlers," William explained. "We were watching for trucks. Instead the cattle were slaughtered right here and the meat was taken across the lake by boat."

"Whoo!" Peter whooped, "Just like a TV story, isn't it, Daddy? Are we going to catch the bad guys?"

"We're going home to call the police right now. Let's go." Without hesitation the little group turned their skis homeward. Beryl suddenly broke the silence.

"I don't understand how anyone could do something like that and think their crime would not be discovered."

"Whoever it was thought he was covering his tracks. No remains were left outside the buildings as far as we noticed. He stayed away from our wharf and I'm sure the one he constructed was well hidden from sight as long as the leaves were on the trees," John deduced. "We never entered the building in the summertime. Who would expect that we would go snooping around in a foot of snow?"

"Why did we?" Everyone looked at the taller man as he repeated his question. "Why did we? Doesn't it seem more than coincidental that we should have decided to visit the dilapidated buildings today when we have not gone into them for years?"

"If it's not coincidental," Beryl said, "Then it must be providential. Is that what you mean, Will?"

"Yes. I believe God put that thought into our heads in answer to our prayers. We wanted to know what happened to our cattle. Now we know."

"We still don't know who did it," Beryl said practically.

"We're on our way to finding out though," John assured her. "With all that evidence, the RCMP should have the rustlers nailed down in no time."

"To think that the place where the pioneers learned about God should be turned into a scene of crime," Marie mused. "It reminds me of a song we sang in church on Sunday. I can only remember one line: 'Where every aspect pleases and only man is vile.' Something like that."

Beryl began to sing the old hymn with feeling and the rest joined in, singing the words they knew, humming the rest.

"I have a beef stew in the oven. You might as well come in for supper," Beryl invited as they neared her house. "You can call the police from here, Brother." William turned to Marie.

"What do you say? Beryl's stews are too tantalizing to turn down."

Marie needed no coaxing. The outing had given her a hearty appetite and she accepted readily.

They were finishing the meal when the patrol car wound its way along the driveway.

"The police," Peter said, the colour draining from his face. William laid a hand on his son's shoulder.

"It's alright, Pete," he said reassuringly. "He's coming because I called him."

Peter forced a weak smile. "I know. I just..."

Marie watched the little incident and felt for her little pupil. She wished she could take him in her arms and make him forget that dreadful day last May when Constable Richards brought the tidings of the double tragedy. At the same time her admiration went out to the man who now tousled his son's hair.

"We want to catch the bad guys, remember?"

John met the officer at the door while Beryl pulled up a chair and set a place for him. He accepted the proffered chair, but waved aside the stew and biscuits.

"No, thank you. I'll be off duty in an hour and my wife will have supper waiting for me," he explained. "Besides, I want to get down to business."

William pulled the dirtied slip of paper from his pocket. "A piece of manila envelope," he said, handing it to Todd. "It was on the floor of the old building where we found the evidence of the butchering."

Todd Richards studied the only distinguishable letters on the envelope: *laus Nic.* His eyebrows lifted and his thick lips parted to form a round O as the significance of the clue dawned on him. Without a word he tucked it into his case and wrote something in his ever-ready notebook. After questioning each one about their observations, the officer rose to go.

"We'll be back tomorrow to check the site by daylight," he promised. "Nothing is likely to change overnight."

"The snow is fairly deep. We'll drive you to the place with the truck," William offered.

"Thanks. I'll be here about ten. There is no need to rush. The operation is obviously shut down for the winter anyway with the lake frozen over and the cattle in the stalls. Good Night."

Soon Marie, too, was on her way home, with William in the driver's seat.

"The Charters must be entertaining tonight. The lights are usually out long before this," Marie commented as William eased the car to a stop at the front gate. The atmosphere that greeted Marie as she entered the house, however, was anything but festive.

She paused just inside the door for a moment when a stifled sob reached her ears. She glanced toward the living room to see her landlady sitting upright on the edge of the chesterfield, dabbing at her teary eyes with a crumpled tissue. Crouched in a recliner nearby was the banker.

Not wanting to appear indifferent to any calamity that might have overtaken the woman Marie walked hesitantly into the living room. Relief swept over her at the sight of Stewart on his favourite rocker in the corner. *At least, he has not had a heart attack or anything like that,* she thought. She smiled sympathetically at the couple.

"Good Evening," she greeted them all.

"Good Evening," the banker said in a flat voice.

Marie joined her landlady on the chesterfield and studied the faces in the room.

"Have you had bad news?" she finally asked of the distraught woman beside her. Anna merely nodded, managing a smile.

"I am sorry. Is there anything I can do to help?" she asked sincerely.

Suddenly Anna found her voice. "Why do you spend so much time with that Indian?"

"What? I am afraid I don't understand." She tried to direct the conversation away from the widower and her present embarrassment. "I was visiting the Carpenter house today. We went cross-country skiing to the lake. They told me about John's grandparents, the Smiths." When no one made a comment, she rambled on in an attempt to relieve the tense situation.

"They came here to establish a school and church. Actually, one building served for both at first. You know, like they did in the early years. I found it interesting to see the place where the pioneer families studied and worshipped."

"What did you see?" Burton asked, sitting forward in his chair.

"Not much left to see." Marie waved her hand casually. "What made it meaningful was just that this was the spot where the first missionaries lived. That, and Mr. Cardinal's dream for the future." She checked herself before saying more. Careful to avoid mentioning the clues to the missing cattle, Marie had almost blundered into revealing the plans William had confided to her.

Stewart cleared his throat and flicked the pages of the local weekly to which he was devoting his attention. "It says here cold weather is coming," he said.

Thankful for the change of subject Marie leaned back and let out her breath slowly. Then she suddenly remembered that she had not heard her landlady's tear-jerking news. In fact, Anna herself seemed to have forgotten it in her disgust over Marie's friendship with the ranchers. Marie chided herself for her confusion. Here she trying to say something to justify her day at the Double C, instead of finding out what the sad news was.

"The news you heard today, Anna, do you want to tell me about it?"

Anna waved her slender hand at Burton. "You tell her."

"I just informed them that I will be leaving in a week's time," Burton smiled patronizingly. Marie's first reaction was surprise. The next moment she wanted to throw back her head and laugh. Instead she tried to think of something appropriate to say. She asked the first question that popped into her head.

"How long have you been at your job, Burton?"

"Two years."

"Your move must be a promotion, I am sure. Let me congratulate you." She rose and extended her hand. Burton eased himself out of the easy chair and shook her hand heartily.

"I will be managing a bigger branch in Edmonton," he informed her.

"I am sure that branch is getting a good manager," she complimented him. *I can say that honestly,* she told herself. *He seems to pay attention to his work.* They chatted for a few more moments and then Marie said goodnight.

"What a day this has been!" she breathed in a half-whisper as she entered her room, hoping Oli would hurry back. She had so much to tell her. Then remembering Burton's upcoming departure, she threw herself on her bed, buried her head in her pillow, and laughed.

18

FIRE AT DAWN

The clock radio roused William from a sound sleep on Sunday morning. He was glad this was Sunday, the one day out of seven when he could break from his regular routine to spend time in physical relaxation and spiritual refreshment. The Lord's Day, as he preferred to call it, had always been a special time for Deedee and himself. With a yawn he rolled over in his queen-sized bed and stretched out his arms. How big the bed seemed, and how empty! A wave of loneliness swept over the young widower at the memory of the good times he had shared with Deedee.

Determined not to give way to the feelings threatening to engulf him he rubbed his eyes and sat up, flinging his legs over the edge of the bed. From force of habit his eyes turned to a plague on the wall. *Lo, I am with you always, even unto the end of the world,* the verse read. He quoted aloud the familiar words that had so often comforted him in recent months, thanking God again for His unfailing presence.

Before heading for the corrals William stepped into his son's room. Peter lay curled up on his pillow, his hands tucked under his head. Gently William moved him around and pulled his blanket over him, dropping a kiss on his brow. For a moment he paused beside the bed, praying again for his son, so small for his six years, yet so full of life.

As the rancher opened the door to the outside he was greeted by the smell of burning wood. Smoke hung heavy in the air. To the east he saw flames leaping upward. In their eerie brightness he discerned the outline of what had once been the cedar-log church. The next moment a column of black smoke blocked out the scene as the structure collapsed. Then ugly flames leaped up again like monstrous fingers reaching for the nearby trees. In an instant William sprang into action. With a prayer for help on his lips he rushed into the house to rouse John and Beryl. John was awakened by the ring of the telephone. Through the bedroom window he detected the red reflection against the sky as soon as he opened his eyes.

"Answer the phone, Honey," he shouted as he launched for his trousers. "Fire!"

Beryl's hand shook as she lifted the receiver. Quickly she offered to take any further calls and to look after Peter. John hurried from the house, grabbing his parka from the closet as he rushed through the back porch. He pulled it over his bare torso as he ran.

As William flung himself out of the door he saw John head for the four-wheel-drive truck to break trail to the scene of the fire.

"I'll bring the ice saw," William shouted to him, pointing toward the tool shed. John must have understood his actions if not his words and honked the horn in reply as he drove from the yard.

Beryl's first phone call was to the Bruce residence. The ranch hand answered on the first ring. Beryl's message was brief.

"Joe. Fire on the lake shore. Come at once."

"Aw, those good for nothing buildings," Joe said indifferently. "Bill was goin..."

"Joe, the timber," Beryl interrupted, "Hurry."

"Oh, I never thought of that," he replied, but Beryl had already dropped the receiver into its cradle.

After dialling for the nearest police and fire department, Beryl called Dick Taylor at the store to arouse any one in Echo Valley who could help. Then she turned to the kitchen to prepare coffee and sandwiches for the volunteers roused from their warm beds. From her window she watched Echo Valley's little fire engine follow John's ruts in the snow. More vehicles soon followed. They had seen the angry flames licking the sky and were now driving out to assist in whatever way they could.

Beryl took more bread from the freezer and made more sandwiches. She was closing the lid on the large picnic hamper full of foodstuff when she saw the truck roll up to the door.

"How is everything going?" she asked anxiously as John came through the door, his face and clothes smudged with soot. He shook his head.

"The trees caught before the fireman got there," he said through dry lips.

"Thank God for the snow. At least the fire can't spread along the ground. Wherever the trees are close enough together the flames leap from one to the other." He reached for the glass of water Beryl was holding out to him.

"Those spruce burn like kindling. I came for the tractor and power saw. We'll try to cut down the trees where they are sparse to make a firebreak." He downed the water.

"I'm glad you thought of whipping up something for the men to eat." John touched her cheek lovingly and dashed from the house with a sandwich in his hand. Beryl turned to the mirror, rubbing the sooty spot he had left on her face. The telephone rang.

"Probably Peter! I forgot about him," Beryl said suddenly as she reached for the phone. "Hello. Oh, yes. Get dressed and come over here for breakfast." She saw Peter coming toward her as she loaded the food into the truck John had left.

"You'll have to eat your breakfast on the way," she called. "Jump in quick."

As she guided the truck across the pasture she heard the fire engines approaching. Through the smoky air arose an answering cheer from the volunteers at the fire.

Beryl honked the horn to announce that food and drink were on hand. One by one the grateful men made their way to the truck, eager for a drink to slacken their thirst. Their bloodshot eyes were rimmed with soot, their voices harsh from the irritation of the smoke, while drops of perspiration drew little lines down their grimy cheeks. They reached for the food and drink with numb fingers and gulped it down hurriedly.

Beryl stayed on the site, pouring coffee whenever someone paused for a few minutes. Peter handed out sandwiches and cookies. Although Beryl had filled every thermos jug and every other suitable container in the house she was draining the last cup from the large urn when Peter said, "The sandwiches are gone, Auntie."

Beryl glanced into the hamper. "Give out those last cookies. Then we'll go home for more." This proved unnecessary as at that moment several vehicles pulled up. New reinforcements rushed over to the fire chief to find out what they could do to help. Meanwhile, several women, including Marie, joined Beryl and Peter, each with a box of lunch and hot drinks.

"Like manna from heaven," Beryl called out. "What a relief!"

"It's the least we could do," Mrs. Taylor assured her. She went back to the truck for a box of men's winter mittens. "Dick brought these from the store. Thought the men's mitts would be soaked and stiff by this time."

"How thoughtful! Remember to thank him for us," Beryl said. Gratefully the men exchanged their frozen mitts for a new pair when they came for a drink.

Through the smoke Beryl saw John emerge from the trees and walk toward her with fast strides. He looked around at the little group, his tired face relaxing into a smile of gratitude.

"Thanks, all of you."

"How does it look, John?" one of the ladies asked, "Are you gaining or losing?"

"I say we're gaining. We picked a path where the trees were scarce and removed them." John pointed to the fire engine circling around the burning trees. "They are starting to move into the cleared area now. Attacking the fire from both sides," John explained between gulps of coffee. He put his hand on Peter's shoulder.

"Could you throw some feed to the cattle when you get time?"

"Sure, Uncle."

"I'll help," Marie volunteered.

"Some more of us can go with you if we can be of help," Mrs. Taylor suggested, "While the rest look after things here."

"Your daddy is heading up the tree cutting," John told his nephew in answer to the question in the boy's eyes. "He will come for a drink as soon as I get back." With that he rushed away and was swallowed up by the smoke.

William and his hired man converged on the site together, each with a handkerchief tied over his face. The owner nodded a greeting to everyone in general, his anxious eyes locking with Marie's for a moment as he wearily lowered himself onto one of the straw bales the women had thrown on the snow for seats. Wrapping one arm around Peter who bounced to his side, William reached for a cup with the other.

Joe Bruce remained standing, saying nothing as he pulled off his makeshift mask and gulped down his coffee and sandwiches. His face was drawn, his eyes glazed with anxiety. Without a word he turned and disappeared again behind the haze of smoke and water spray.

"Peter and I are going home now to feed the stock," Beryl told her brother, "We're taking help along. Then we'll cook up a hot meal for whoever will still be around.

"Thanks. This will be licked soon, I hope," William replied, waving his arm toward the fire scene.

"Thank God," Mrs. Baxter breathed. Turning to Beryl she added, "I know you must all be feeling anxious. Can we help by going for more food?"

The sun was lowering in the west by the time the fire fighters began to disperse. Only a few volunteers remained on the scene to keep watch in case of any fresh outbreak. Will was standing alone in the lingering shadows, surveying the blackened area before him when the fire chief walked up.

"You did a remarkable job of cutting a firebreak in record time," he said. "If the fire had managed to get into that dense growth it would have been beyond our control."

"Thank God for all the help we had," William said sincerely. "And the fact that there was a strip that had only a few large trees. At one time that must have been a firebreak to protect the buildings in case of a forest fire."

The fire chief gave a little laugh. "It worked in reverse this time. It protected the forest from the burning buildings."

Caught up in the tension and mystery, Peter listened intently to the conversation of the adults around the supper table that evening. When William was getting on his wraps to drive Marie back to Echo Valley, Peter tugged at his sleeve.

"Daddy, can I go along, please?"

"You have stayed up too long now, Son, but I suppose a few minutes more won't make that much difference. Okay, get ready."

William saw Marie to the door and chatted briefly with Anna who sat in her rocker, knitting an afghan. When he returned to the truck, he found Peter crouching on the floor, his face buried in his arms. William tugged at his son's cap teasingly.

"Whatever are you doing down there?" he asked. Peter looked up with eyes wide open.

"I saw him, Daddy, and I didn't want him to see me."

"Saw whom, Peter?"

"The man that gave me the watch. He was coming along the sidewalk."

19

REACTIONS

On Monday morning Marie's classroom buzzed with talk of the fire. Peter, looking ill at ease, did his best to field the questions of his curious classmates.

"How did the fire start?" a wide-eyed Sally Knott wanted to know.

"I don't know," Peter answered quietly.

"Well, it couldn't just start by itself," his classmate persisted. Randy Taylor, who had picked up the comments of the early morning customers at his parents' general store, elaborated.

"Someone must sure hate your dad so he started the fire."

"No. It were no one else," Mitchell spoke for the first time from his seat at the back of the room. "Indians start their own fires."

Marie felt relief at the sound of the school bell. "Take your seats quickly," she said, eager to terminate the discussion. She stood to face the class with a lack of enthusiasm, drained of energy and angry at the insinuations she had overheard.

Marie considered talking about the fire, then decided to shelf the idea. By the time she had taught a lesson in counting to the first grade and multiplication to the second class, her mind was made up.

"Everyone, put away your books," she announced toward the end of the class period, "and gather in our story corner."

Desks were swept clear of books and pencils almost instantaneously. Eighteen eager youngsters rushed to their favourite spot. When they were all gathered in a circle Marie placed a tiny chair next to Peter's and sat down.

"You all know about the fire at the lake shore yesterday," she began. She told how shocked the owners had been, how hard the fire fighters had worked to put out the flames and how serious the loss would have been if the fire had gone unchecked. She mentioned how kind and helpful the people of the community had been, including the parents of many of them.

"You have heard people express different ideas about the fire, but remember, they are only guessing at how it started. The police are trying to find out what caused it. Until they find the answer let's not talk about it any more. To repeat stories we hear is to spread gossip," she ended.

"Now we have something good to talk about. Christmas is coming." Marie had time only to mention the subject before the bell sounded, but it was enough to divert the conversation away from the fire. During the recess break that followed the children talked excitedly about subjects like decorations and gift exchanges that the word Christmas had conjured up in their minds.

Relaxing in front of the television set in the Charters' living room that evening Marie wondered why she had felt such compulsion to squelch all talk about the fire. Defending her motherless pupil from further hurt was important to her, she admitted, but there was something more.

Arson, Marie was sure, but who? Why? Did anyone know of the discovery made by the ranchers and herself? The whole thing loomed so sinister, so repulsive: the slaughtering of the cattle, the theft of Mr. Nicole's valuables, the attempt to involve an innocent child. She was sickened by the ugliness of it all.

Burton ambled into the living room. He acknowledged Marie with a slight nod and settled into an easy chair, his attention drawn to the hockey game on the television. After a few minutes he turned to Marie, as if he had just thought of something to say.

"I hear there was a fire on the Indian's ranch yesterday."

"I would have expected everyone had heard about it before now," Marie replied.

The banker lit a cigarette and turned his eyes back to the screen as if the subject of the fire was of little concern to him. The thought came to Marie that Burton had not put in an appearance at the scene, although as far as she knew he had been in town all weekend.

He may have been busy packing for his move, she told herself, *but why had he not heard about it like everyone else?*

Some time later Burton crushed his half-smoked cigarette in the ashtray and, without looking at Marie, asked, "Any clues yet on how it happened?"

Then in the next breath, "Oh, look at that play!" His attention was back on the hockey game. Marie remained silent, her eyes on the screen.

Finally Burton asked again, "Did you say if there's any clue?"

"I have not heard whether the police have found any clues."

Burton seemed not to hear her reply. He was watching the game, emitting short exclamations as the puck was passed from player to player.

"So they have no clues," he said at length. "I have heard of fires being started by the sun reflecting off broken glass. Could be something like that." He glanced at his watch, yawned, and stood up to stretch.

"Supper must be about ready," he said. He turned toward the dining room where Anna was setting the table. "It was kind of you to invite me again tonight," he told her.

"Oh, we're glad to have you eat with us," the hostess beamed. "We're so sorry that you're going soon."

Olivia tripped into the living room. Settling herself in the armchair she idly picked up a brochure Burton had dropped.

"Fly with the sunshine to Brazil," she read aloud from the cover of the leaflet. "Brazil! Now, that would be an interesting place to go. Maybe Grant and I should consider that for our honeymoon spot," she joked.

Her musing was cut short by Mrs. Charter's announcement that supper was ready.

"Having Burton for supper seems to have become standard procedure around here," Marie complained in a low voice as she and Olivia mounted the stairs together after the meal.

"No need to worry, my friend." Her dark-haired companion held up four fingers. "Only four days left till he moves out."

"You remind me of my first graders on the first day of school. Ask them a question and up come the fingers." Marie gave a short laugh. "But you are right, Oli. Four days is not so bad, taken one at a time."

"I know what you mean, though." Olivia followed Marie into her room at the head of the stairs. "And it's almost as bad when he is not there. Then we listen to, 'Burton this and Burton that.'" She hoisted herself onto the desk and sat swinging her legs. "He really has that woman brainwashed." Her face brightened.

"I'll tell you what, Marie! Why don't we go out for supper one day this week?"

"Sounds great," Marie responded. "Whether there is a Burton Greenfield to avoid or not, I could go for a relaxing time out." She sat down on the bed and kicked off her shoes.

"I guess I have been letting him get to me lately. Especially today. Telling me he heard about the fire at, of all places, 'the Indians' ranch.' As if they are nameless people. Then he suggested that it could have been caused by the sun shining on glass. I wanted to snap at him, remind him that the fire broke out before dawn. I bit my tongue instead. It is not kind of me to feel like that."

"You have a right to your feelings," her friend consoled. Marie shook her head.

"I read something about that just last week. The article said we are not responsible for the annoying actions of others. But we are responsible for our reactions to them. I do not need to let him bother me."

"That's expecting a lot of yourself, Marie. To remain unruffled no matter what others do to you. Do you think that's being realistic?"

"In my own resolve it would be impossible. But, remember, I told you how Christ's Spirit comes to live in a person who accepts Him. Well, it's His power that can keep us calm. We can depend on Him instead of letting ourselves get uptight."

Olivia slid off the desk. "I guess I better go. I want to make some phone calls before I go out. I'm going to Nancy's place tonight. She's having a few friends over and she asked me to come." At the door she turned around. "About that meal out, why don't we make it even better? How would you like to go to Calgary instead of Sundre? We could leave right after school."

"Oh, Oli, what a great idea! We'll do that." Marie jumped up and threw her arms around Olivia. "It's been so long since we've been away from this place."

"We need to break out of our rut," Olivia agreed. "We'll work out our plans later. Got to go now."

20

Unexpected Encounter

The hostess led Olivia and Marie to a little table in a far corner of the restaurant. Marie looked around with obvious pleasure as she pulled out a chair and sat down.

"I am so glad you thought of coming here, Oli," she enthused. "Just look at that view!"

Olivia laughed. "Want to know how I found this spot? I checked the Calgary yellow pages by the hall phone. I was looking under 'Motels' for a place to stay and I noticed the number for Riverside Motel encircled in red. I decided somebody must like the place. Underneath someone had written, 'Close to Chow's Place.' So I phoned it, too."

"You were lucky, Oli. This is a lovely place to eat."

"How do you know, Marie? You haven't eaten yet."

"Oh, I know I am going to enjoy my meal in this attractive atmosphere. I expect to enjoy the whole weekend, in fact. I am glad we decided to come to Calgary for a change."

"So am I," Olivia agreed. "And I am glad we decided to stay till Sunday. I want to show you some good shops tomorrow."

"And we'll forget about everything else and have a real holiday," Marie added.

"Right. We won't think of anything connected with Echo Valley, not about Mrs. Grimm, or Nikolaus Nicole, or any problems with the kids at school, or the fire, or Burton Greenfield, or..."

"Especially Burton Greenfield," Marie interjected.

They both laughed. Like youngsters let out of school, they were determined to make the most of their weekend in the city.

When the waitress had taken their orders Marie excused herself. In the hallway leading to the ladies room she passed a door that was partly open. It was marked *Private*. Just inside she caught a glimpse of a man in white talking to someone in a plaid jacket.

I thought that flashy topper of Burton's was one-of-a-kind. Obviously, the manufacturer was successful at selling at least two of those outlandish jackets, Marie smiled to herself. A big woman coming toward her apparently thought the smile was intended for her and acknowledged it with a pleasant nod.

As Marie neared the office door again on her return a familiar voice floated out to her. She stopped instinctively.

"I told you I can't bring any more meat," the voice was saying. "Just pay me for the last order so I can go."

"Yes, yes, I pay," came the reply. "But why you bring no more meat?"

Marie turned on her heel and fled back to the washroom. As the heavy door closed behind her she leaned her back against it and put her hands over her face. They felt cold to her burning cheeks.

"Oh, you...you...you...," she muttered through clinched teeth, then fell silent. She could not think of an appropriate name for the man she had overheard.

Someone pushed against the door and Marie quickly moved to a sink. She turned on the cold water tap as another patron entered. Marie washed her face, praying inwardly for God to calm her spirit. When she felt more composed she contemplated returning to her table.

I can't walk past that office door and risk being seen, she decided. *I will slip out a back door and make my way around the building.*

Cautiously she opened the washroom door and peered down the hall. All was clear. And yes, there was an exit light at the end of the long passageway. Clutching her purse under one arm, she made a dash for the fire escape door. It opened easily to her push. She stepped out and quickly closed it behind her, breathing a sigh of relief as she turned around.

Only then did she see the red Ferrari parked in the alley directly in front of her. Getting in behind the wheel was Burton. Marie stood rooted to the spot momentarily, the blood draining from her face. Then she whirled around and grasped for the door before she remembered that fire exits are not equipped with outside doorknobs.

The car was facing toward a side street so Marie turned in the opposite direction, running along the wall of the building, her boots sinking into the snow. Without a backward glance, she dipped into the tight space between the buildings.

A cold wind whistled through the narrow confines, chilling her coatless body. As she edged along the space between the tall structures her dress caught and snagged on the rough concrete walls. At the front street she peered around the corner stealthily before stepping out onto the sidewalk. She paused again outside the main door to brush off the snow. Below zero temperatures and fear of being spotted by the culprit, however, soon drove her inside.

The waitress was placing two seafood and salad dinners on the table as Marie approached. Olivia looked up, startled to see Marie's shivering form.

"Marie, what happened? What..."

"We're getting out of here!" Marie said through chattering teeth. She grabbed her coat from the chair and draped it over her arm. "Hurry, Oli!" Olivia's eyes shifted from Marie's shocked face to the inviting dinner before her, then back to Marie.

"Do we have to leave? Can't you sit down and tell me what happened?" She stood up and put a consoling arm around her friend's shaking shoulders. "Did someone attack you?"

"No, no. Nothing like that."

"Our table is secluded here. This is a pretty good place to talk," Olivia suggested. Marie looked around at the empty tables nearby.

"I guess we might as well," she conceded. "He's gone now anyway." She slipped into the chair. "I just wanted to get as far away from him as I could."

"Then there was someone?"

"Burton."

"Burton? Here?" Olivia gasped in surprise. "You mean he followed us here?" She started to laugh, but the laugh died on her lips as she looked at Marie's distraught face.

"Burton?" she asked again. "What did he do? It would take more than just seeing him to get you this upset. What happened?" Marie blurted out the story.

"Oh, Marie, you have stumbled onto the answer!" the would-be sleuth said when Marie finished, "At least, part of it. Who would have guessed that Burton..." She paused as the waitress came to offer them coffee. Then she asked, "Well, what are we going to do now?"

Marie considered the question. "I would like to make a phone call right away." The waitress returned, leaning across the table to add a few more sugar packages to the already-full sugar bowl.

"Who do you want to call?" Olivia asked as soon as the girl had gone. "The police?"

"Don't you think we should talk to Bill first?"

"I should have guessed that was your intention," Olivia said. A sly grin began tugging at her mouth. "Maybe we can find out something more on our own. Burton doesn't know we're onto him so he's not likely to disappear. Just think, Marie, the criminal we've been trying to trace has been living under the same roof with us all this time and we never even suspected him." Olivia spoke in a low voice, but her excitement shone in her eyes. "But at least, you have redeemed yourself by catching him in the end."

"Pure coincidence."

"Boy, I wish I would happen to be with you when you incidentally stumble onto your discoveries. I'm the one always wanting to be the detective and you end up being the one that finds the clues." A new thought came to her. "Marie, why don't we talk to the chef? We can find out if he was partner in crime with Burton or innocent victim."

Marie hesitated. "What if we arouse suspicion? We could foul things up for the police."

"Oh, we'll be tactful. We are bound to get some fresh information. Come on, Marie. This is our chance."

The waitress came again to ask if they were enjoying their meal. As soon as she had left they laid their plans. By the time they made their appearance at the kitchen door a feeling of excitement had overpowered Marie's earlier apprehension.

"We'd like to talk to the chef," she said to the youth turning steaks at the barbecue pit.

"Samuel Chow? He's having supper right now. In the restaurant." He pointed over the counter with his long fork while keeping his eyes on the sizzling meat. The chef saw the girls approaching his table, his leathery face wrinkling into a big smile.

"What can I do for you?" he asked pleasantly.

"May we have a talk with you?" Olivia began.

"I be pleased to talk to you." He waved his hand toward the chairs across the table. The self-appointed investigators sat down.

"I am Olivia Barr. This is my friend, Marie Stumbur."

"Pleased to meet you." The chef was still smiling. "What can I do for you?" he asked again.

"We would like to ask you some questions about an acquaintance of ours, Burton Greenfield." Chow's face went blank. "Who?"

"Burton Greenfield," Olivia repeated.

"Don't know him."

The girls shot side-glances at each other.

"Why are you asking?"

"I saw him in here earlier," Marie was speaking now. "I thought you might know him."

"Oh, Lady, many people eat here. New faces all the time. I don't know them. I'm busy in kitchen. I don't see much people."

"He sells meat. We thought you might have bought meat from him." Olivia tried in vain to keep her voice casual while taking a daring plunge. The man's eyes took on a decided look of suspicion. He studied their faces before speaking again.

"A meat salesman?" he asked finally.

"Yes. Name is Burton Greenfield," Olivia persisted.

The Chinese shook his head. "Never heard of him."

His gaze continued to flit from one face to the other. "Why you ask? You come to inspect meat?"

"No, we are not inspectors." Marie dismissed the thought with a wave of her hand. This discussion was proving unproductive. Realizing their questions had kindled distrust she decided to end the visit.

"Thank you for your time, Mr. Chow," she said, rising. Adding a hasty, "Good-bye," she retreated hurriedly with a reluctant Olivia in tow.

"Well, what do you make of that?" Olivia asked under her breath as they left the cafe. Marie shrugged in mute reply.

21

SLEUTHING

Marie and Olivia checked in at the Riverview Motel and carried their bags into Room Fifteen.

"Well, we really blew that interview," Marie moaned, pushing back the curtains and opening the window to let in some air. She dropped into an overstuffed chair below it.

"Oh, don't write it off," her optimistic friend encouraged. "We did learn something from that little meeting with Samuel Chow."

"Yes, we learned that his name is Samuel Chow. That's about it. But, then that might add authenticity to our story," Marie said half-jokingly.

"That's true. Besides, denying that he knows Burton tells us a lot about the man."

"Like?"

"Like that he's a liar, for one thing. And that he is probably in cohorts with Burton Greenfield. Why else would he deny knowing him after you saw them together?"

Marie held up her hand. "Hold it, Girl. Don't you think Burton might be operating under a pseudonym?"

Olivia was nonplussed. She hung up her coat and stretched out on the bed.

"You're right. It seems logical that Burton would use an assumed name to carry on his illegal business. I had not thought about that."

"Anyway, we can tell Bill what we have learned so far." Marie reached for the telephone on the stand beside her.

"We better report this to the police right away," the rancher said when he had heard the story. "I will talk to Todd Richards and let him take it from there. Thanks for your help, Marie...and Marie, don't do anything foolhardy," he added before hanging up. "I don't want you getting yourself hurt."

Marie laughed. "Don't worry about me. I am not venturesome enough for that. Besides, who would want to hurt me? Burton didn't even see me. At least," she added slowly, "I hope he didn't see me."

"Bill Cardinal will be calling later tonight," she informed Olivia when she hung up.

"In the meantime let's go for a drive along the river," Olivia suggested. "With all the houses decked out in Christmas decorations, it should be a beautiful sight."

Olivia guided her car along the riverside street, then circled back to pull up at the Chow Restaurant again.

"No," Marie objected. "No more interviews."

"We won't," her companion promised. "We'll have a drink and, well, look around. We might get some ideas."

"Well, okay," Marie agreed half-heartedly.

She glanced around the cafe anxiously as they entered, but recognized no one apart from the girl who had served their supper. Although they were led to a different section of the eating area, Marie was aware that their former waitress was constantly observing them from across the room. Several times she approached their table with the coffeepot. Each time Marie and Olivia told her they were not having coffee.

Over their milkshakes, Olivia talked excitedly about her wedding plans, having agreed with Marie not to broach the subject of the cattle rustler while in the cafe.

"Did I tell you that Grant will be home from Africa in time for Christmas?" she asked.

"Several times a day," Marie teased. "But I understand. I know how excited I would be if I were in your situation." Her voice held a note of longing.

I have no plans after the end of this term, she thought. *Once the final report cards are handed out, what then?* She shrugged and pushed away her glass.

"Let's go," she said, trying to shake off the depressive mood that was settling on her. "Bill may be calling soon. We best get back to our room."

The Riverview Motel was set well back from the street. The rooms were strung out in a straight line facing the South Saskatchewan River across the street. Single light bulbs over the doors cast a yellow glow over the snow.

Olivia had turned the blue Mazda off the street onto the drive that ran along the front of the motel. She suddenly screeched to an abrupt stop.

"Oh!" Marie gasped, "What happened?"

Then she saw what Olivia had seen. Parked in the circle of light in front of their room was a red sports car.

Olivia slammed the gear shift into reverse and backed recklessly into the street. Once parked on the curb out of sight of the motel she turned to her companion.

"What do you think he is doing in our motel room?"

"How would he even know we were staying there unless... unless he saw me sneaking out of the cafe and trailed us?"

"But why? What could he possibly want from us?"

"If he saw me behind the cafe, well, I guess I must have looked mighty suspicious." Marie gave a nervous laugh. "If he saw me he would have known at once that I was trying to hide from him."

"But what if you did overhear him talking to the chef? Even if he suspects that you know his secret, what can he do? He can't wipe out what you heard unless..."

"Unless he wipes me out? Forget it. Burton wouldn't go that far."

"Oh, I know. I'm getting morbid over this thing." Olivia sighed and touched Marie's shoulder. "Forget I said that."

"That's okay," Marie replied kindly. "We both got carried away. Our imaginations are working overtime." She slumped down in her seat and leaned her head back, closing her eyes.

"Dear God," she prayed silently. "In my heart I have been calling, 'Help us, help us,' but I have been so busy trying to figure this all out I have not been listening to You. Lord, calm us and direct us." The girls sat in silence for a few moments.

"Maybe we should leave the car here and walk back," Olivia suggested. They were walking away from the car when Marie latched onto a new thought.

"Burton may not even know we are around. He may have checked into the motel and been given the room next to ours. Or," she added sheepishly, "that may not even be his car."

"True, there must be more than one red Ferrari," Olivia agreed. "But we'll be cautious just the same."

They rounded the corner of the motel just as a stocky figure emerged from the motel and walked toward the red car. Marie clutched her friend's arm and together they dashed back the way they had come.

"Quick, Oli, get the doors unlocked," Marie urged unnecessarily. "There's no place else to hide."

Olivia fumbled with the keys for what seemed a long time to Marie before she opened the door and slid behind the wheel.

She reached over to open the passenger door. Marie leaped in and before she had time to close the door behind her, Olivia was coaxing the car into the stream of traffic. They drove in tense silence for several blocks.

"Was that him?" Olivia asked when she found her voice.

"That was him alright."

"You're sure?"

"I'm sure. There may be more than one red Ferrari, but a red Ferrari and that hideous jacket together is too much to be mere coincidence."

"Could you tell which door he came out of?"

"No. They are so close together. It could have been the one next to ours. Then again, it could have been ours."

Olivia turned the car around and drove back to the motel. Seeing the red car gone, she pulled up to the curb and stopped.

"What do we do now?"

"We better leave the car some place else," Marie advised. "If he checked into the motel he'll be back." They decided on the restaurant parking lot.

"When we get back to our room we will soon know whether anyone has been snooping around," Olivia said on their walk back.

"In that case we'll call the police," Marie said quickly. She hoped her adventurous sidekick would not have other ideas. To her relief Olivia nodded agreement.

"If we see nothing unusual we will conclude he is living next door," she added, "And we'll settle down to wait for him to come back."

As they stopped in front of Room Fifteen, Marie noticed a light in the window next to theirs. "Someone must be staying there," she whispered.

Her fingers trembled slightly as she inserted the key in the lock to their room and opened the door. Hesitantly she reached in for the light switch before stepping through the doorway. Together Olivia and Marie examined the contents of the room, peering behind the shower curtain and under the beds, at the same time laughing at themselves for doing so. "Everything seems to be as we left it." Relief echoed in Olivia's voice. She immediately seated herself at the desk to write a letter, content to keep to their room for the rest of the evening.

Marie prepared for bed. Then wrapping her velour robe around herself, she curled up in the big chair with her Bible on her lap. She flipped the pages to find the place where she had left off reading that morning.

Psalm fifty-five, yes, here it is, verse twenty-two. She read slowly, thoughtfully, trying to absorb the message: *Cast thy burden upon the Lord, and he shall sustain thee. He shall never suffer the righteous to be moved.*

"Thank You, Lord. I needed that reminder," she answered silently. She read on. "'I will take refuge in the shadow of your wings until the disaster has passed.'"

Marie's thoughts wondered back a dozen years and many miles to the summer holidays she had spent at her cousins' farm. She remembered a mother hen that had appeared with a dozen downy chicks in tow. The city-bred girl had ached to hold one of the little balls of yellow fluff in her hands. Each time she attempted to catch one, however, it would duck under its mother's wings.

Marie felt a new closeness to the God who provided protection for her. The ring of the telephone interrupted her meditation. She caught up the receiver. Olivia spun around in her chair, eager to learn of any new development. Marie listened intently for several minutes with only an occasional question or comment.

"The police will take Greenfield in for questioning as soon as they can locate him," Bill Cardinal told her, "But they don't seem to have any idea where he might have gone after he left the restaurant."

Quickly Marie related having seen Burton at the motel.

"I will inform Todd of that immediately," Bill assured her, "But how about you, Marie? Are you going to be okay? I feel badly that Double C's problems are disrupting your weekend holiday."

"Don't worry about us," Marie answered lightly. "Olivia and I are tickled to have a part in bringing in the cattle thieves."

"You are a good sport, Marie," William replied, "and a great help. If it turns out that Burton is the criminal you and Oli deserve the credit for rounding him up."

"How like Bill," Marie mused as she replaced the receiver. "He gives everyone the benefit of a doubt. 'If it turns out that Burton is the criminal, you and Oli deserve the credit for rounding him up,'" she quoted.

"Oh, he's the criminal alright," Olivia said with finality. "What else did the man say? I mean, you only need to tell me the part of the conversation that has to do with Burton."

Olivia stood and paced around the room, vigorously brushing her short, curly hair while Marie related her conversation with the rancher. The telephone rang again. Olivia waved her hairbrush in its direction, indicating for Marie to answer.

"What was that all about?" she wanted to know as soon as Marie hung up.

"That was the police. They will be watching the motel tonight."

"Alright," Olivia exclaimed. "This could be an exciting night."

Marie checked her watch. "Maybe we should get some sleep. It's eleven-thirty now and Burton may not come back as long as our lights are on."

"If he knows we are here, that is," Olivia reminded her. "Okay, we'll douse the lights, but I won't sleep a wink. I might miss some excitement."

"We will keep our ears tuned for the sound of the Ferrari," Marie said. "We'll probably hear it in our sleep."

After she had turned off the light Marie pushed the curtain aside for a lingering look around. The air was calm and a soft snow was falling. Leaving the window open slightly she closed the curtains again and crawled into bed. Before long the sound of soft breathing from the next bed indicated to Marie that sleep had quickly overtaken her friend.

22

Footsteps in the Night

For Marie sleep did not come easily. For a long time after she went to bed she laid on her back, watching the changing shadows cast on the ceiling by the headlights of the passing cars. Her mind kept sifting through past incidents, trying to sort out what would prove significant evidence for the police. *Like Burton's dislike for the Cardinals. I suspected all along that he was responsible for the rumours that Indians can't be trusted. Now I see why. He did not want their word to be believed if he was ever caught.*

Marie smiled to herself in the darkness as she recalled the community reputation of the owners of the Double C Ranch. *If Burton thinks he can cast suspicion on Bill he will soon find out differently.*

A slight movement outside her window brought Marie back from her state of semi-drowsiness. Slowly she raised her head, her senses now fully alert. She was certain she had heard the crunch of footsteps on the soft snow outside. Yes, there it was again. So close to her window was the movement she scarcely dared to breath. How she wished Olivia would wake up, but she could not call her for fear of being heard by the person outside.

After several moments the footsteps moved on. When they paused again Marie heard the sound of keys rattling. She held her breath, her eyes glued to the door only a few feet from her bed. A sigh of relief escaped her lips when a minute later she detected the sound of the door next to theirs being pushed open.

Stealthily she reached for the phone and pushed the button for the motel office. In the tense wait that followed Marie listened with one ear for further developments in the adjoining room. The sounds were soft, but there was no mistaking them. Someone was rushing around on the other side of the wall.

Was anyone awake in the office? Marie pressed the button twice more before a sleepy voice came on the line. Ducking under the bedclothes to muffle her voice Marie spoke in a half-whisper, "Please connect me with the R.C.M.P. Fast."

"Is something the matter?" the sleepy woman asked. "Maybe we can solve it, whatever..."

"No. Give me the police. Quick." This time Marie's voice was louder, more urgent.

"What is it?" the night clerk wanted to know.

"Listen. There is someone in Room Sixteen. Someone the..."

"Of course there is. All the rooms are occupied tonight."

"I said I want to talk to the police. Right now." Marie tried to sound authoritative. It worked on her pupils. She hoped it would have the same effect on the half-awake clerk.

"If you send the police on our guests..."

"Listen to me," Marie interrupted. "Your guest is wanted by the police. If you do not connect me right now..." She was on the verge of shouting into the phone, but checked herself.

"If you do not connect me with the police at once you will personally be held responsible if the man escapes."

The woman suddenly came awake. The next moment Marie heard a strong voice saying, "Royal Canadian Mounted Police."

When she had given her message she returned the phone to the table and sat up in bed, her eyes fastened uneasily on a narrow gap between the curtains. She regretted leaving a slit open between the drapes even though it wasn't wide enough for anyone to see in.

Some minutes passed before she heard the door open again. There was the sound of footsteps on the walk. Then a lone figure came into view. For one moment he paused and turned toward the window. Marie cringed as the light shone full on Burton's face. *He can't see me*, she told herself.

As the banker hurried on, swinging a large suitcase at his side, Marie dropped back on her pillow. She tried to evaluate the events that had just transpired.

One thing is sure. He knows we are here and he knows we are on to his tricks. That must be why he left. The police did not get here on time. Is there a chance they will catch up with him? With these questions still chasing around in her mind, Marie finally drifted off to sleep.

23

AN UNEXPECTED TWIST

A draft of cold air aroused Marie the following morning. She opened her eyes to see Olivia standing in the open doorway.

"Good Morning. You are up bright and early this morning," Marie greeted her drowsily, "Already dressed and raring to go."

"Bright, but not early," Olivia replied, closing the door. "I have never known you to sleep so late before. And did we miss some excitement last night! I just discovered something."

Marie sat up and stretched. "I didn't know it was this late. We will have to rush to get our Christmas shopping done today." Olivia sat down on the edge of Marie's bed, a gleam in her dark eyes.

"I said I just made an exciting discovery."

"Oh, what?" Marie asked innocently, deciding to tease her friend before telling her of the night's happening.

"Well, you know how you thought the sound of Burton's sports car would wake us up?"

"I am sure if he had pulled up to the door the way he usually drives we would have heard him." Marie got up and wrapped her robe about herself. "Besides, his headlights would have shone right in my face through that crack. I couldn't have missed that."

"That's where he fooled you," Olivia said excitedly.

"How's that?"

"Take a look out the door and..." Olivia's comment was cut short by the ring of the telephone. While she answered the call Marie strolled to the bathroom.

"Marie," Olivia called as soon as she had hung up. "Marie, that was the police. We are wanted at the police station at eleven to answer some questions."

Olivia prepared instant coffee, heating water on the burner provided by the management.

"Do you think coffee will do us? We have no time to stop for breakfast."

"Just fine. There are some snack biscuits in my bag," Marie called from behind the closed door. "We can finish those."

Minutes later the two rushed out the door. While Olivia manoeuvred her car through the Saturday traffic Marie drew a packet of printed cards from her purse.

"What are those? I thought we had left school work behind," Olivia reminded her.

"These cards? These are Bible verses," Marie explained. "I carry them with me to read whenever I have some spare moments. I make a point of reading my Bible every morning, but since I overslept this morning I am glad I have these along."

"Really! Don't you think God would excuse you for missing your reading on a morning like this? After all, you didn't know we would be called to the police station."

"It's not that God wouldn't understand. I do not want to miss it." Marie laid the cards on her lap and turned to Olivia. "Because you are my friend I enjoy hearing what you tell me.

Since God is my best Friend I do not want to miss what He has to say to me."

As Olivia made no further comment Marie turned her attention back to her reading.

Constable Todd Richards was talking to a young officer behind the desk when the girls walked through the front door of the police station. Marie felt relief at the sight of the familiar face. He came to meet them at once, introducing them to Constable Clyde Remus.

The constable rose to shake hands. "Thank you for your cooperation," he said. "Our suspect is now in custody, thanks to your help. Please be seated."

While Marie sipped the coffee the receptionist handed her she was hit by the realization that Burton was in jail. The thought saddened her.

And I put him there, she theorized. Then she analyzed the concept and decided it was not her that put him there, but his own wrongdoing. Still, the thought was a depressing one. Not the idea that he got caught, she concluded, but knowing he was guilty. Marie became aware of Constable Remus' eyes on her and she turned her attention to his words.

"Our men were cruising the area during the night," he was saying, "but it is possible that they would have missed him had it not been for your phone call."

"Our phone call?" Olivia asked. Marie's lips formed a silent exclamation at the perplexed look on her friend's face. She chided herself for neglecting to enlighten Olivia about the night's episode. Her intention had been to merely play innocent for a few minutes before relating the story of Burton's return for his suitcase. The idea had struck her as funny at the time. Then the call had come from the police, spurring them into action, and the subject had been dropped. She looked at Olivia now, hoping for understanding.

"The ranchers will be coming in shortly," the officer continued. "We called you in early because we want to talk to you each separately."

He led Olivia into a private office. While Marie waited she prayed silently for her. She also prayed for Burton and that she would be free from any feelings of malice.

The front door swung open, admitting the owners of the Double C Ranch. William strolled across the lobby floor to where Marie sat waiting with his usual quick, decisive step. "Good Morning, Marie," he smiled down at her. "How are things shaping up?"

Briefly Marie filled him in on the happenings since she last spoke to him. William placed his hand on her shoulder. "You are a real brick." It made Marie feel amply rewarded.

"How would you and Oli like to join us for lunch as soon as we have made our statements to the police," William asked. "This business here should take only a few minutes."

"Thank you," Marie smiled her acceptance. "If that is convenient for Oli, I'd like that."

Constable Remus called her away then. As she turned to go down the hall she saw an R.C.M.P. officer ushering a frightened Samuel Chow into the lobby. *He is such a pleasant man,* she thought, *I do hope he is innocent.*

Interviews over, the group gathered in the lobby. "Everyone set for a good meal? Let's go," William said, leading the group toward the door. The receptionist was speaking on the telephone as the party passed her desk. "Cardinal?" she called after them, holding her hand over the mouthpiece.

William swung around. "Yes?"

"Sergeant Bradley wants to talk to you."

"What's this all about?" Beryl asked.

William shrugged nonchalantly. "Probably some minor technicality. I hate to hold you all up though."

"Never mind. I'm sure it will only take a minute," John said. "Likely something to sign."

Even as he spoke a stern-faced officer appeared through a side door and strode toward the waiting group.

"He looks mad enough to chew us all up," Olivia said in an aside to Beryl who was standing next to her.

"You can say that again," Beryl nodded in agreement.

"Which one of you is Cardinal?" Sergeant Bradley's eyes flashed from William to John and back to William.

"I am," William offered, looking into the officer's face. "Anything wrong?"

The two men were of equal height, but the officer's deep-set chest and burly arms indicated that he was decidedly heavier. His voice and mannerism matched his solid physique.

"Is that your truck parked in front? The one with the *Double C* insignia on the door?"

"Yes, it is," the rancher answered undisturbed. "That is, the company owns it. I drove it here."

The official's eyes were shooting fire at William as he dropped his bombshell.

"Samuel Chow confessed everything. He signed a statement saying that he bought meat from William Cardinal. He identified that truck as the one used to deliver the meat to the cafe."

A look of unbelief flitted across William's face. "I beg your pardon, Officer. This must be a misunderstan..."

The sergeant held up his hand for silence. "You are under arrest for selling meat illegally and for laying false charges. I will read you your rights." He unfolded a sheet of paper and read the statement. Refolding it he returned it to his hip pocket and without another word indicated with a wag of his head for the accused to follow him.

William turned to speak to his companions, but the officer cut him off. Grasping William's arm Bradley gave it a hard yank.

"Get going," he demanded.

The sergeant's words had fallen on the ears of the listening party with a heavy thud. Now they stood in stunned silence as he steered William through the doorway from which he had emerged a few minutes earlier. The heavy door squeaked in protest as it slowly closed behind them.

"What do we do now?" Beryl wondered aloud.

John took her hand in his for reassurance. "I will see if there is anyone we can talk to." He turned to the reception desk. "May I speak to Sergeant Bradley, please?"

"The sergeant is busy," came the curt reply.

"Could I talk to Constable Todd Richards? The officer from Sundre? He was here earlier."

"He has left."

John was not about to give up. "Is there anyone else I could talk to? Is Constable Remus available?" For a moment the girl peered at him suspiciously through the strands of blonde hair that kept falling over her face. Then she slowly reached out and pressed the intercom button.

"Constable, someone from the cattle rustling case wants to talk to you. Do you want to see him?"

"Send him in," the voice came over the intercom.

"Go on in," the girl echoed with a toss of her head.

The hands on the big clock on the wall crept up to one o'clock before John came back.

"Let's go for some food," he called to the women. "You can leave your car here, Oli, till we get back. What little I learned I'll tell you on the way."

Silently the quartet filed out of the building, still trying to comprehend this unexpected twist of circumstances. Marie was the first to speak.

"Let's go back to Samuel Chow's place. Maybe we will learn something more." Her suggestion was readily accepted. Marie slid into the back seat of the Charters' car beside an unusually quiet Olivia. In the midst of the confusion Marie had been too dumbfounded to notice her friend's lack of enthusiasm. Now as they drove toward the eatery she wondered why no comment was forthcoming from the would-be detective. Then she remembered her earlier mistake.

"Oli, I apologize for not cluing you in on what happened during the night. I meant to, but then the police called and we had to rush." She shrugged. "Well, I forgot. Honest."

"Why didn't you tell me before that?" Olivia blurted unexpectedly. "Instead you made me appear a fool in front of the police. I can't understand you. It looks to me like you want the recognition for having captured the criminal single-handedly."

Marie's mouth fell open in surprise. Never had she seen her friend so upset and unreasonable.

"Horrors, Oli, I know how you love sleuthing. I just happened to land in the middle of all this. I got involved despite of myself." She shook her head. "I'm so glad to have you beside me. Without you, I guess I would have run from it." Olivia still looked unconvinced.

"How come it was you who happened to notice someone into the school? How come you found the watch? How come you discovered the blood? How come you happened to walk out just when Burton was talking to the chef?" she asked candidly. "How come you noticed Burton come back to the motel after you told me to go to sleep? How come you...?"

"Oli," Marie interrupted. "Oli. That was all coincidence. That is what it is. Coincidence."

"How many coincidences do you expect me to allow you? How come you didn't wake me up? Did you forget that, too?"

"Oli, I had left the window open a wee bit, remember? I was wishing you would wake up, but I didn't dare call you. I pulled the covers over myself when I phoned to muffle the sound for fear that whoever was out there would hear me. Believe me. Please, do. We need you to get Bill out of this mess.

She caught Olivia's arm impulsively. Gradually Olivia's face began to relax.

"Okay, maybe I was letting my imagination run away with me again," she admitted. Marie smiled a forgiving smile and took Olivia's hand in both of hers.

"I'm glad you understand. I don't want to lose your friendship over something like this. Or anything else," she added.

In the front seat John was discussing William's predicament with his wife. "We'll wait to see what we find out at the restaurant, if anything, before we decide what to do next."

Marie leaned forward eagerly. "If Samuel Chow had bought the meat from Bill like he claimed, what would there have been to confess? He would not have been guilty of anything, would he?"

"The only thing he confessed was that he had bought meat that had not passed government inspection," John explained. "The statement he made was that he was buying meat from the Double C Ranch because it was superior quality, even if it had not been graded by government inspectors. If his story is believed in court he will pay a fine, that's all."

"There is no way he could get away with accusing Bill, is there?" Beryl wanted to know.

"Not likely, but he does have the banker behind him. Burton apparently charged that Will had been cashing checks from Samuel Chow at the bank, Remus told me."

"The skunk," Olivia muttered.

"So by confessing to a minor offence he hopes to get off the hook for cattle rustling," Beryl spoke accusingly.

"He may not be involved in the rustling," John reminded them.

"Is cattle rustling considered a serious crime?"

"Yes and no, Marie. In the early days of ranching in the west cattle rustlers would drive off whole herds," Beryl said. "It was the ranchers' livelihood. It was a major crime alright."

"They used to get strung up in trees for that if they got caught, didn't they?" Marie asked, remembering cowboy stories she had read.

"While it is true that in the United States the cattlemen sometimes lynched the thieves if they could catch them," John agreed, "That was never the case in Canada. In our country no one was ever hanged for cattle rustling. When the laws were put on the books in Ottawa the punishment for rustling was set at seven years' imprisonment, maximum sentence. That law has never been altered."

"Neither is it ever enforced any more," John continued. "The fact is, if a hunter is caught shooting a doe he loses the carcass, his vehicle, his gun, and his hunting license, besides paying a steep fine. He could drive off a rancher's herd and pay a few hundred dollars and still fill enough freezers to keep him in meat for years to come." He pulled into a parking place at the Chow Restaurant. "Well, here we are. Now let's keep our eyes and ears open for anything unusual."

24

MORE PUZZLES

John chose a round table in the centre of the room. "With one of us facing each direction," he explained after everyone was seated, "We have a view of the whole place." The waitress offered them coffee.

"That's the same girl that waited on our table the first time Marie and I were here," Olivia informed John in an undertone as soon as the blonde was out of earshot. "She's terribly nosy."

"Do you think she knows something?"

"It's possible," Olivia shrugged.

"Then we better watch what we say when she's near, in case she's in cahoots with the boss." Marie shook her head.

"I still think the chef is innocent. Of anything more serious than buying meat that had not been government inspected, that is."

Olivia was not that lenient. "How can he be? We already know he signed a false statement. Doesn't that imply that he is in league with Greenfield?"

"Not necessarily," Marie began, "When he bought the meat..."

Olivia nudged Marie's knee. "Keep your voice down," she whispered, "Our ever-ready waitress has her hearing aid turned way up."

"Thanks for the reminder," Marie continued in a hushed tone, "Maybe the restaurateur thought the man he was dealing with was William Cardinal. Olivia and I already suspected Burton was operating under an assumed name. He could have been crafty enough to use Bill's name to throw suspicion on the victim."

She paused while the Charters considered that possibility. Beryl's face brightened.

"Then maybe if the chef saw both men he would identify which one sold him the meat."

"Chow will be brought in to identify Bill before this case is through, I'm sure, but the Sergeant seems so sure that Bill is the criminal that he may take his time about it."

"Hey, Girls, is this our man?" Beryl asked as a Chinese in a white smock emerged from the kitchen. Marie glanced around to see Chow walking toward the table where she and Olivia had first met him.

"That's him," she exclaimed, "That's Samuel Chow."

"I think I'll pay him a visit," John said, "Unless you two want to follow up your first contact with him."

The girls waved aside the suggestion. "We'd get nowhere with him because he is suspicious of us," Marie explained. "But wait a minute." She held up a hand as a new idea hit her. "Do you have a picture of Bill you could show him?"

"I have a mug shot of him right here," Beryl said. She brought out her wallet.

"Great," John said, "Now if any one would happen to have a shot of Burton as well..."

"I do," Olivia remembered. "I just had some pictures developed. They came in the mail before we left Echo Valley yesterday. I slipped them into my purse and forgot all about them." She was rummaging through the contents of her handbag. "There should be several of him at the farewell party Mrs. Charter threw for him. I took them for her sake. Yes, here they are."

From her favourable spot Beryl watched the elderly man smile as he looked up from his plate of steaming noodles to greet John with a handshake and proffered chair. Her opinion of him began to soften.

"My name is John Carpenter. My wife and I operate the Double C Ranch together with my brother-in-law, William Cardinal." At the mention of William's name the smile on the chef's face was replaced by a look of suspicion.

"What you want?" he asked quickly.

"Hopefully I can clear up a misunderstanding. You see, because of your statement this morning, William is at the police station right now getting fingerprinted and photographed and whatever else they do to a suspect."

"That bad, hey?"

John handed the pictures across the table. "Can you identify William Cardinal on any of these pictures?"

Mr. Chow squinted at the picture of William and shook his head. He laid it carefully on the table and looked at the next print, a look of recognition dawning in his eyes.

"That is William Cardinal," he exclaimed as he pointed at a man with a birthday cake. He studied the remaining pictures. Each time the exposure included Burton's profile he pointed it out.

"Do you recognize anyone else?"

"Yes, that one. She came to talk to me." Chow held up a picture of Marie. "And her." He pointed out Olivia's face on another shot. "They came to see me. I think they made trouble." He handed the pictures back to John.

"Mr. Chow, this is the person that caused the trouble." John laid Burton's picture on the table. "He is not William Cardinal. This is Burton Greenfield."

"But...but...he had papers," Chow gasped, "He showed me identification. His name on cards. And the truck with the sign..."

"His papers were forged, I'm sure," John said. "I don't know how he got the truck, but we'll find out. You can help by coming back to the police station with us now. Will you do that, Mr. Chow?"

"I work till four."

"After work, then?" The white head nodded uncertainly. "I'll meet you at the police station after your shift. I apologize for disturbing your meal, but this is urgent. Thank you for your help."

The elderly man shook John's hand again before turning his attention to the noodles that were fast cooling off.

"I'm convinced he thought he was telling the truth when he signed that statement for the police," John reported to the others on their drive back to police quarters. "He's confused now, not knowing whom to believe. He'll identify the men when he comes to the station after four o'clock."

"Two more hours till Bill can be cleared!" Marie exclaimed. "Is there nothing we can do?"

"Maybe Sergeant Bradley will talk to us now," Beryl hoped aloud.

"Won't they let Bill out when they have finished taking down all the necessary information?" Olivia wondered.

"They probably will, but I'm sure we all want to see him walk out cleared before we go home." Her statement was echoed by three exclamations of agreement. Marie tried to compose herself.

"We may find that Bill has straightened things out for himself by the time we get back there," she philosophized. Her optimistic statement, however, was soon to be proven false.

Constable Remus listened intently as John related his visit with the chef. "Just tell that to the Chief," he said, ushering the party into the sergeant's office.

Sergeant Bradley refused to consider the testimony. "I have just gone over the information we have on file: Cardinal's son in possession of the stolen watch, the envelope with Nikolaus Nicole's name on it showing up on the ranch, the cattle butchered right there, Chow testifying that he saw Cardinal's ID. He identified the truck. The only ones coming forward in the Indian's defence are his few personal friends."

John spoke up quickly. "Sir, we are the only ones who know that he is charged. Remember, the chef did not recognize Bill's pic..."

John's admission to contacting Chow had obviously angered the officer. "You would do well to leave the investigation to my men," he said, his eyes flashing. "I will hear what the man has to say for himself when he arrives." His voice was heavy with sarcasm, "And if I find that he has been threatened at all..."

The unfinished sentence sent shivers down Marie's back. Then her anger rose up in protest at this gross injustice. *I will face Burton with his dastardly action. Tell him what I saw and heard. Surely he will make some comment that will incriminate him and free Bill.* She said this only in her mind.

Aloud she said as she stepped forward, "Sergeant Bradley, may I speak to Burton Greenfield?" It was more of a demand than a request.

Surprise showed on the chief's face. "That is not possible," he said after studying the determined face before him for a full minute. "Greenfield has been released."

25

A Mysterious Disappearance

For the second time that day William's defenders filed silently from the police station. When the door had closed behind them Constable Remus approached his superior. "Sergeant, if that woman were falsely accusing Greenfield would she request to speak to him in person?" he asked.

"I already thought of that," the man in charge replied curtly. He kept his eyes diverted from his subordinate.

Seated in the Charter car in the parking lot, Beryl was the first to speak. "I know we have been praying quietly about this whole mess, but I think it would be good for us to pray together."

John agreed at once. "Will you lead us, Beryl?"

With bowed head, Marie joined silently in Beryl's request to God for wisdom and patience. "Thank You for the assurance that You are with us and with Will. We know You will make this all turn out right. We leave the matter in Your hands. Teach us to trust You and to anticipate the outcome. Amen."

Marie was aware of Olivia fidgeting beside her. She felt a tenderness for this close friend to whom God was still a stranger. When Marie glanced in her direction after the brief prayer Olivia's face was turned to the window. It was sometime later when she spoke.

"Surely Burton's fabricated story cannot hold up for long," she said. "Why would he even think he could get away with it?"

"It threw suspicion off his track long enough for him to take off. By now he has probably hit the trail," John answered.

"And you can be sure it is not to Edmonton to take up his new post there, if there ever was any truth to that claim," Olivia stated decisively.

She suddenly turned to face Marie. "He'll probably clear the country. Remember that brochure on Rio De Janeiro I found in the living room? He could have already been planning his exit route."

"As long as Bill's chart is wiped clean," Marie said, "That's the main thing."

John consulted his watch. "In the meantime I'll take the truck and pick up the tractor parts we were going to get. If you like you can do an hour's shopping before four o'clock."

Marie recalled the long list of purchases she had hoped to make while in Calgary. "Still game for a quick shopping spree, Oli?" she asked.

Olivia shook her head absently. "The rest of you go ahead and do what you want to do," she said. "I'll take my own car. I want to make a phone call first."

"I think we better stick together," Beryl replied. "How about making your call from the mall?"

On the short drive to the mall Olivia was uncommunicative. While Beryl and Marie exchanged ideas on what to look for in the stores Olivia sat lost in thought. Inside the doors to the shopping complex the women paused beside the pay phones.

"You two go ahead," Olivia said, "I'll probably catch up with you before long."

"In case we get separated," Beryl cautioned, "let's meet back at the car at four."

Beryl and Marie made their way along the corridor, stepping into several shops to see the displays and make a few minor purchases. "Funny that Oli has not caught up to us yet," Marie commented as they stopped beside a table outside a toy store to watch battery-operated dogs perform.

"Do you think there's something wrong?" Beryl asked, "That maybe Oli is not well or something?"

Marie looked at her friend across the toy table. "You noticed it, too? She certainly has not been her cheery self."

"Perhaps we should start back the way we came. It's almost four o'clock any way," Beryl suggested. "If she's looking for us we'll run into each other."

When they reached the door through which they had entered the mall they bought a soda drink and sat down to wait.

"It's four o'clock now," Beryl said a few minutes later. "Let's go. She may be waiting for us at the car."

As they approached the car Beryl spotted a slip of paper tucked under the windshield wiper. Anxiously she unfolded the brief note.

"Don't wait for me. Will meet you at the police station," was all it said.

"But why?" Marie wondered aloud, "Why did she go back?"

"Or did she?"

Marie studied Beryl's face, trying to fathom the implication of her words. "You mean...?"

"Oh, I don't know!" Beryl gestured. "I don't know what to think. You hear those awful stories of girls disappearing and with Burton on the loose..."

147

Fear struck at Marie's heart. "Let's hurry back," she urged. "She may be there waiting for us." Then more to console herself than Beryl, she added, "Olivia will have a perfectly logical explanation, I am sure."

They drove the short distance to the police station without conversation. They met John in the parking lot. Quickly Beryl showed him the note.

"Her car is still here where she left it when we went for lunch," he said. "She can't have gone far."

A shiny Cadillac came to a stop beside them and Samuel Chow slowly emerged from the passenger side. He had exchanged his white smock for a dark suit, but his eyes held the same look of distrust and uncertainty John had seen there earlier.

"I'm glad you came, Mr. Chow." John shook the worried man's hand, then addressed his companion, "And thanks for bringing him."

The well-mannered youth returned the greeting and introduced himself as the chef's son, David.

"I'll be there shortly," Marie called to John and Beryl as they followed the Chows into the police station. "I want to walk a bit." She wanted a moment to be alone, a chance to think over the new developments and to check over Olivia's car for clues, not knowing what it could possibly reveal. In deep concentration she circled the parking lot, feeling at a loss.

I'm like an unseasoned sailor in a flimsy boat in the midst of a stormy sea, she allegorized. *Peculiar things are happening to people close to me and I feel like a helpless bystander, not knowing what to do.*

Like a blaze of light breaking through dark clouds, the words she had read and reread that morning on the way to the station burst on her mind. She leaned against Olivia's car as she dug into her purse for the packet of printed cards. Eagerly she read the short verse again, as if seeing it in print gave it added thrust:

Casting all your care upon Him; for He cares
for you. (1 Peter 5:7)

That morning she had found comfort in those words. She had thought of them again as she had listened to Beryl pray. The thought struck her now that although the problems were still mounting God's promise remained the same. He was still inviting her to leave them all with Him.

"Oh, there you are!"

Marie jumped at the sound of Beryl's voice close by.

"I didn't mean to startle you. I thought you might like some company."

"Thank you, I'm ready to come in with you now. Besides, my feet are getting cold."

Nothing had changed in circumstances as far as Marie knew, yet she felt a new lightness as she walked into the building with Beryl. John met them at the door.

"Have you heard any news yet?" Marie asked.

"Not yet," John answered.

"We are not allowed to talk to Bill till the sergeant is through questioning the Chows. They are still in his office."

"Did you tell anyone about Olivia?"

"Yes, I told Constable Remus right away," John assured her. "He thinks there is no cause for alarm yet. But he is alerting the men on patrol to watch for her. Because of her part in apprehending Greenfield they will keep a lookout for her while he is on the loose. Fortunately I still had her pictures with me. That may help. Marie, can you recall anything Olivia said that might give us a clue as to where she has gone?"

Marie shook her head slowly. "No-o, not really. She did seem preoccupied all day though."

"Did anything upset her?"

"No, except that she was put out with me this morning because I...But that was settled."

"Because what?" John probed.

"Oh, it seems so silly now. You see, I had neglected to tell her I noticed Burton come back to the motel during the night and she got thinking I was trying to get recognition for capturing him single-handedly. It was really not like Oli to take offence, but it was my error and you know how she likes sleuthing. I guess this hit a sore spot. But I apologized and, anyway, I can't see where that has anything to do with her disappearance. Oli is not one to carry a grudge."

"But she was still bothered?"

"She seemed reserved. Now that I think of it, she has been more like that lately."

"Do you think she was planning to do some investigating on her own?"

"Possible, but more likely something came up and she acted on impulse. She may have seen Burton and decided to follow him. Something like that..."

"Will," Beryl sang out, rushing to meet her brother as he emerged from a door across the lobby. Will threw his arm around her as they strolled to where John and Marie stood talking. While John and Beryl pitched questions at Will, Marie stood by speechless. As she nervously wiped her hand across her face she discovered her checks wet with tears. With a reassuring smile William handed her a white handkerchief.

She turned to wipe her eyes as an excited Samuel Chow approached, David and Sergeant Bradley close behind. The Orientals bowed to the group, apologizing profusely. Their apologies were accompanied by invitations to come back to the cafe for a meal on the house.

When the Chows had left, the sergeant cleared his throat. He swallowed hard and brushed his forehead.

"I was mistaken, too," he admitted. "I apologize." Obviously, that was a difficult word for him to say. "But you must realize we can't take chances," he continued. "I needed concrete evidence before I could dismiss the charge."

Too bad the same rule didn't apply in Burton's case, Marie thought, but she held her tongue.

William graciously offered his hand. "I accept your apologies, Officer." The sergeant shook his hand, did a sharp about-turn, and marched back to his office.

"Well, I guess we are free to go now," William said. He felt suddenly very tired. "I left home just this morning, but I feel like that was ages ago. First a quick bite, then Double C, here we come."

"We have to locate Olivia first," John informed him.

"Olivia? What happened to her?"

"Let's take the Chows up on their invitation for supper," William said when he had heard the story of Olivia's disappearance. "Maybe we'll get some leads there." An obliging David Chow personally waited on his new friends. Marie glanced about for the blonde-haired waitress, but saw no sign of her. She questioned David about her.

"Pauletta Fleet? She walked out in the middle of her shift this afternoon without any explanation. Why are you asking?"

"I wondered if she knew anything about Burton's business deals. She hung around us a lot. Do you think she might have some information?"

"I do not think so. I know my father would not confide in his employees about his business. But I will ask him."

A moment later the senior Chow approached their table. "What can I do for you?" he smiled. Marie repeated her question.

"No, no," he assured the group. "I told Pauletta nothing. But that man Burton, he ate here often. She waited on tables. It is possible they talk."

The foursome looked at each other. "Do you have any idea where she can be reached?" William asked.

"I can give you her telephone number," David offered.

"No answer from Pauletta," William announced when he rejoined the group. "But I notified the police of her possible connection with Greenfield. This time I think the sergeant took my word seriously."

Apart from promises from David and his father to watch for clues regarding Olivia's whereabouts, the group was no closer to finding her. Outside the restaurant Bill turned to face the others.

"Try to recall anything Olivia did or said that might give us a clue. Anything at all."

Marie put her mind into a slow replay as they walked to the car. Suddenly she stopped.

"Yes, there was something she said. Remember, John, in the car. Something about Burton clearing the country. The brochure about Brazil that he left behind..." She looked at the faces anxiously watching her. "Don't you see? She probably took off to the airport!"

26

KIDNAPPED

Olivia chaffed inwardly. Why was she feeling so depressed, so out of it? Was it because Marie was beating her at the detective game? Maybe if she could track Burton down on her own, inform the police about his whereabouts… Once they realized he was their man, of course. By the time the three women arrived at the mall her mind was made up. She would telephone the airport to find out the time of the next flight to Brazil.

"We do not fly directly to Brazil," a crisp voice replied to Olivia's question. "But we will take you to Lima, Peru, and arrange a flight for you from there to Rio De Janeiro. The plane will leave for Vancouver at fifteen thirty-seven. From there you fly on…"

Olivia hung up and ran from the building. With no time to explain her sudden departure to her friends, she merely scribbled a hasty note. While shoving it under the windshield wiper of Beryl's car she waved frantically at a passing taxi with her free hand.

"Airport," she panted, clambering into the back seat. "My plane leaves at three thirty-seven."

The driver let out a low whistle as he put the cab in motion. "I'll do my best," he said.

"If my hunch is right our suspect could be taking off on that flight," Olivia muttered to herself as the taxi came to a screeching halt in front of the air terminal. Throwing a bill onto the seat, she bolted into the terminal. With her eyes on the sign *Canadian Pacific* over the ticket counter, she made her way toward it, dodging in and out among the people in her way.

Suddenly she stopped short. An audible gasp escaped her lips. Ducking behind a man standing in line she cautiously peered around his massive frame at the couple checking in suitcases. Olivia had almost walked up beside the two before she had recognized the man in the tan sports jacket as Burton. Now from a mere three feet away she watched him grasp the arm of the young girl beside him, steering her toward the loading gate.

"Well, if it isn't our nosy waitress," Olivia muttered.

Just then the ticket clerk left his post. The waiting customer, casting suspicious glances at the girl who had taken refuge behind his broad back, joined another queue. Olivia took advantage of the moment. Quickly she stepped forward and tore the destination tag from the large brown suitcase she knew to be Burton's.

There, I have concrete evidence, she congratulated herself, tucking the tag into her coat pocket. Then, remembering that Burton would recognize her in her grey wool coat, she stuffed it hurriedly into a locker.

In the ladies room she attempted to disguise herself by parting her hair in the middle and dusting it heavily with talcum powder. She tied her red scarf over it, knotting it securely under her chin. While she ordinarily used makeup modestly, she now slapped it on in total abandon. With her purse tucked inside her shirtwaist dress, she buttoned her new sweater over it. She smiled at the misshapen figure in the mirror. Then, donning her dark sunglasses, she left the ladies room. Her body sagging, her hands shoved deep into her dress pockets, she limped toward the loading gate.

Olivia spied her quarry and fell into line a safe distance behind them. To her surprise the suspects paused before the security door, engaged in serious conversation. Then Burton planted a kiss on his companion's cheek and hurried away. He passed so close to Olivia that for a moment her heart stopped beating. Although he flashed a glance in her direction, no flicker of recognition dawned in his blue eyes. Slowly Olivia let out her breath.

When she next turned her gaze toward the security door the girl with the bleached hair had disappeared through it. The self-appointed detective hobbled after Burton, determined to find out where he was going. Across the crowded lobby and through the automatic doors she trailed the familiar figure, not taking time to retrieve her coat for fear that she might lose his trail.

In the parking lot she shivered from the subzero temperature. Feeling more conspicuous and vulnerable outdoors, she increased her limp, keeping close to the parked cars. Every few steps she paused as if in pain. Through the rails of a cattle truck she watched Burton get into an old model car at the far end of the lot. As he put the car in motion she caught the first two letters of his license plate.

Concluding there was nothing more she could do, she hurried back toward the terminal to remove her disguise and retrieve her coat. Then she would rush back to the police station to report her new findings and meet her friends.

It was at this precise moment that the Cardinal car pulled into the parking lot. "I better go in alone," Bill volunteered. "If

Burton should be in the terminal he will not spot one of us as readily as if we were all together."

The seconds ticked away ever so slowly for the anxious trio waiting in the car. *What is taking so long?* Marie questioned. *Why can't Bill find her? If Olivia's not here, then where is she?*

"Here they come!" they all sang out in unison as Bill and Olivia emerged through the doors of the terminal. "Oh, thank God."

With a squeal of delight Marie leaped from the rear seat of the car and ran to meet them. Scurrying around vehicles and banked-up snow she cut across the parking lot only to lose sight of Bill and Olivia.

As she paused momentarily she heard a vehicle approach from behind, screeching to a stop beside her. Before Marie realized what was happening strong hands seized her arms and unscrupulously propelled her into the car. She landed in a heap in the front seat.

"Get over." The harsh command was accompanied by a blow to her ribs. Marie let out a cry and crowded against the far door, grasping frantically for the handle.

"Oh no, you don't." Her captor caught her arm and held it in a vice-like grip while he steered the car out of the parking area. Once in the main stream of highway traffic he released his hold on her.

Silently Marie massaged her bruised arm as she stared into the driver's face.

"Burton," she gasped.

27

NIGHTMARE

"Where's Marie?" was the first question asked on both sides when William returned to the car with Olivia. A quick check of the parking lot revealed nothing. Paging her in the terminal was also futile. John contacted airport security while William put in a phone call to the office of the Royal Canadian Mounted Police.

"Maybe we should notify the Chows," Olivia said, rummaging through her purse for her address book, "Just in case Burton shows up there." She headed for the nearest pay phone. When she returned, the men joined her and Beryl in a secluded corner to share their information and to pray for wisdom in planning a course of action.

"Burton is the prime suspect this time," William told the group. "Sergeant Bradley is putting out an alert with the city police as well as the RCMP. They will be on the lookout for his car."

"Oh, no!" Olivia gasped. She explained that instead of his red sports car she had seen him get into an old model sedan.

"The nosy waitress! They probably came to the airport togeth-er. It could have been her car he was using for his get-away. Also he was dressed very conservative. Brown trousers and jacket. The police need to be told."

This time it was Olivia that placed the call to the sergeant, filling him in on all she had seen. "I tore the destination tag off his suitcase," she confessed. She read the information to him.

"We are all wanted back at the police station," she an-nounced when she rejoined the group. "They want to interview us in the event we recall something we have not told them yet."

On route to the station, Olivia suddenly remembered that they had not checked out of the motel.

"Do you think he may have taken her there? Maybe we should go back..." The words got stuck in her throat. She blew her nose.

"Anyway, I will have to go back for our luggage. And if we don't find her, I will stay at the motel tonight and wait for her."

"It's gallant of you to offer, but we won't take a chance on losing you, too," William stated. "If anyone stays in that room tonight it will be me, but we better let the police make that decision."

"The motel is under surveillance," Sergeant Bradley said when William spoke of going back. "We will retrieve your lug-gage for you. From now on let my men do the investigating."

"If I had done that in the first place Marie would not be in trouble now," Olivia spoke softly. The thought of returning to the Charters' house did not appeal to Olivia. Beryl seemed to sense her uneasiness and was quick to speak up. "Why don't you come home with us for the night, Oli?" Then if any word comes from Marie, the Charters won't need to be disturbed by the phone call. Besides, we don't want them to get suspicious of what's going on."

"Anyway, we hope to have Marie back before long." Will tried to sound optimistic.

Meanwhile, in the front seat of the 1984 Reliant car, Marie stared helplessly at the man beside her.

"Where are you taking me?" she blurted at last. "Why don't you leave me alone?"

"That's what I'd like you to tell me!" Burton burst out with a volume of profanity. "Why are you following me? What business do you have spying on me? Well, you got me into trouble with the police once. You and those goody-goody friends of yours." He looked at the defenceless girl huddled against the passenger door and a harsh cackle rose from his throat. "Thought you were smart, didn't you? You and your sleuthing game. I was going to pick up Olivia. What a fool! Thought I wouldn't recognize her if she made herself look ridiculous." He laughed again. "But then you came along. Even better. Now who's in trouble?"

"What are you going to do to me?" Marie made herself ask it again.

The question evoked another string of cursing. "You stupid woman. You're nothing but a pack of bother. Now I have to lose time getting you out of the way."

Marie knew her friends would not be long in notifying the police of her disappearance. The police would be out looking for her. But they would be looking for his red Ferrari, she remembered. That thought caused a lump to form in her throat so big it almost choked her. Her eyes scanned the unfamiliar countryside now fast fading in the gathering darkness.

"Lord, You know where I am," she whispered. "You will never leave me." The thought brought reassurance.

"Where are you taking me?" she asked again.

As if in response to her question Burton pulled onto the shoulder of the highway and stopped. Marie's eyes widened in horror as she watched him whip off his necktie. Holding her arms tightly together he twisted the tie around them, securing it to her belt. With one sweep he yanked her red scarf from around her neck and rolled it into a blindfold.

"Not so tight," Marie protested.

Burton only laughed.

They drove in silence after that. Marie leaned back in her seat, fighting to control her fears. Surely Burton would not kill her. Not the man who lived under the same roof with her. Oh, she had never liked him, but she had not imagined he could be a murderer.

"God, You are my only way out of this mess," she prayed in an undertone. "Show me what to do." The thought came to her that if she kept calm she might have some effect by reasoning with him. "Lord, help me keep my cool and reason my way out." She was not aware that she was verbalizing the words.

"What are you saying?"

"I was just thinking, Burton," she began almost casually. "You managed to get away today, but that's only for a short time. The R.C.M.P. will soon catch up with you."

"Not much chance," Burton threw back at her. "I'll make sure you won't be running to them with any more tales."

"Without our leads it might have taken them longer, but sooner or later the game will come to an end."

"You are the one that's playing games," Burton spat out. "I can be out of the country in short order. Besides, what do they know except your stories and what is that to go on? Nothing. Nothing at all. I have a good reputation. No marks on my record. Your Indian friend is the one that's the suspect now." He broke into a mirthless laugh. "Sure got even with that religious blimp for putting the police on me."

Marie decided not to tell Burton that William had been released. That might only drive him to more desperate action.

"Burton, that is only a temporary out for you. The police will investigate and find out the truth. My absence will only intensify their efforts and increase the charges against you."

"Shut up you..." Marie pretended not to hear the outburst. She fought for control of her emotions, praying fervently for wisdom.

"You will be an immediate suspect in my disappearance. Who else would have reason to want to get me out of the way? The very fact that you nabbed me affirms your guilt. So the better you treat me the better your chances, Burton."

"And let you witness against me? Not on your life."

Marie sensed that her words were beginning to have an effect on her captor. She continued, "If you take me back safely that will speak in your favour."

"You expect me to return you to the cop shop? Fat chance."

"'Take me back to Echo Valley if you like. Or to the Double C Ranch or to my motel room in Calgary. If you hurt me that will say more against you than anything I could say in the witness stand."

No response.

"Okay. I won't witness against you. I promise."

Despite Marie's decision to keep track of the turns they made she had long since given up. It seemed to her that they were constantly weaving back and forth. She had no idea what direction they were heading or how long they had been driving when she noticed the car losing speed. Then suddenly they spun around in a circle and picked up speed again.

A ray of hope sparked in her mind. Had Burton decided to take her back, she wondered. She could only wait to find out, thinking it wise not to push her luck by too many questions.

Her stomach growled on empty and her need for washroom facilities was pressing. Surely Burton would stop for gas before long. Finally the sound of traffic died away and Marie knew they had left the main highway. When the loud barking of a dog reached her ears her heart leaped. They were coming to a farmyard, a home, a family, help.

Then her heart sank again. A dog's bark might not mean a welcome. Greenfield stopped the car and got out, closing the door behind him.

"What's going on?" a male voice shouted. Then she heard Burton talking rapidly, but although she strained her ears she could pick up only a few words of the conversation.

"Be gone...more loads...come back..." The stranger's voice was tense.

A door slammed and a woman's voice called loudly, "Who is it, Joe?"

"It's okay," the man shouted back. "Just go inside and wait." The door slammed again. The men's voices faded into the distance. Momentarily alone, Marie crouched down to get her head close enough to her hands to undo the blindfold. Suddenly the car door flew open. Burton screamed at her, accompanying his curse with a blow that sent her sprawling against the dash.

"You idiot, Greenfield. Don't you know when to quit?" the stranger yelled.

As Marie struggled into a sitting position she heard the gurgling sound of the car's fuel supply being replenished. Soon Burton got behind the wheel.

"Burton," she said simply. "I need a washroom."

He ignored the statement. The man beside the car spoke up.

"Let her go, Greenfield."

Burton merely swore.

"Let her go." The voice was louder this time.

"Go then and be quick about it," Burton hissed through his teeth. He reached across and opened the passenger door.

"You will have to release my hands, Burton."

It was the stranger who came around the vehicle and untied the knot. Marie rubbed her arms vigorously till they tingled with renewed circulation. Then swiftly she reached for her blindfold.

"No," Burton yelled.

"How can I see where to go?"

The two men led her, unseeing, though the deep snow. As Burton pushed her through the doorway of a long-unused outhouse, he hissed in her ear, "Don't you come out of there with your blindfold off if you know what's good for you."

"Will you please close the door?" she pleaded. The stranger obliged while Burton repeated his threat.

As soon as the door closed she reached for her blindfold, but checked her action when she heard Burton shouting, "I'll count to ten. Then I haul you out."

As he pushed his victim back into the car the man she did not know commanded, "Listen to me, Greenfield. Be back at two."

Burton grunted in reply. "The weakling suddenly getting authoritative," he muttered as he put the car in motion. Marie shivered from the cold. Wearily she leaned against the headrest, thankful that at least Burton had not remembered to tie her arms again.

The continuous motion of the car made her seasick. Driving, driving, uphill, downhill, around curves, turning, turning. Her head throbbed from the tension, the heavy blindfold adding to the pressure. She willed herself to relax and eventually drifted between sleep and wakefulness.

The sudden cessation of movement brought Marie to full consciousness. She continued to feign sleep in hope that she would glean some information about her whereabouts. Once Burton was out of the car she rolled the window down enough to allow the sound of voices to filter in. But no one came to talk to Burton. No dog barked in welcome. She heard only the sound of Burton's feet crushing the snow, then the slamming of doors and all was quiet.

A moment later she heard his footsteps returning and his callused voice ordering her out of the car. She slid from the seat and made her way around the vehicle on shaky legs. Ignoring the pull on her hair, she yanked off the blindfold and hurriedly wrapped it over the back bumper.

"Make it snappy. What's taking you so long?"

"I...I'm coming," she stammered, her voice conveying the fear that was almost choking her.

Burton grabbed her arm as she appeared around the car and propelled her through the garage into the deserted farm house. Alone inside the dark building with her captor Marie shivered. She felt along the wall for a light switch and flicked it on. Nothing happened.

"The power is off," Burton said flatly. "But you can stay here tonight, or as long as you enjoy it here." His mocking laugh bounced off the walls of the empty house.

He stepped closer to her and grabbed her shoulders with both hands, his stubby fingers eating into her flesh. His face loomed over her menacingly in the darkness and his breath was hot on her face as he spoke.

"Remember, I have your word that you will not testify against me, should it ever come to that."

"I promise," Marie answered meekly, her voice barely audible.

"Don't forget, I can do a lot worse to you than this," he hissed, giving her a violent shake. With that he pushed her from him and walked out of the house without closing the door behind him.

28

Alone

Marie pushed the door shut with a bang and leaned her quivering body against it. She heard the car door slam and through the window she watched the headlights disappear behind the dense growth of cedar.

"Anybody home?" she cried into the darkness. The words echoed through the empty house. There was no response. Sinking down on the floor in a heap she broke into sobs. She cried from the relief of knowing Burton had gone. She cried from weariness and uncertainty. And she prayed.

Casting all your care upon him, for he careth for you. She repeated the words to herself and found comfort in the fact that God knew her whereabouts. He was there with her. It was this assurance that had sustained her through the long drive. It was God who would help her out of this predicament. Her tears spent at last, she wiped her wet face on the sleeve of her coat and got up. Standing in the middle of the empty kitchen she listened to the quietness. Her own heartbeat sounded loud in the darkness. Slowly she felt her way through the house.

At last she laid down in the corner of what she supposed was a bedroom and tucked her purse under her head. Without bedding she could not find a comfortable position. She kept shifting from side to side to no avail. Tossing her bumpy purse aside, she tucked her hands under her head instead. She heard the hum of the furnace and thanked God that she had warmth, even though the lights were shut off.

"Probably due to the more humane attitude of the man I heard talking to Burton," she told herself. "He did not approve of Burton's actions. Will he come back for me? Not much chance. Better not count on that. He's likely a partner in crime. Probably glad to have got away. No, he won't come back."

Marie was speaking aloud. "It's less spooky to hear a human voice, even if it's just my own," she told herself. She looked at the watch on her wrist, but could see nothing so she tucked her hand back under her head and listened to its tiny pulse. The watch had been a gift from Marc. The thought of him gave her new impetus. She would get out of here.

"I know my friends are praying for me, Will, Beryl and John. By now they have probably alerted other Christians to pray." She found comfort in the thought. "And they will have notified the police about my disappearance hours ago.

"I will wait till daylight," she decided, "Then I will walk out. You will lead me, God." She continued to talk quietly to God as the hours wore on. At last she fell asleep.

When she awoke again the first glimmer of dawn was creeping over the earth's edge. At first she stared absently into the semidarkness, conscious only of her aching limbs. Then gradually the tangled memories of her night's experience crept into her memory. She moved to get up, and then froze as she heard a door being pushed open. Every nerve was taut as she listened to someone stalking through the house with hurried tread.

This was not Burton, she concluded, but someone in cowboy boots. She held her breath as the footsteps approached the bedroom where she crouched in the corner, petrified. The door swung wide and for one instant she saw the form of a man etched in the doorway. Then as suddenly as he had appeared he retreated, leaving the way he had come.

The back door of the house opened and shut again. A moment later she heard the beat of horse hooves galloping from the scene. When the sound had faded away in the distance she got to her feet and looked out of the window.

"Who was that?" she asked as she peered into the early morning mist. "Did Burton send someone after me? Or was that the mysterious stranger that was here the first time we were here? Perhaps this early morning caller would have proved to be a friend in need. He may have been a knight in shining armour looking for distressed maidens to rescue and I missed my chance to be whisked away to safety."

She went in search of the electrical control panel. She found it at last in a dark corner of the garage through which she had entered the house. She threw the switches and instantly the place was flooded with light. Next she turned to the bathroom. After a quick wash she stood near the heat register to dry. Then pulling her clothes over her still partially-damp body she continued her investigation.

A few cooking utensils and dishes were all that a search of the kitchen cupboards yielded. "Even if I have nothing to eat, at least I can have a drink before I start walking," she told her growling stomach. She filled a cup with water from the tap and drank thirstily.

In the basement her eyes roved over the concrete walls and floor in search of some clue. Storage shelves on one side held a few paint cans and empty bottles. Marie checked them carefully for a name or address, but found nothing. Through a door at the far end she entered what was obviously a root cellar. The bins had been emptied of vegetables and the shelves along one wall held only empty fruit jars. Disappointedly she climbed the stairs again.

When the garage revealed nothing she stepped out on the stoop. A small barn stood not far from the house and Marie turned her steps toward it. As she stepped cautiously into the dim interior she was greeted by the pungent, warm smell of a barn housing horses in winter. It, too, was now empty.

Outside again she followed a path to a barrel with the stench of burning garbage still hanging over it.

"Maybe I will find an old envelope or discarded school book with an address on it," she reasoned. Picking up a stick she stirred the charred contents of the container. The ashes and carbon billowed upward, stinging her eyes and nostrils. She threw down the stick in disgust.

Back in the house Marie checked the contents of her purse and pockets for anything that might aid her survival. "I have paper and pen. Why didn't I think of this before?" she spoke as she scribbled a note to leave in the house for anyone who might enter.

"Time to venture into the great unknown," she said, as she fastened the note to the door with a pin. "I will follow the lane through the trees. Once I get into the open I am bound to see some kind of landmark that will show me which way to go."

Turning off the lights and shutting the door behind her, she started determinedly along the trail. The air was pleasantly calm and the snow had been packed smooth by the moving trucks, but the feeling of uncertainty and the weakness from lack of food soon slowed her progress. She began to thank God for His blessings to her as they came to mind. There were so many. Soon she found herself humming a tune.

As she came out of the shelter of the trees she shielded her eyes from the brightness of the sun while she scanned the countryside. The vast expanse of hills and valleys stretching out before her made her feel very small and insignificant.

The tracts of the heavy traffic now twisted sharply to the right winding their way through a valley to meet the horizon beyond. In the opposite direction she saw buildings and she turned her footsteps toward them. The road was less packed making walking more difficult, but having a destination in sight gave her a new burst of energy.

She hurried on. Only a horse had broken trail toward the ranch houses since the last snow and she followed its tracks.

As she drew nearer to the yard it took on an aura of famiiliarity. Slowly her numbed mind began to recognize the ranch houses. She questioned whether her imagination was playing tricks on her. *Can this be real?* she wondered. *Is this what it looks like or am I dreaming? Am I really on the Double C Ranch?*

29

Excitement at the Double C

Peter spent the night at the Carpenter house so William would be free to leave if any word of Marie should come during the night. Bouncing out of bed the moment he opened his eyes Peter ran to the kitchen.

"Where's Uncle John?" he shouted.

"You are up with the birds," Beryl said, emerging from the master bedroom, "But your uncle was up earlier. He rode over to Bruce's place to find out why no chores were done yesterday while we were in Calgary." Just then John burst through the back door, reaching at once for the hall telephone. Beryl rushed to him.

"What happened?" she asked anxiously.

"They are gone," John said simply. "I'm calling Todd Richards."

"What do you mean, gone, Uncle John?" The pyjama-clad youngster crowded close to his uncle to make sure he would miss none of the excitement. "You mean like moved?"

"I mean moved," John replied. "Furniture, car, horses, everything. Gone. The place is empty."

Olivia had emerged from the bedroom and stood open-mouthed listening to the exchange.

"Isn't that akin to signing a confession that he was connected with the cattle rustling?" she asked.

"Could be. Oh, Good Morning, Todd," John replied to the voice on the telephone.

Quickly he told the officer of the Bruce's disappearance. "It's my guess he's heading back to Montana, but he may not have made it over the border yet."

"I'll see that the custom's people are alerted at once," Todd answered. "They could nail him at the point of entry."

"The police will be here later," he said as he hung up, "In the meantime I'll help Will with the chores." He was out of the door before he had finished his sentence.

Peter dressed in record time and joined the men at the corrals. After his other chores were done he spent a long time brushing the yearling that was going to be his riding horse once it was old enough to break. His Shetland pony nickered and Peter ran to the box stall where his regular mount was impatiently turning circles.

"Here I am, Shaggy." He gently stroked the animal's ears. "I didn't forget you." He slipped a halter over Shaggy's head and led him to an empty corral for a run. He was closing the gate when he saw someone coming along the trail through the pasture. He did not recognize the stranger plodding determinedly through the snow, her face half hidden by her turned-up collar. Peter climbed the rails for a better look.

"Daddy," he called, "There's someone coming."

William halted in his tracks as he studied the approaching form.

"That's Marie!" With a shout of welcome he ran along the trail to meet her. "Thank God, you're safe! What happened?

No, never mind that. You can talk later. Come on in for breakfast."

With tears of relief streaming down her checks Marie clung gratefully to William as he assisted her across the yard. Open-mouthed, John followed. Peter, bouncing ahead in excitement, was holding the door for them by the time they reached the house.

"Auntie, Miss Barr, look quick," he shouted, "Miss Stumbur is here!" Instantly both women ran to hug the bedraggled guest. "Thank God, you're back," Beryl cried in unmasked relief. She stepped back for a better look at Marie. "You look like you have been through the wringer. Let me help you out of your coat."

While Marie washed up, William put through a call to the police of Marie's arrival. There was relief in the officer's voice as he replied.

"Wonderful. I was organizing a neighbourhood hunt, but I can call that off now."

Before breakfast John prayed briefly, thanking God for Marie's safe return.

"We prayed so hard that you wouldn't get hurt," Peter volunteered.

"I know. I thought of that. That my friends would be praying, I mean. Maybe that's why he let me off in the end. Thank you. Thank you, all of you."

Now that the ordeal was over and she was safe in the company of her friends Marie felt a numbness settle over her. As soon as she had eaten she retreated to the spare room for a rest.

Constable Richards and an assistant arrived shortly and drove immediately to the vacated bungalow. When they returned from their investigation everyone gathered around the fireplace to hear the report. Marie appeared in the doorway looking her usual self. She waved a cheery greeting and sat down on the chesterfield.

"Where were you last night, Marie?" Olivia asked, glad that at last she was free to verbalize the questions that were waiting to tumble out. "The way you looked this morning I doubt that you slept a wink."

"I slept alright. It was probably the long fast that made me tired. That, and the uncertainty."

"Marie, will you start at the beginning, where you got out of the car at the airport and relate to me everything that happened from then on?" Constable Richards asked.

His interviewee reflected briefly on her recent flirtation with imminent danger before launching into the story that kept her listeners spellbound.

"I feel almost as if I were there with you," Olivia said when Marie finished her vivid recital. "Oh, I'm so glad you came away as well as you did." Impulsively she threw her arms around the girl beside her.

"You are fortunate to have friends like this," Todd said. He closed his notebook. "Thanks for sharing this information, Marie. When Burton's trial comes up I'll make sure you will not be required to testify. The evidence against him is overwhelming anyway."

"Has Burton been apprehended again?"

"He was picked up during the night. It must have been just after he dumped you in that empty house." The officer chuckled. "I got to hand it to you, Marie. That was smart thinking under some pretty grim circumstances. You can be sure he didn't get very far with his license plate covered up with a red scarf. Congratulations."

"Thank you," Marie answered. "You see, I had a long time to plan that while he was driving me around and around the country."

"Oh, I almost forgot." The officer handed a package to Olivia. "These are the pictures John left at the police station

173

in Calgary for identification purposes. I made reprints for the court so I can return yours."

"Pictures? Can I see them?" Peter asked.

"Certainly, Peter." Olivia handed the colour prints to him. He began laying out the pictures on the table.

"You will remember not to put fingerprints on them, won't you, Peter?" William admonished.

"I'll be careful, Daddy," Peter replied. The next instant he brought his index finger down with a thud. "That's him!" he shouted. "Yap, that's him. Right there."

Constable Richards was putting on his parka when he heard Peter's shrill announcement. Quickly he returned to the family room. "That's who, Peter?" he asked, leaning over the boy. "What do you mean?"

"That's him. That's the guy that said I could keep the watch. That man, right there." Peter jabbed at the picture again.

The Constable's lips formed a circle as he drew in a deep breath. "Are you sure, Peter?"

"Sure, I'm sure. I didn't much see the man, but he was wearing that jacket. I know."

"Thanks, boy," he said, rumpling Peter's hair. "Thanks. I will talk to you again. Now I have to get back to town."

30

PETER'S STARTLING REQUEST

Marie and Olivia stayed at the ranch till Monday morning. Back at school they settled into a busy schedule of classes and practices for the upcoming Christmas program. They did not return to the Charters' house till after classes were dismissed.

Over the supper table that evening no mention was made of their venturesome weekend in Calgary, but Marie suspected that their landlords had heard the story from other sources. If the Charters were uninformed of the charges laid against Burton, Sundre's weekly paper brought the case to their attention the following Wednesday.

The community buzzed with the news, speculating on the details and the eventual outcome. Still the elderly couple made no reference to Burton Greenfield. Olivia mentioned this fact as she and Marie were walking home after school one day. "After she has been bragging Burton up sky high I guess she's embarrassed to discover he's a crook," she said.

"Embarrassed and hurt, too, I would think, to be deceived by someone she trusted," Marie added. "I feel sorry for her."

"I say she had it coming," Olivia returned, "and I hope she learned her lesson."

Being a man short at the Double C Ranch, William and John rushed from their houses in the cold predawn of the Alberta winter to begin the feeding process. The three owners discussed the situation one evening after the chores were done.

"I was thinking of driving over to the Wilson ranch in the morning," John said. "I hear the new owners have moved in and won't be needing Allan Boschy. Apparently they have a family of boys that can handle the work. I was thinking we could take Allan on temporarily and, if he pans out okay and he wants to stay on, then we can work out a permanent arrangement. What do you think?"

"That would be great, just great. Aaron Wilson told me Allan is a responsible fellow and a hard worker. He expected to make Allan foreman of his operation. That was before he got sick and had to sell out."

"I will go over and talk to him right after chores, then."

"If he is not ready to start right away, what do you want to do with Peter?" Beryl asked. "I know you pack his lunch and leave breakfast on the table for him. Still for a six year old to have to get himself ready for school is expecting a lot."

"I know. It bothers me that he has to be alone sometimes when he wakes up. Are you offering to go over in the mornings?"

"I was thinking the simplest arrangement would be to let Peter sleep over here," Beryl suggested. "Only till we get help," she added quickly when she saw her brother was about to object.

"I don't know if I was thinking more of myself than of Peter. The house is mighty empty without him," William admitted. "But you are right. That might be the best arrangement for the time being."

"What you two need over there is a woman," John tossed out offhandedly as William was about to leave. He turned his head.

"I know that. I know that better than anyone. But Deedee is gone...gone. We have to live on and we are doing the best we can."

"Of course you are," John replied quickly. "You are doing very well at keeping house for Peter and we should find a replacement for Joe soon." When William had said good night and closed the door behind him, John turned to his wife.

"I guess my suggestion was premature," he said sheepishly. "Still, I didn't expect such strong reaction. He and Marie have been getting along so well together I rather expected he was thinking along those lines himself. I thought I'd give him a little push in that direction."

"I know," Beryl said understandingly. "I guess the memory of Deedee is still so fresh on his mind that the idea of another woman is unthinkable to him."

"How would you like to sleep over at Auntie's house tonight?" William asked his son the next morning. He had come in from the corrals to have breakfast with Peter.

Peter scraped his bowl with the spoon. "Do I have to?"

"Why not, Peter? I thought you enjoyed being over there."

"I do, but, well, I like being at home with you and... Daddy, why can't I have a mommy?"

William dropped his spoon into his porridge so that the milk splashed over the side of the bowl. "You know why, Peter. Your Mother went to heaven."

"I know, but can't God give me another one?"

"No, that wouldn't be the same. It would never be the same. Forget it."

"Jimmy got a new mommy."

"I know."

"He says you get used to a new one. He said no two mommies are alike, but they can be just as good without being the same. That's what his daddy told him and Jimmy says his daddy was right."

"I don't want you discussing our private affairs with Jimmy or anyone else. Get that?" William said sharply. Peter looked up with hurt in his eyes at this unusual reaction from his parent.

"Are you mad, Daddy? Please, don't be mad. I never talked about you. Honest. Jimmy told me he has a new mommy and I said, well, I said I wish I could have one, too." He slid off his chair as he talked and snuggled close to his father. "I didn't know that would make you mad."

Shamefacedly William hoisted the child onto his knee and held him close. "I'm sorry I got upset with you. There was nothing wrong about talking to Jimmy like you did. I can't blame you for wanting a mommy, Son." He spoke softly, his lips against the boy's dark hair. "It's just that I think about your Mother so much I can't think of anyone else taking her place. She was so much part of my life."

"But couldn't you get a mommy just for me?" Peter looked pleadingly into his father's face. William shook his head.

"Oh, Peter, look at the clock. Get your jacket and cap. The bus will soon be here." William was helping Peter into his boots when the yellow school bus drove into the yard. He handed Peter his lunch kit.

"Bye, Dad," Peter called, throwing a kiss over his shoulder as he ran out the door. William watched the bus drive away, then pulled on his parka and walked thoughtfully back to the corrals.

31

THE BOSCHYS ARRIVE

The next morning John and Beryl drove to the neighbours to welcome them to the community and enquire about Allan. Having a family of boys themselves they had dismissed him and he had returned to Calgary.

John dialled the Boschy number as soon as he got home. Allan was delighted with the offer of another ranch job and agreed to drive out the next morning.

William was feeding cattle when Allan pulled up to the corrals in a red pickup truck. He jumped from the vehicle waving his hat in jovial greeting as the rancher walked toward him.

"It is good to see you again, Allan," William said, shaking his hand. "And good to have you here to give us a hand. If you want to get settled I will direct you to your quarters so you can unpack your things." The rancher pointed to the luggage and camping equipment stowed on the back of the pickup.

"I'm in no rush to unpack. If you like I'll help you finish up with the chores first," Allan offered. "I can throw my stuff off after my sister arrives."

"Your sister?"

"Yeah, Marilyn is coming out to help me set up house as she calls it. Me now, I'd just as soon roll up in my sleeping bag, but Marilyn insists I live more dignified. Personally, I think this provides her with a place to dump all the odds and ends of family furniture she doesn't want to move to her apartment."

The chores done, William led Allan to his office to discuss the job. Allan looked with amazement at the computer terminal against one wall.

"That panel is not hooked up yet," William explained. "That is our rainy weather project. When it is finished the feeding process will be fully automated."

"No kiddin'. You won't be needing a man then?" Allan's face grew serious

"To the contrary. We're doing this so we'll have time for other projects. In fact, we hire one or two extras each summer beside our full-time man and we intend to do so again. Next spring there'll be more fences to put up and a well to dig for drinking water."

William was still discussing the work with his new employee when a white Lincoln Continental glided to a stop in front of the office. William rose from his chair, but even before he reached the door he heard the click-clack of heels on the cement walk outside. The door swung open and a trim figure in a western outfit stepped in, her beautiful face wreathed in smiles.

"Hi, Sis," Allan greeted her casually. The woman gave a slight nod in his direction, but her eyes were on his boss.

"Oh, Billy, how wonderful to see you again," she gushed as she moved toward him, her clothes crackling with their newness.

"And to see you. It has been a long time since you last visited Echo Valley," William replied. "I heard about your mother. Let me express my condolence."

"Thank you, Billy. How thoughtful of you." She gripped his extended hand in both of hers. Cardinal pulled up a chair for her.

"How is your work going?" he asked.

"I have not been working lately. I took a three month leave when Mother took sick. After her decease I took a Caribbean cruise with friends. Now I am disposing of the house and closing the family business. Since I am not expected back in my office till after the new year I thought I would help Allan get moved in and maybe spend some time in the country with him, soaking up the peace and quiet of the surroundings." Her deep blue eyes studied the view through the window.

"It is beautiful out here away from the rat race of the city. Your layout is really something, Billy," she spoke admiringly. "You obviously are a great success."

"I was about to suggest to Allan that I would show him to the house where he will be living. Do you care to come along?"

"I wish I could stay on right now," the lanky youth apologized when they had unloaded his belongings, "But Sis here thinks it important that I go back for another load."

"That's quite alright. If you have much more to bring out you are welcome to use one of our trucks. Our policy has always been to allow our men to use our truck when..." William stopped short in mid-sentence. "That's it!" he breathed. "Yes, that's it." He smiled sheepishly at the sight of the quizzical expressions on the faces before him.

"Pardon me," he said casually. "I just thought of something, but it is really quite irrelevant. As I was saying, you can use the big truck if that will save you extra trips. We can go back for it right now. Then you can stop at my house for a cup of coffee and a sandwich before you head back to the city."

"Oh, that would be great. Thank you. I am dying to see the interior of your house, Billy," Marilyn spoke enthusiastically.

As she stepped from the truck she paused to evaluate the Cardinal dwelling. "This is a beautiful structure, Billy, and I am sure the inside must be as beautiful."

"I suppose you go around sizing up buildings the way I look at cattle. One's work has a tendency to become a part of one's thinking," William said laughingly.

"I suppose so, but I have always appreciated beautiful buildings. That is why I went into architecture in the first place."

Marilyn passed through the large porch into the family-dining area. "This plan must be your original. It is well laid out. I expected your place would be like this. You have good taste," the woman said, eying her surroundings critically.

"You give me too much credit, Marilyn. Mom and Dad built this house," the owner reminded her with a laugh. "The plan came out of their heads and the material mostly off the property, timber and rock. All I put into this was muscle. When my parents left the ranch Deedee and I were glad to move in. Deedee loved this house from the first time she saw it."

"Of course," Marilyn shrugged, "Who wouldn't? This place has real potential."

As soon as the Boschys had left Cardinal telephoned the police quarters.

"Hi Todd. This is Cardinal. About Greenfield using our truck to deliver meat to Calgary. I can explain that."

32

WOMAN TO THE RESCUE

William walked slowly toward his house at the end of his day's work. He was hungry, but not in the mood for cooking. Canned beans would have to do. After all, beans were what was generally considered a cowboy's fare, at least in story books. As he opened the back door, however, he was greeted by the tantalizing aroma of beef steak. He stopped short, flexing his nostrils.

"Surprise," a female voice floated from the kitchen.

"This is a surprise," William agreed, poking his head around the corner. "I thought you were over at the other place getting Allan set up for housekeeping."

"I couldn't help thinking that you must be starving for a good home cooked meal after all these months of batching," Marilyn Boschy cooed as she walked toward him.

"Oh, I can't complain about starvation rations. My sister sees to that." He took off his parka. "And I'm pretty good in the kitchen myself when I have time. But tonight I thought I would have to be satisfied with beans."

He looked through the doorway again, his gaze sweeping over the big, stone fireplace, its flames crackling merrily. A card table covered with a lace cloth stood in front of it.

"I must say that even if we eat substantial meals as a rule, we do not often dine in such elegance. Thank you for this treat. You will have to add two more plates though, for Allan and Peter."

"Allan is going into town," Marilyn answered, her eyes twinkling up at him.

"One plate for Peter, then," William replied as he disappeared into the wash room.

"Oh, right," Marilyn murmured after William had closed the door, "You have a kid." As Marilyn turned back to the supper preparations Peter burst into the house with his usual bounce.

"Daddy, what's for sup..." He caught sight of the stranger taking English scones from the oven and stopped. He surveyed her silently. "Who are you?" he asked finally, looking around the room. His eyes grew round as they fell on the festive table with two tall blue tapers flanking a low bowl of flowers in the centre. "Wow, this looks special."

Noticing there were only two place settings he added, "Is this just for Daddy and me? Oh, that's nice." He rubbed his stomach and licked his lips in anticipation.

"What's wrong?" he asked a moment later when his presence had not been acknowledged. "Oh, I know," he said suddenly. "I'm not supposed to come past that door with these things on." He retreated to the porch to shed his outdoor wraps.

"It's like Christmas, isn't it, Daddy?" Peter commented during the meal, "Kinda special."

"We have Marilyn to thank for that," his parent replied. He turned to the woman across the table. "I must say you are a superb cook, Marilyn."

"I enjoy cooking," Marilyn replied. "I often have friends over to my apartment in Calgary for gourmet suppers. Next to architecture, my career choice would have been something in the line of food preparation."

"I hear you have done very well in your chosen field."

"Thank you. Now that I have moved up in the firm, however, I spend more time shuffling papers than actually designing." She gave a world-weary sigh. "I have made a few ripples in my profession, but in time one wishes for a change. Right about now I would be willing to ditch it all for a simpler life." William helped Marilyn clear away the meal while Peter stretched out on the rug in front of the fireplace with a pile of picture books in front of him.

"We have a whole evening ahead of us," Marilyn commented, wiping the cupboard top. "You don't have anything planned for tonight, do you?"

"It happens that I do. A group of young people come here every Monday evening for a Bible study." He looked at the clock above the mantle. "In fact, they will be arriving any time now."

"Arriving here?" Marilyn asked incredulously. "Isn't that what churches are for?"

"That is where Bible studies are traditionally held, I suppose, but home Bible study groups are becoming common. This is an informal sort of fellowship around the big table, everyone digging into the Book to find out what it has to say. You are welcome to join in. Allan, too."

Marilyn brushed a dainty hand across her forehead. "Oh, I would love to, I am sure, but I have a long drive ahead of me. I have to get back to Calgary tonight. Some other time, Billy."

The group of jubilant young people who arrived at the Cardinal house a few minutes later saw a brisk figure in a blue mink jacket emerge from the front door. Tossing her beautiful head as she passed the chattering group she slid quickly behind the wheel of her car and sped away.

"Because of extra activities the week before Christmas our meeting next week will be the last till after the new year," William announced at the end of the meeting. "Someone suggested we make it a social event. What is your opinion?"

"That would be a good time to invite our friends," Nancy volunteered. "They can meet the group and if they like it they can join the studies when we start again." The decision was quickly reached to make the occasion a potluck supper. When Marie shared the plans with Olivia back in her room Olivia consented at once to be her guest. Marie went to bed full of excitement.

The next morning she arrived at school early to prepare materials and patterns for the Christmas decorations the children would make later that day. Nikolaus Nicole met her in the hall. He was the first to speak.

"Good Morning, Marie. I've some good news and I want you to be the first to hear it."

"Good Morning, Nikolaus," Marie smiled, blinking away her astonishment. "I expect the good news is that you got your jewellery back."

"Not yet, but I do have good news. Since you had a hand in bringing it about I thought you should be the first to know." Nicole lowered his voice although no one else was in the building.

"The R.C.M.P. called me last evening. They have charged Burton Greenfield with the theft of my antique jewellery. He was the only one that knew I had taken it out of my safety deposit box in Sundre. I should have thought of that myself."

"You were not the only one fooled by him," Marie answered. "I hope you get it back soon."

"He still denies taking it. Constable Richards thinks his girl friend may have carried it into hiding or to a foreign Market. It is possible some pieces may be stowed away among his possessions. The police are still investigating."

"I will be happy to hear when you get everything back, Nikolaus, really happy for you," Marie said sincerely. "Especially since I was the only one in the school when the loot was stolen. Now that I think of it, the loud banging of the door and the heavy footsteps were like Burton's, not yours. I should have checked, but I guess I was too preoccupied with my own problems at the moment."

"Don't blame yourself. You didn't know about the keepsakes, of course." Then he smiled. "You must wonder why I emptied my safety deposit box in the first place."

"I wondered," Marie admitted, "But it's none of my business so you don't need to tell me."

"You see, I had hung onto these family keepsakes," Nikolaus continued as if he had not heard her. "I had promised my parents that I would not part with them, ever. Some of these heirlooms had been passed down for generations and they wanted them kept in the family. But I needed money badly. Do you understand?"

"Yes, but you do not have to tell me."

"I decided loved ones alive are more important than promises to those dead. Right?"

"I guess you're right," Marie said slowly, looking puzzled.

"So I took the jewellery case out of the bank last week because I had an appointment with an appraiser in Calgary for Friday evening." He shrugged. "Well, anyway, things are working out."

"I can't believe it," Marie said under her breath as she watched him walk away. *He is actually walking with a spring in his step. I don't really know what that was all about. What I do know is that it makes him happy and that is really something.*

33

FATHER'S DECISION

"Oh, I didn't realize how much I had missed you all. It's so good to see you again." Marie expressed her pleasure at being home for the Christmas holidays as she hugged each family member in turn.

"Oh, Oscar," she laughed as her brother ducked to escape her embrace. "Just because you're a teenager now doesn't say you can't welcome me home." The youth fled the scene and Marie went in hot pursuit, bounding up the stairs after him. A few minutes later they both returned to the living room, panting and laughing.

"I will get you before the holidays are over," Marie teased. "But right now I am interested in something to eat. My stomach tells me it's supper time and the aroma floating in from the kitchen tells me something good is cooking."

"Mom made your favourite, creamed chicken and mashed potatoes with mushroom gravy," Ruth filled in.

"Supper is ready to dish up now. Come set the table, Ruth." Mrs. Stumbur turned to the kitchen with Ruth shuffling after her on leaden feet.

"Come on. I'll help you," Marie offered. She took Ruth's hand playfully and escorted her through the door.

Once supper was out of the way Arnold brought the boxes of Christmas decorations from the basement storeroom and everyone gathered around, lifting out tinsel, coloured balls, and strings of lights.

"Oscar and I wanted to trim the tree last week, but Mom made us wait till you got here," Ruth explained.

"It was kind of you to wait for me. I always think of putting up the decorations as part of the Christmas celebration," Marie said, "Although I would have no cause to complain if you had gone ahead without me, seeing I already had a chance to help with the trimming of four trees this season. We had a tree at school, of course, and at the Charters' house. Then I helped with the tree for the program at the church and our Bible study group decorated the tree at Bill's house. We had a social time afterward instead of our regular study."

When the last bauble had been hung and the empty boxes removed to the basement, Oscar lit the artificial log in the fireplace and the family gathered around popping corn and firing questions at Marie, while she filled them in on the latest happenings in the Echo Valley robbery case.

"Boy, I wish I could be there," Oscar thrilled. "Just think, you're living out an old western. Who would have guessed that my sister would turn out to be a private detective."

"Time to call it quits for tonight," Marie said at last, stifling a yawn. "The past few weeks have been packed with activity and I am tired tonight."

"Aw, tomorrow is Sunday. We can all sleep in."

Marie shook her head. "No, Ruth, I have a better suggestion. Why don't we all get up in time to go to church together?"

"Boy, you really have gone fanatical," Oscar commented. "Church even when you're on holidays."

"Oscar," his mother reprimanded him sharply, twisting her hands self-consciously. Her husband rose from his favourite chair and stood looking into the dying embers.

"I support Marie's suggestion," he said at length. Slowly he turned around to face his surprised family. "It would be a good idea for us all to go to church in the morning." He looked at Marie. "I don't think any of us have been to church since you left. This would be a good time to get on track."

"But Dad, you never insisted that we go before," Ruth countered.

"Then this is the first time," her father responded.

Julie waylaid Marie a few minutes later as she carried the cups to the kitchen sink.

"This Bill Cardinal you mention so often," she said hesitantly, "Is he someone special to you?"

"Not in the way you think, Mom," Marie answered seriously. "He is a friend. I suppose I could say he is a special friend. I wrote you about how his wife died in the accident with Marc, remember? So we have that in common, the fact that we both lost the one we loved. Then he showed me what it means to be a Christian. After I accepted the Lord..."

"Okay, okay," Julie silenced her, "But you didn't accept this...uh...religion just because of him...because you wanted this Bill, I mean?"

"No way. Jesus Christ means more to me than any man ever will. Just knowing..."

"I was just wondering," Julie interrupted again. "You were the most conscientious one in the family...about going to church and all. I just can't understand why you suddenly decided that our religion wasn't good enough for you any more. I know your dad says it is not a cult you are mixed up with, but I can't help worrying."

"A cult? Oh no, not a cult. And it's not a new religion, Mom. It is a personal relationship with Jesus Christ. It is living for God instead of for myself."

"You already said that...in your letter."

"Would you like me to explain it to you the way Bill told me?" Marie asked, turning to face her mother. She noticed her mother bristle.

"No, no. Just forget it."

Kneeling beside her bed that night Marie prayed again for each member of her family in turn. "God, while I am at home I want them to see that Jesus lives in me. The Bible says there is a time to speak and a time to refrain from speaking. Show me the difference so that I will keep quiet when words are not necessary, and so I will speak when I should."

As she prepared for bed she thought of her mother's question again. *Bill Cardinal is just a friend,* she told herself. *It's true, he is a special friend. A very special friend. He cares what happens to me. I care about him.* She paused in front of the mirror to give her hair a quick brush. *In fact, I care an awful lot about what happens to him.*

A surge of emotion welled up in her as she evaluated her own attitude toward Bill. *He is special to me, more special than I realized,* she told her reflection, *But that's just because of what he has done for me. It may be that someday he will love again, but he doesn't think of me in that way. When he does decide to marry again I expect she will be someone really special. Anyone deserving of a man like William would have to be an exceptional person. He would not settle for anything less.*

34

THE HOUSE

Slender, pink fingers of sunlight were reaching gingerly over the eastern horizon as the Greyhound bus wheezed to a stop in front of Echo Valley's general store. The driver swung down the steps, turning to give a hand to the only passenger disembarking. Marie turned up her coat collar, wrapping her scarf tightly around it, while she waited for him to retrieve her suitcase from the baggage compartment.

"Here you are, Miss." He handed her the large bag. "And a happy new year to you."

"Thank you, and a happy new year to you, too," Marie replied. "And thanks for the trip," she added with a wave of her hand as she turned down the familiar street toward the Charters' house. In the grey-white crispness of the January dawn, her gaze automatically followed the road that wound like a black ribbon through the snow-covered countryside to the ranch below. Her eyes rested fondly on the area in the valley marked by the glow of vapour lights.

Double C Ranch is like an oasis in the desert to me. The way they have taken me in...Beryl and John...and of course, Bill.

She recalled the feelings of aloneness and confusion with which she struggled when she first came to the area. She wondered now how she would have coped if Bill had not been there, if he had not proved to be the friend she needed...If, in fact, he had not introduced her to Jesus Christ...

As she turned in at the Charter gate she breathed a silent prayer of thanks to God for what He had done for her. She set her suitcases down and turned the lock. The door groaned on its frosty hinges as she pushed it open. Closing it quickly behind her, she removed her boots and climbed softly up the stairs to her room. She was about to crawl into bed to catch an hour's sleep before breakfast when she heard a car door slam outside. Surprised, she looked out of the window to see Stewart Charter plugging an extension cord into his car. *I must say this for the man,* she mused as she stretched out on her bed, *the operation of selling plants and seedlings certainly keeps him busy.*

Olivia arrived at the school only minutes before the nine o'clock bell. "I hope Mrs. Grimm didn't notice me come in," she sighed as she rushed through the front door. "But nothing ever escapes her keen eye." In the hall she met Nikolaus Nicole, beaming broadly. Olivia shook his hand as they exchanged a quick greeting in passing.

"Talk to you later," she said over her shoulder as she rushed toward her classroom. Even in her haste she observed a remarkable change in Nikolaus. The ringing of the bell, however, cut off any chance to reflect on the change.

Not till classes were dismissed for the day did Marie and Olivia have an opportunity to share the experiences of their Christmas holidays. Olivia bubbled happily about her reunion with her fiancé as they drove home together. Suddenly she caught her breath and tramped down hard on the brake.

"Look at that, Marie!" she exclaimed excitedly, pointing at a small house they had often admired as they passed. A moving van was parked in the driveway. "Oh, Marie, this could be a dream come true!" she enthused. "Let's stop at the store and find out." When Marie did not reply immediately, Olivia continued, "Don't you see? We could rent that."

"I don't know," Marie spoke slowly. "Maybe that's not such a good idea."

"What do you mean, not such a good idea? Why, don't you remember how we talked of finding a place to stay by ourselves, do our own cooking. You were as enthusiastic about the idea as I was."

"Oh, I know. The thought was appealing, all right, but I rather like our present arrangement, now that Burton is out of the picture. I've become accustomed to having my meals served, no dishes to wash. Besides, I wonder how the Charters would feel about our leaving now. When we moved in last fall they naturally expected us to stay for the term. They are probably counting on that extra income. Probably don't make a lot of money with their small gardening business, selling seeds and slips or they would not bother with boarders in the first place."

"But, Marie, I thought this was the answer to our dream."

"I know, but I hate to disappoint them. Wouldn't they feel like we were unhappy with them if we suddenly moved out? And after all, they do treat us awfully well."

"They do that. But..." Olivia fell silent.

"Oh, don't look so crestfallen," Marie said quickly. I'm not writing it off entirely. I guess there's no harm in inquiring about it." They walked across the street to the general store. Dick Taylor greeted them cordially.

"You own that house across the street, don't you?" Olivia asked excitedly. "We saw the moving van and wondered whether you are looking for new tenants. Marie and I w..."

Olivia paused when she saw Dick shaking his head. "You mean you are not renting again?" she asked.

"Those movers are not moving furniture out. They are moving it in. The Custers moved out during the holidays. Decided to go to the city. Closer to their family and medical help when they need it. They were getting on in years."

"We are too late then," Olivia stated flatly.

"Just as soon as Nicholas Nicole heard it was being vacated, he spoke for it," the congenial grocer told them. He pointed across the street. "Their furniture just arrived from Montreal."

"Their furniture? From Montreal? You mean?"

"That's right," Dick said. "Nicholas flew east for Christmas and apparently they worked out their problem. Anyway, she's flying out tomorrow morning. Nick is going to Calgary to meet her."

"Whoopee," Olivia gave a shout. "Great going, Nicholas Nicole! That explains why he was walking on air today."

"That's right," Dick said. "This is more like the Nicholas we knew when they first came to Echo Valley." He shook his head again. "Just didn't adjust after she took off."

"Where has he been living?" Marie wondered.

"Right here," Dick pointed to the rear of the store, "In a little room at the back. Ever since she left." The subject was dropped as other customers entered the store.

"I still don't understand what the loss of his jewellery had to do with all this," Olivia said to Marie when they were back in the car. "But I am convinced there is a definite connection."

"I don't understand it either," Marie answered slowly. "He tried to explain it to me once, but I was just as confused when he got through." Her face brightened. "But he's getting his wife back and I guess that's what really matters."

"You know, I feel so excited about Nicholas and his mystery that I don't really mind about the house." Olivia slammed on the brakes at the curb in front of their boarding place when another idea hit her. She slapped the steering wheel with her open hand, inadvertently honking the horn loudly. She ignored the honk.

"Why don't we write all this down? By the time we have recorded all the mysteries around here we might have the puzzle figured out. It would make a good story, don't you think?"

In the days that followed Marie and Olivia had numerous occasions to meet Monica Nicole. As they became acquainted they soon put the puzzle together.

The young bride had difficulty adjusting, not only to life in the foothills of the Canadian Rockies, but also to being without money. Soon after they were married, Nikolaus had invested what money they had in shares in a business that proved to be fraudulent. Monica had begged him to sell the family jewellery, but Nikolaus remained determined that the old treasures were to be passed on to future generations. Only when she had learned of his decision to sell them for her sake did she realize how much he really wanted her.

35

Spring

The days, weeks, and months slid joyously past for Marie. Almost before she realized it, the Chinook winds thawed the winter blanket of snow. Children in rubber boots and splash pants delighted in finding the deepest puddles. As Marie and Olivia walked to school one morning they saw their first crow of the season.

"When I was younger, Ruth and I always had a contest. We would keep count of the first hundred crows we saw, but I don't know if either of us ever won. By the time we got half way there the crows were so numerous that we lost interest."

The signs of spring popping up all over, and Easter only weeks away, stirred feelings of loneliness in Marie's heart. The fact that Olivia was blissfully enthralled in marriage plans brought back vivid memories of her own situation from a year ago. She wondered if she would ever get over missing someone she loved so much. Or if she would ever want to. Every harbinger of spring seemed to arouse new longings for Marc.

It was on a sunny day in early April that Marie and Olivia met Marilyn Boschy for the first time. They were walking down the church steps after the Sunday morning meeting when William caught up with them. He stopped to greet them. Almost immediately a mink-clad stranger detached herself from the surrounding group of acquaintances and made her way to his side.

"Billy dear, don't forget I made lunch reservations for us at a restaurant," she reminded him without looking at his companions.

"No problem, Marilyn. We have plenty of time to get there," William answered casually. Drawing the newcomer into the circle he made the introductions.

"Glad to meet you," Marie smiled. She hesitated, wondering whether to address this sophisticated person by her first name or to use a more formal term. She added a belated "Marilyn," as she shook hands.

"How do you do?" Marilyn responded as she surveyed the two briefly. Then she abruptly turned her attention back to William.

"Dear, you will be hungry by the time we get there. Don't you think we should get going?" William checked his watch.

"Our reservations are for two o'clock. By that time I will be ready to do justice to those lobsters, but there's no rush. Excuse me for one moment." He turned to Olivia.

"Oli, are you aware that Burton Greenfield's preliminary hearing is coming up in late May or early June? You may be required to take the witness stand." Turning to Marie he added, "Apparently the police are going to let you keep your promise to him not to testify against him. They think they have enough evidence against him anyway."

"I have been thinking we need to talk about some of the details to be sure I have the facts straight. If it's anything like TV they will go, 'And what were you doing in the early morning of

December the sixteenth,' and on and on." Olivia laughed. "It should be exciting if I don't blow it."

"You are right. We must get together to review the events. We will talk about it after Easter."

"Billy, we really must be going now." Marilyn slipped her hand through William's arm. "Come on, Dear."

"'Billy dear,' of all things," Olivia muttered as she watched the rancher being whisked away toward the shiny Lincoln. "'Billy dear, we really must be going now,'" she mimicked. "Who does that woman think she is, anyway? I have heard him called William, Bill, Will, and I don't know what else, but 'Billy dear?' I bet he has not heard that since he was a kid."

Marie made no reply as they started the brief walk to the Charters' house.

"What's the matter, Marie? Is that woman getting under your skin?"

"Oh, no. Why do you ask that?"

"Oh, you know why! The way she spirited Bill away as if she owns him. Doesn't that bother you?"

"I guess she is trying to impress him alright, but Bill is big enough to look out for himself." Marie gave a short laugh. "I must say this for her, she has good taste."

The following evening Olivia and Marie drove to the ranch together for the weekly Bible study. Although Olivia attended an occasional Sunday worship service, she had not accompanied Marie to a Bible study before. Despite Marie's numerous invitations, she had always received a negative response. In fact, Olivia had avoided any comment on the subject of Christianity since that evening when Marie had explained to her how she had come into a personal relationship with Jesus.

Why had she agreed to come this time? Marie wondered. Was it just because I was leading the study as she claimed or was her heart softening toward the gospel?

Marie's prolonged silence annoyed Olivia.

"Come on, Marie. Admit you are ticked off with that woman."

"You mean Marilyn? Don't worry, Oli. She is wasting her time," Marie spoke seriously. "If Bill some day decides to get involved with another woman it won't be someone like Marilyn."

"Then why so quiet?"

"If I am being poor company it is because I was thinking. Thinking and praying, too. You know, it is kind of scary to lead part of the study tonight."

"Kinda scary," Olivia echoed. "But why? Speaking comes easy for you."

"But I'm doing the Bible study. That's different."

"How's that?"

"Well, this is different because it is on a spiritual level. The Bible says we can't understand spiritual things unless the Holy Spirit helps us. Just a minute, I will find the place in the Bible where Jesus told his disciples why He would send the Spirit. Then I will read it to you."

"Never mind, Marie. You don't have to start your lecture before we get there." Olivia had cut Marie off more abruptly than she had intended. She did not understand why the subject always irritated her whenever it came up. She was beginning to wish she had not come.

"Well, at least I don't see that woman's flashy limousine around," she said with a sigh of relief as they pulled to a stop in front of Bill's house.

"No, Marilyn has a job in the city during the week. Her brother says she likes to come out to spend the weekends with him because she enjoys the country."

"Yes, I bet she enjoys the country," Olivia spoke in a mocking tone, "Especially when a good chunk of that country is owned by an eligible widower."

"Oh, here's Allan now." Marie waved at the young man coming across the yard. He tipped his broad brim in return.

The girls waited beside the car till he came abreast of them. Marie introduced the two.

"Howdy, Lady." He spoke with a studied casualness as he shook Olivia's hand. "When I was goin' to school I never dreamed the day would come when I'd be pleased to see a schoolmarm, but here's two of them I'm glad to know." He smiled boyishly as he steered them through the door, his humour shining through his eyes.

"Help yourselves to something to drink from the counter, coffee, tea, or fruit juice," Bill said. He took their coats.

With cup in hand the newcomers joined the group already seated around the large table. After prayer, the host opened his Bible to the book of Philippians. Everyone listened quietly while he pictured the relationship between the author and the infant church at Philippi. He explained that Paul was a prisoner of Rome. His friends helped him write the letter while he was under constant surveillance. He knew the need of the Christians for instruction in the faith they had so recently embraced.

"To learn what exhortations the Apostle Paul gave to those fledgling believers and how that advice applies to us in our modern-day society, we will have to read the book itself," Bill said. Marie held her Bible close to Olivia so she could follow along as each one read a verse. Then Bill called on Marie to expand on what she had learned from studying this section.

As Olivia listened to Marie she wondered how her friend could find so much meaning in these words that had said nothing to her. Marie's words in the car came back to her. *This is different because it is on a spiritual level. The Bible says we can't understand spiritual things unless the Holy Spirit helps us.*

As everyone was leaving, William waylaid Marie at the door. "This is a tough month, isn't it?" he asked quietly.

Marie nodded.

"I know. Maybe I can help you. After the holidays I want to take you for a drive. I have something to give you. How about the eighteenth?"

"April the eighteenth," Marie repeated slowly. "Yes, that would be good. Thank you." She smiled up at him then and their eyes met in a moment of understanding.

Marie knew that over Good Friday and Easter, now only days away, memories of last year's holiday with Marc would hound her. Fortunately, she would be with her family. When she returned to Echo Valley, Bill would be there to keep her company on the first memorial of Marc's death. Her spirit was buoyed up by the promise that she would not be alone on what could well be the darkest day for her since she had come to terms with her loss. William had recognized their mutual need for comfort on the anniversary of the accident and had given her something to anticipate.

Best of all, she had the promise of Jesus, *Lo, I am with you always.*

She looked forward to the Easter break and found herself humming cheerily as she finished marking school work and packing her suitcase. Mr. Charter was going into Edmonton and offered her a ride immediately after school on Thursday.

36

GOOD FRIDAY

The Stumbur house was wrapped in quietness when Marie awoke on Good Friday. Quickly she showered and dressed. Then, tucking her packet of Bible verses into her sweater pocket, she slipped from her room for an early morning walk around the familiar neighbourhood.

As she tiptoed down the hall she noticed a shaft of light under the door of the den. *Who would be awake this early?* she wondered. *Maybe Mom got an inspiration to write.*

She tapped lightly on the door. When no one answered she concluded that the light had been left on the night before. She pushed open the door to reveal her father sitting with his back to the door, his face buried in his hands. Immediately concerned, Marie stepped toward him.

"Dad, what's wrong? Are you not feeling well?"

Arnold Stumbur started. Slowly he turned around in the swivel chair, a smile creeping over his wan face.

"Marie, I didn't notice you come in. Good Morning."

"You are not sick, are you? You look rather pale. I mean..."

"No, I'm not sick." Mr. Stumbur ran his hand through his dishevelled hair. "I have just been sitting here thinking over my past life."

"I apologize for disturbing you then. I better go," Marie spoke undecidedly, "and leave you alone to your reflections."

"No, sit down, Marie." He father pointed to an easy chair. "I'm glad for a chance to talk with you alone."

Marie sat down and waited for her parent to begin. Instead he lapsed into reverie. Marie did not disturb him. In time she began to wonder whether he had forgotten she was there. What had brought about his present state of mind she did not know, but she sensed that a battle was waging within this man who had always appeared so strong and self-controlled.

He had been a good man. His wife had been secure in his love and had often said so. "Arnold told me when we were dating," Marie had heard her say, "that when he married it would be for life. He said he didn't mean a marriage that would merely exist for the full duration. He intended to enjoy it to the end."

Her mother's confidence had spilled over to the family. Although Marie had seen some of her friends distressed by unstable home conditions she could not recall ever entertaining doubts about the continuity of her family life. If guilt caused his present perturbation it was not due to mistreatment of his family, she was sure. But she also knew that a good life alone did not bring peace of heart. No life was complete without God at the centre. *There is none righteous, no, not one,* came to her memory. *For all have sinned and come short of the glory of God.*

Watching her father run his fingers through his mop of red hair, her heart went out to him. Although Marie found the room temperature comfortable, drops of perspiration glistened on her father's forehead. *Does he understand God's gift of salvation?* she wondered. *Does he know God's forgiveness? I have never heard him or Mom talk about it.* She prayed silently for them.

"Wasted," she heard him murmur, more to himself than to her. "Twenty-five years, wasted." His hand shook as he wiped it across his face. "I have not done it, not in twenty-five years." He fell silent again.

"Do you want to talk about it?" Marie asked.

Arnold Stumbur straightened up, a look of resolution settling on his face.

"When I was a kid," he began, "I had this friend. Oscar was his name. Oscar Barnes."

"I remember you named Oscar after an old friend. Was that the one?"

"Yes, him. We spent a lot of time together, the two of us. His family took me along to Sunday School. Then one summer when I was about thirteen or fourteen I went with them to a Bible camp at Thompson Lake. We had a great time, swimming, boating, softball, all kinds of things. And every morning we had church, singing hymns, Bible lessons, the whole thing. In the evenings we gathered around the campfire for more singing and testimonies. Kids would tell how they had accepted Jesus. Oscar, too. I knew I didn't have what they were talking about, but I kept telling myself I had done nothing wrong. No real crimes.

"Then one night the preacher talked about that very thing. I still remember that meeting. He said God's Son died in our place. He said murder was not the worse sin we could commit. The most serious crime is to reject Jesus Christ. He made us and loved us. He died to pay for our sins. To refuse to accept His gift was the meanest thing we could do. That night I prayed to become a Christian." Marie gave a little gasp.

"Then you do know what it means to be a Christian!" she exclaimed. "I never knew that."

"That is because I never told you. I told no one, not for the past twenty-five years." His head dropped. "Twenty-five wasted years," he ended in a sob.

"God will forgive that, too," Marie heard herself speaking into the pause that followed, "Just like He forgave you in the first place."

"Yes, I keep telling myself that. I have been talking to Him about that this morning. But I am so ashamed. I love Judy so much and yet I never told her. Not in twenty-five years. I turned my back on God. Lived a life of compromise because I was scared."

The fireman shifted in his chair, flexing his limbs. "I never meant it to be like that. After I became a Christian I was really happy about it. I joined the young people's group at the church. I became friends with the kids there. My activities during my teens centred largely around the church.

"Then this beautiful girl came on the scene. I was working as a packer at a grocery store and she came to work there. When she started paying attention to me, wow, I went all out to impress her. When I found out she had no interest in church I didn't have the guts to tell her what it meant to me. I should have told her right off that I was a Christian, but I kept putting it off. I was afraid she would drop me if she knew.

"At first I kept going to church and young people's. I made up excuses why I was tied up certain nights. Then things got pretty serious between us and I decided I wanted her at any cost. I promised myself I would explain everything to Judy after we were married." He shook his head again.

"I did suggest that we go to church together and she went along with the idea. I thought if she heard the gospel..." He cleared his throat. "It didn't work out that way. The only church she knew about was little more than a social club. Since I had not admitted to having any church affiliation before, I just went along with her choice. We went more or less regularly at first..."

"Ruth tells me you have all been attending church regularly since Christmas. I was glad to hear that." Stumbur nodded.

"You know, Marie, when you wrote about your decision to follow Christ, I was so happy for you." He smiled self-consciously at his attentive daughter. "I wanted to tell your mother then what I believed. I wanted to start over, but I felt so ashamed of myself. Then I saw her nervous reaction to your letter and..." He paused again. "Well, I chickened out."

"When you made that decision at Christmas time to go to church, you meant to tell us then?"

"I had made up my mind to do it while you were home. When you suggested we all go to church I thought that was the right moment to come out with it. But...it's a hard thing to turn around after sliding along for so long. I..."

"Oh, here you two are," Judy said as she emerged through the doorway. She kissed her husband. "You must have been out of bed for hours, Arnold. I suppose you are hungry by now."

Marie volunteered to look after breakfast. She walked out of the room and closed the door behind her.

"I have something more important to do first," Arnold said. Judy stepped back, eyeing her husband.

"Is something wrong, Arnold? You have been so restive lately. Are you ill?"

"To the contrary. Come sit down with me and I will explain." He led her to the chesterfield and sat down beside her. Taking her hands in his, he looked earnestly into her face as he began his story.

37

EASTER

"I have decided that from now on we will all attend church together," Arnold Stumbur told Ruth and Oscar at the breakfast table. "I want to find one that sticks with the Bible and preaches salvation. Come Sunday, we will check out the place I used to go to." Arnold and Marie were excited at the prospect, Julie apprehensive. As for Ruth and Oscar, this sudden switch of directions in their family life left them confused.

While the Stumbur family rolled out of their beds on Easter Sunday to dress for church, the congregation of the Echo Valley Community Church had already gathered in the church yard. Standing in a semi-circle between the building and the graveyard the believers watched the sunrise as they sang joyously of the resurrection of Jesus Christ.

Up from the grave He arose,

With a mighty triumph o'er His foes.

He arose a victor...

William's heart thrilled with the message these songs conveyed, his strong baritone voice blending with the rest. Beside him Marilyn Boschy stifled a yawn behind her carefully-manicured hand. She could not recall a time she had roused herself from her bed at such an unearthly hour for the purpose of going to church. *But if that's what it takes I can do it,* she told herself. She heard the next hymn announced and the singing continued.

I serve a risen Saviour,

He's in the world today...

Marilyn shifted uneasily, trying to balance on her toes to keep her high heels from sinking into the soft soil beneath her feet. A coolness crept through the early morning air and she pulled her white stole tighter around her shoulders. William noticed her shiver and stepped closer to shield her from the breeze. She glanced up at him then, her face suddenly wreathed in a grateful smile.

The trail across the pasture should soon be dry enough for Willy to drive me to the lake, Marilyn thought. She was eager to tour the location of the future resort and size up its possibilities. The visit to the spot had to be postponed because of the spring thaw. *That is one thing that will have to be taken care of right away. The construction of an all-weather road will have to be given first consideration,* she determined.

She was thrilled with the prospect of some new excitement for the community of which she expected to soon be a part again, and she had encouraged Bill in his plans ever since he had first mentioned them to her. *To think that Will has decided to open up his lakeside property is even better than I dreamed.* Marilyn smiled to herself. *Life on the Double C need not be drab after all. In fact, it could become quite exciting. The right planning and the right advertising will attract many influential and interesting people. I will see to that.*

She tried to remember what Will had said about wanting the resort to be a ministry for God. She knew he had high ideals and motives. Of course, providing a place for recreation and relaxation would be a service to fellow men. *Just like I'm making a meaningful contribution by designing beautiful buildings,* she thought.

> *"Beneath the cross of Jesus*
> *I feign would take my stand,*
> *The shadow of a mighty Rock*
> *within a weary land."*

Marilyn remembered that song, too. This had been her mother's favourite. For that reason Allan had insisted it be sung at her funeral. Why were they sticking with those old outdated hymns? The new tunes they sang in her church in Calgary were not so, well, disturbing.

> *My sinful self my only shame,*
> *My glory all the cross.*

The singing stopped at last. The preacher's voice penetrated Marilyn's thoughts.

"I am the resurrection and the life..."

He was reading from the Bible now. The words stirred memories in Marilyn's subconscious and held her attention momentarily.

"'He who believes in Me, though he may die, he shall live. And whoever lives and believes in Me shall never die.'"

I remember hearing that in this very church when I was growing up in Echo Valley. My Sunday school teacher had us memorize that verse. Well, I believe it. I know Jesus died so I can go to heaven some day. But I don't know what that has to do with standing out here where the wind and the dampness can make havoc of my hair. And at such an unearthly hour! Imagine meeting for an Easter service beside a cemetery. I wonder what the reaction of my city friends would be if they could see me now.

Marilyn had not attended church often after moving to Calgary, had not had time with all her other involvements. She had made it a practice to go at Easter though.

But it was never like this. She recalled the spring fashions and padded pews in an attractive sanctuary artistically arrayed with fresh flowers. She considered that much more appealing than this. That particular church complex in Calgary gave her a special sense of satisfaction because she had starred in the designing of it. For that reason she had frequented the meetings more often after the new building had been erected.

Now Marilyn's eyes swept over the adjacent graveyard. *Easter is meant to be a joyous occasion. These morbid-looking grave markers are monuments of death. This is a place of death: Dead bodies under the ground, last year's dead grass on top. Everything is the same drab colour.* She found it all very depressing. She looked back at Pastor Baxter.

"'In a moment, in the twinkling of an eye, at the last trumpet. For the trumpet will sound, and the dead will be raised incorruptible, and we shall be changed.'"

The aged pastor continued to quote Scripture throughout his sermon. As Marilyn caught snatches of it she marvelled at his brilliant memory.

"Instantaneously these graves will spring open. Tombstones will topple as all believers in Christ Jesus are caught up. What a day that will be! What a reunion with those who have crossed over before us!" Eyes grew misty as they looked over the low stone fence to where their loved ones lay buried. William wiped his hand across his eyes and cleared his throat. Peter turned around to look at him. Instinctively William reached out his hand and drew the boy closer. Marilyn witnessed the emotional moment and was irritated by it.

Deedee has been dead for almost a year now. That marriage is over. Why does the preacher talk about reunions anyway?

"What a welcome will be ours from our Saviour who loved us and gave Himself for us. What a joy will be ours when we behold Him face to face, the King of kings and Lord of lords."

The brief service over, the worshippers turned to greet one another.

"What a wonderful service," William spoke in awe. "I am glad we decided to gather out here this morning. It seemed an ideal setting to be focusing our attention on the resurrection. Don't you think so, Marilyn?"

"I must agree it certainly is an innovative idea. Pastor Baxter is quite ingenious. Remarkable, really."

"You will both be staying for the pancake breakfast, won't you?" Mrs. Baxter asked as she shook hands with Marilyn and William.

"I am sorry I will have to forgo that, Mrs. Baxter. I must hurry home to do the chores, but I am sure Marilyn intends to stay."

"I would love to, Mrs. Baxter, but I can't see Willy going off to slave without at least having a good breakfast cooked up for him. I better do that for him."

"Don't think of it, Marilyn. By the time I have looked after the cattle Beryl and John will be back. Then we are heading out to spend the rest of the day with mom and dad."

"Please convey our greetings to them," Mrs. Baxter said, "We miss them so much. And do drive safely." She patted his arm motherly as he turned to leave.

"Marilyn, I am so glad you are able to be with us today," the pastor's wife continued. "I know many people here will be glad for a chance to renew your acquaintance."

Former neighbours and school chums were already coming to talk with Marilyn. The next thing she knew she was being swept along with the crowd toward the church doors.

38

THE GIFT

Back in Echo Valley after the glorious Easter weekend with her family, Marie's thoughts naturally travelled ahead to the Friday night outing with William. Her excitement mounted as the week wore on. By the time Friday came around her heart was bubbling in anticipation. Olivia noticed the extra effort Marie was putting into preparations for the night out and offered to style her hair.

"What do you think your gift is going to be?" she asked candidly. "Must be good if he has to make a special occasion of the presentation."

"Supper in Sundre, that's gift enough," Marie countered. "I don't expect him to give me anything on top of that."

"That is not the way I interpret what I overheard him saying to you," Olivia sang out as she brushed Marie's hair up into a bun.

"Olivia! Bad enough to have my friend eavesdropping on me without reading more into what was said than what was intended. What he meant was that he was taking me out for dinner. That's the gift." Marie sobered as she continued. "It was a year ago today that Marc and Deedee were killed. Bill knew we would both be lonesome and he wanted to do something to keep us both from becoming depressed."

"I'm sorry, Marie." Olivia was silent while she stepped back to survey Marie's reflection in the mirror. "This gives you a dressed up look. I think it looks great on you. What do you think?"

"I like it. Thanks, Oli."

"Good. Now just wait and see if that rancher of yours doesn't reach into his pocket for that little present." Marie swung around in her chair.

"Oli, you're a dreamer. Bill has never even implied anything like...like engagement!"

"Marie, my deductions are not ungrounded. The special attention he pays you. Always concerned about your welfare. Stuff like that. And I'm not the only one to notice. When Bill drew you aside to talk to you when we were leaving Monday night I happened to catch Beryl's eye and she gave me a quick wink. She was thinking the same thing." Marie opened her mouth to protest, but Olivia raised her hand to silence her.

"And that woman, Marilyn Bushy or Bossy, or whatever her name is. She obviously considers you a threat to her schemes. Why else did she think she had to rush Bill away?"

Marie felt the warm colour creeping into her face and turned away to hide her emotions. She realized Olivia was putting into words thoughts that she had not allowed herself to think. Could it be that Olivia was right?

At the sound of the doorbell Olivia slid from the desk where she was perched.

"Good luck, Marie," she said with a knowing smile, planting a quick kiss on Marie's cheek. "I will see you in the morning," she threw over her shoulder as she breezed from the room.

Marie tingled with excitement. She drew in a deep breath and let it out slowly. Then, turning to the mirror, she checked her reflection one more time before sedately descending the stairs.

William was standing just inside the door, exchanging small talk with Stewart Charter. As he opened the door for Marie, the older man rejoined his wife in front of the television set. The click-clack of Mrs. Charter's knitting needles never missed a beat.

The evening air was calm and clear. The temperature was pleasantly warm for April. Marie leaned back in her seat and watched the landscape glide past.

"A perfect night to be out," she sighed contentedly.

"That it is," Bill agreed. "We could not have asked for better weather."

Gradually the light faded from the sky, and the outline of the trees and fields grew dimmer. Here and there vapour lights lit up the yards of the farmers and ranchers along the highway.

Conversation flowed spontaneously, the occasional lapse into silence neither awkward nor embarrassing. *Bill's free and easy manner could put anyone at ease,* Marie thought. And he made any subject interesting.

"It is no wonder you and Marc became such good friends," she heard herself saying. "He was interested in everything, too. I learned a lot from being with him. He was always interesting and fun. We laughed a lot. And he was considerate. So considerate and kind."

The man beside her nodded understandingly. Marie rattled on.

"You are a different individual, quite different, yet you have all those same wonderful qualities. All the things that matter..." She suddenly caught herself and stopped short. William looked at her then, smiling.

"Why, thank you, Marie. That was a wonderful compliment."

Marie studied his face, wondering if he guessed what she was feeling. Yes, William Cardinal had all the qualities that matter most to a woman. He was all she wanted in a husband. She valued especially his devotion to Christ. For the first time since Marc's death she had allowed herself to think of marriage again.

"Have you considered getting a car of your own, Marie?" Bill asked casually, breaking the silence that had settled over them.

"Very much. When I was home for the holidays my dad took me to several second-hand car lots, but we didn't come across anything we were happy with. Dad said he will keep his eyes peeled for a vehicle in good condition."

"What do you have in mind?" William tapped the steering wheel with his hand. "Are you interested in something like this?"

"I am afraid I would have to settle for something smaller. And older." Her eyes swept over the interior of the Mazda mini-van. "Something like this would be out of range for my bank account and I have made up my mind not to finance."

"A wise decision," her companion smiled.

"I do hope Dad finds a good car soon. He is going to phone when he does. Then I'm going to Edmonton to pick it up," Marie explained. "I will be glad when I can offer transportation to Oli for a change instead of the other way around. Of course, now that Grant is back in the country I don't expect she will be in Echo Valley much on the weekends."

"Did she hit out for Lethbridge today?"

"No, Grant spent the day scouting around for a job in Calgary, so he is coming to Echo Valley this evening. When Anna heard Oli's fiancé was coming she offered the basement bedroom for him to stay tonight."

"That was thoughtful of her."

"It was," Marie agreed. She wondered silently at her landlady's excitement over Oli's romance while turning into an icicle every time she saw Marie as much as leave the house with William.

"They are going shopping for the wedding tomorrow. Oli has been compiling the longest shopping list I ever saw," Marie chuckled. "She filled up about two feet of adding machine tape."

At the restaurant the conversation drifted to plans for the resort. This subject occupied William's mind a good part of the time, but he shared his dream with few others, only his family, a few close friends at the church, and Marie. More and more the two of them would discuss the plans whenever they were together. Marie had become the sounding board on which William tried out any new ideas.

From the project's conception Beryl and John had supported the idea. John would take over the management of the ranch in the spring, freeing William to head up the new undertaking. Allan Boschy's common sense and enthusiasm for ranching and anything related, including hard work, made him a boon to the Double C. The owners had no qualms about entrusting him with many of the ranch's responsibilities. Over plates of steaming rice and lemon chicken William updated Marie on the latest developments in the plans.

"I mentioned the project to Marilyn a few days ago. She was immediately enthused."

"Marilyn?"

"Yes, Allan's sister. She is an architect, as you probably know. I happened to mention the resort only briefly and she surprised me by offering to make drawings. She has considerable experience in designing lodges, motels, cafes...Different layouts that she says have a lot in common with the type of buildings we need for what we have in mind."

"Does that mean you will save some money?" she asked, not knowing just what to say. She hoped her question was not too far out of line.

"We had not intended to have this done professionally since we expect to keep everything simple. But like Marilyn pointed out, having someone do the job who knows about this type of thing can save us some headaches later on. Besides, someone who understands our purpose as well will be that much more of a help. She said she wants that part to be her contribution."

He paused, smiling. "It's wonderful how everything is working out. Allan becoming available just when we needed a man, then Marilyn happening along. That was another god-send."

"How soon will the blueprints be ready?"

"Oh, she will have them completed by the time we are ready to start construction. The next time she comes out to spend the weekend with Allan I intend to take her to see the site. She needs to see the natural setting before she can make any suggestions."

This Marilyn must be a different person than I took her to be, Marie decided.

When William and Marie arrived at the car after the dinner, William paused. His eyes were on Marie as he reached slowly into his pocket. Marie watched him and her heart skipped a beat as she remembered Olivia's words. What he drew from his pocket, however, was a set of car keys. He dangled them in front of her.

"For you. Happy Motoring, Marie." Marie stared at him blankly while he went on to explain. "I bought this car just over a year ago to use as a family car and for Deedee. Big enough so we could take friends. I usually use the pickup when I go by myself or with Peter. And if some day I change my status..." Bill paused without finishing his sentence. "Well, anyway, I have decided to give it to you."

"But...but you could sell it... use the money to get the retreat centre going. I... I..."

"I know. I thought about that, but it seemed appropriate for you to have it. I wanted to do something for you today. It's kind of a memorial gift." He placed his finger under her chin and tilted her face up so she was forced to meet his gaze. "Remember I told you I wanted to give you a present today? Well, this is it. Don't you like it?"

"Like it? I like it fine," Marie stammered. "I… I'm just dumbfounded, that's all."

"I thought maybe you were bothered by the fact that it's not new."

"Oh no, not at all." Marie ran her hand along the fender. "That only makes the gift that much more meaningful."

"I appreciate that. I thought you would understand."

William held out the keys again. This time Marie took them.

"Thank you, Bill." Her eyes twinkled with a moistness of which she was not aware. "Thank you. I don't know what else to say."

"No need to say anything more." William opened the door and Marie slid behind the wheel.

"My own car," she whispered, petting the wheel. Her hands were clammy with excitement.

"I will be glad to navigate."

Marie could hardly contain her excitement until the next morning to show Olivia and Grant her car.

"Mark my word, my dear, men don't go around handing out cars as casual gifts. Your next gift will be a sparkler. Bill is definitely in a whirl over you." *If Olivia is right…*Marie relished the thought. It occupied her mind over much of the weekend.

At church on Sunday morning, however, she noticed the attention Bill directed to the woman at his side. As Marie started home she heard her name called. She turned to see Marilyn detach herself from Bill's arm and come toward her.

Marie wondered what the woman that had avoided her up to this point suddenly wanted to say to her.

"Marie, Billy told me he gave you the car that his wife used to drive," she said through smiles. "I want to congratulate you."

"Thank you, Marilyn. I was quite surprised to get it."

"Oh, I am sure you were. But that is the way Billy is, always feeling sorry for the less fortunate. I suppose he was tired of having it sit around anyway, and he knew I would not want the old thing. I would not accept anything that had belonged to another woman. But then, those who have to depend on charity can't be choosers, can they?"

"Thank you for your congratulatory words," Marie said without a smile as she turned to leave. Marilyn's words left a bitter taste in her mouth.

39

Change of Plans

Marilyn's late model Lincoln coasted to a stop in front of the Cardinal residence. Even in a jogging suit the young woman looked eloquent as she strode briskly up the walk. William swung open the door for her.

"Hello, Billy," she greeted him. "I can't tell you how happy I was to get your call." She planted a light kiss on his cheek. "I had been waiting for the moment that you would say we could check out the lake site. I am so excited about your novel plan." Marilyn paused for dramatic effect.

"A ministry to your fellow men. What a wonderful way of looking at it," she spoke slowly, reflectively, as she walked the full length of the room and back. "How like you, Billy, always thinking of others." She stopped directly in front of him, her face turned up to his. "I can hardly wait to get started."

"Then I won't ask you to contain your enthusiasm any longer. Let's go!" William escorted her out to the truck parked in the driveway just as Marie and Olivia pulled up in front of Charter house.

"That woman again," Olivia muttered, making no attempt at hiding her feelings toward this stranger who had suddenly intruded into her circle of friends and was treading on what Olivia considered Marie's turf.

"Oh, they are probably heading for the site where Bill plans to erect some new buildings. He told me Marilyn offered to do the architectural drawings for him." She was trying to convince herself rather than Olivia. Olivia grunted in reply. Peter rushed up to greet the teachers.

"Hi, Peter," Olivia greeted him. "How come that woman is with your dad?"

"Oh, she's with Daddy all the time. She fusses over him, but she doesn't much like me, though."

William could not wait to show Marilyn the site and tell her of his dream. Deedee's dream, actually. It was she who first had the inspiration and had opened his eyes to the potential before them. His desire had been to fulfil her vision, the vision she had passed on to him.

Surely now the Lord was working out the circumstances to help him get this project underway. Double C Ranch needed a man just when Allan Boschy was available. Employing him had led to the encounter with Allan's sister. Marilyn having time off to help get the project underway was truly a provision from the Lord. Her training in real estate and architecture would be invaluable. Just the person he needed right now to discuss the mechanics of the project, the buildings, things like that. That was the area in which she felt she could share her expertise.

She had understood immediately when he talked of the ministry aspect, he reflected. Today they would discuss in detail the avenues of ministry he had in mind so she'd know just what was required. He could just imagine her enthusiasm when he explained all the possibilities for helping others that this place presented. Bill led Marilyn to the spot that had become hallowed ground to him.

"Deedee rode out here one day to check on the cattle," he began. He would tell her the whole story of how the dream came to be. "She reined in the horse right here..."

His eyes swept the scene before him, envisioning what Deedee had shared with him. He did not perceive the smile slipping from Marilyn's face or the slight jerk of her body.

How distasteful! Why does he bring me out here to talk about his dead wife? she protested inwardly. *He will have to give up talking about that woman. I will see to that.* When William turned to face her, Marilyn beamed a winsome smile at him. She appeared completely composed.

"The world is full of people who don't know where to turn with their problems. Here hurting people will find a place where they can be alone, a place where there will be someone to listen when they want to talk, someone to pray with them, to council. Here they will have a chance to learn what God has to say to them."

"What do you mean?" Marilyn interrupted. "What kind of hurts? What kind of problems?" Her voice sounded hollow.

"Whatever their hurts are. I am thinking about the products of broken homes, men and women deserted by their spouses, young people left homeless, those struggling with addictions, loneliness."

"You do not mean it. You do not mean you are turning this beautiful spot into a...a rescue mission. You do not intend to fill this place with derelicts and drunks!" Her face had turned white under her makeup. "That is not what you are saying, is it?"

"Not exactly," William said slowly, his arm falling to his side. He stood still, momentarily nonplussed.

"I'd not thought of a rescue mission in the same sense as the rescue missions in city slums. That's what you meant, isn't it? Not all the people who need help are found in the gutters, Marilyn. I am thinking of a rescue mission of another sort, a place to help people before they hit bottom. I mean the ordinary people on the street, in places of business, in schools and universities, and in the homes. They undergo grief and loss. They have hang-ups, battles to fight. Sometimes we all need a place where we can get away from the stress of everyday life."

"I see what you mean," Marilyn said sweetly, her smile back in place. "But do you not think you are carrying this moral thing a bit too far? You could certainly be more effective if you toned down the religious part a bit. I agree that it is right to worship God and all that, but it is possible to go overboard, to become fanatical."

"Marilyn!" William was aghast. "Marilyn, don't you see? It is not a matter of being moralistic or religious. It is a matter of extending help where help is needed."

"Oh, that is all very good, but you have your own life to think about, Willy. You cannot expect to change the world single-handedly."

"But I can do what I can," William answered calmly. "Now, shall we look over the site?"

The two of them walked over the grounds, discussing the most suitable spot for the four-winged building that would house the general office, family-style dining room, and chapel. There would be smaller rooms for prayer and counselling. Marilyn pointed out some factors to be taken into consideration in choosing the exact spot. William made notes as they discussed the best location for the buildings, but he knew the project had lost its appeal for Marilyn.

Marilyn, too, realized her candid comments had been a mistake. She had become too sure of herself and those few unguarded moments, she knew, would curtail her progress in winning the man she was determined to marry. It would take time to regain the ground she had lost, but she was not defeated. She knew how to turn on her charms.

Back at the house William changed his clothes and hurried to the corrals. Marilyn whisked about the kitchen, preparing the supper she had so carefully planned. She knew how to tickle a man's palate.

If the way to a man's heart is through the stomach, like the adage my mother used to quote, I will cook him a meal that will make him forget the little incident at the lake. It is a good thing his kid is at Beryl's place. I hope he jolly well stays out of the way till we have had dinner. That will give me ample time to smooth down any ruffled feathers.

Marilyn's thoughts were interrupted as Peter burst through the door. Dropping his jacket in the porch he made his way to the kitchen where Marilyn was taking a pan of biscuits out of the oven.

"Hi," Peter greeted her. He had come to accept her presence in their house these past two weeks. For the most part he stayed out of her way, but right now he was thirsty.

"What are you doing here?" Marilyn demanded.

"I came in for a drink of water." He clambered onto the counter and stood up to reach a glass. Marilyn swung away from the stove.

"Peter, get down from there. At once." As he hurried to obey, the glass slipped from his hand and shattered on the floor.

"Look at the mess you made." Her voice was louder this time. "Get out of here, you stupid brat. Do you hear me?" She swung her open hand at his head, but he ducked the blow.

"Get out!"

Peter needed no urging. He was already making his escape as fast as he could straight into the arms of the man who had entered the house unobserved. Marilyn looked up to see William standing there, answering her shocked look with a steady gaze.

"I will be ready to serve dinner as soon as I get this glass swept up," she said quietly when she had regained her composure.

"Good. We will clean up. Come on, Peter."

By the time William and Peter were ready to sit down Marilyn had returned to smiles and sweetness. The table was attractively laid, Marilyn's culinary ability had never been more obvious, but the meal was not a festive event. William had seen Marilyn in her true light when she expressed her disgust with his idea of a resort. The incident between her and Peter just reinforced what he had already recognized. Plans for her involvement in the project had vanished. As soon as Marilyn had said goodbye and closed the door behind her, Peter gave vent to his pent-up feelings.

"Daddy, I don't like when she comes here," he sobbed. "She's mean." William sat down in the rocking chair in the corner and drew the boy into his arms.

"I know, Peter. But she won't be coming any more."

Peter's head shot up.

"She won't? How come?"

"Because I don't want her to come any more." A sad smile creased his face. "And she won't want to come any more either."

William felt the boy's body relax as he snuggled down in his father's arms. William sat there a long time deep in thought, absently stroking Peter's hair till the youngster drifted off to sleep.

40

THE BATTLE WITHIN

Marie left the Charter house that evening with mixed feelings. As she turned her car around and headed down the winding driveway she noticed with some feeling of relief that the shiny white Lincoln was no longer parked in front of Bill's place. In the passenger seat beside her Olivia wasted no time in expressing her opinion.

"I've had it with Bill. First he spends all available time with you, leads you on by giving you his Mazda, practically proposing to you, and then he turns around and takes up with that woman."

She was putting into words thoughts that Marie had struggled with since Marilyn's brutal attack on Sunday. Peter's words had reinforced her fears. *Oh, she is with Daddy all the time. She fusses over him, but she doesn't much like me, though.* Marie had not mentioned Sunday's incident to Olivia, yet Olivia had come to the same conclusion. *But Bill does not have to give us an account of his actions,* she thought. It was Olivia that had fanned the flames of hope that had simmered in Marie's heart. Yes, that was it. Or maybe Marilyn had poisoned his mind against her...She closed her eyes and tried to squeeze out these thoughts. It was no use. She could think of nothing else.

Back at the ranch, William roused himself from his painful reflection. He needed to get outside into the fresh air, he decided. Rising to his feet, he strode across the yard to his sister's house with his sleeping son in his arms.

Beryl was stacking dishes into the dish washer. She looked up as William knocked and entered the kitchen without waiting for an answer.

"Beryl, Peter's asleep," he said, "I'm going out for a while. I would appreciate if I could just pop him into bed over here."

"Of course," Beryl responded, "Is anything wrong?" She studied his face. "You don't look good."

"Nothing you can do anything about, Sis, except to look after Peter until I get back. I just got to, well, think some things over. See ya."

Darkness had crept over the ranch, wiping out familiar landmarks as William started across the pasture. Driven by the unsettled spirit within, he walked at a rapid pace, like a man in a rush to reach his destination. Yet he had no specific goal in mind. In fact, he was scarcely aware of the direction his feet were taking him, so absorbed was he in the bitter conflict raging within his breast.

"What a fool I was," he muttered through clenched teeth, "To think that woman could play a part in this ministry!" She had flattered him and he had lapped up the attention she showered on him like an infatuated school boy. He could see now that she had not cared about the things that meant most to him. Her idea of a resort had not been to build a place to help others, but to construct some sort of showcase to attract celebrities.

After walking in a wide arch Bill suddenly found himself under the tree that had become his favourite place to pause and pray. Sinking down on the grass he poured out his heart to God. He confessed his lack of discernment and expressed gratitude to God for saving him from his own impetuousness. He wanted more than anything else for Jesus Christ to be glorified in his life. Using words of scripture he prayed that he would learn to know his Saviour better, to be conformed more and more into His likeness.

Lines from Lanny Wolfe's song came to mind:

I will trade sunshine for rain, pleasure for pain
If that's what it takes to make me like Him.

He repeated the words slowly, thoughtfully, searching his own heart to be sure he meant them. "Yes, Lord, that is what I want more than anything else, to be like You."

William had no idea how long he had lain there, talking to God. Gradually the cool dampness of the earth crept through his clothes and chilled his body. He rose to his feet, dusted himself off, and started homeward with a lighter step.

As he walked he caught himself singing snatches of hymns to his Lord. The realization of his own lack of discernment had brought him to a reassessment of his life goals, a renewed submission to God. He was aware of a deeper sense of commitment, an urgency to help others to experience a joyful relationship with Jesus Christ.

He thought of Marie then and of how far she had come in her walk with God in less than a year. *Funny, I have felt such a sense of responsibility toward her, to help her in Marc's stead. I never realized till just now how much she has given me in return. The newness of her relationship with her Saviour, the innocent way she laps up the Scripture, her boldness in telling others of Him. She has been like a breath of fresh air to me.* Suddenly William stood still.

"I didn't see it," he spoke in an undertone, "While I was trying so hard to help her come to terms about Marc's death and become grounded in the Word that all the time I was being comforted in my loneliness."

Marie more than anything else had helped him through his own bereavement. She had become a sounding board for him. His thoughts, whether new ideas for the resort or some new insight into a portion of Scripture, whatever it was, he had shared it all with her. And she had understood. This sharing had not only strengthened her faith as he had hoped, but her enthusiastic response had been an inspiration to him.

And then there was Peter. The way Peter had taken to her. His teacher in many ways had filled in for his mother. As he walked on he thanked God for Marie. Someday soon when he had opportunity he would thank her personally. It would encourage her to know she was being a blessing.

Back at the Charters' house Marie had plodded up the stairs with weary steps and disappeared into her room. Closing the door behind her she threw herself across her bed and stared up at the ceiling. A deluge of untamed feelings suddenly flooded her breast. Hurt. Embarrassment. Humiliation. Anger. Yes, anger toward Olivia, who had reinforced Marie's fondest dreams. Anger toward Bill, who had made her a special object of his attentions for so long. And anger toward Marilyn, mean, hurtful, selfish Marilyn!

"Oh God, why is this happening to me? Why do I have to go through a second disappointment?" Her thoughts leaped back over the past year to the devastating experience of Marc's death. It had been Bill that had steered her through the stormy waters at that time. It had been he who had guided her to a safe haven in Jesus Christ. Could she fault him now after all he had done for her? Could she blame him for the fact that she had begun to read into his actions intentions he never implied? And could she accuse Olivia for telling her what she herself wanted to hear?

But Marilyn! Why her? After sharing his life with a woman like Deedee, how could he even think of marrying someone like Marilyn? At this point Marie slid off her bed onto her knees, clasping her hands in prayer.

"Oh God, make me willing to release Bill to whatever and whoever You have for him." She felt her self-pity melt as she continued to communicate her thoughts to God. "Right now, Dear Lord, I long to know Your love. I want to feel Your arms around me. Oh Lord, hold me close. I want to experience Your love more than anything else. I put myself into Your hands." On and on she prayed till at last she fell into a peaceful sleep.

41

DEALING WITH DISAPPOINTMENT

"I don't believe it!" Olivia exclaimed when she saw Marie dressed for church on Sunday morning. "I thought not even you would want to go back to that church again, not after the way Bill has treated you. If I were you I would have nothing more to do with his religion."

"I would not give up my faith in Jesus Christ for anything. Even if people fail us, Jesus never fails. As for Bill, well, I can't fault him if I misinterpreted his kindnesses." She paused, her eyes shining with unshed tears. "After all, he introduced me to Jesus and it is Jesus who gives me the strength I need to carry on."

"But how are you going to face him?" Olivia persisted. "And that woman?"

"Not easy," Marie sighed. "I feel ashamed as well as disappointed. I am glad no one knows of my foolish fascination with Bill, except you. But there is a verse in the Bible that says,

'I can do everything through him who gives me strength.' I'm counting on that."

"No, it is not going to be easy," Marie repeated to herself as she walked the short distance to church, "But I can do all things..."

Nevertheless, her footsteps slowed as she neared the church. As she followed the usher down the church aisle she spotted Bill sitting in a pew by himself. She wondered why Marilyn was not beside him. Too late she realized that was where she was being taken. Her eyes stung with the sudden desire to cry and her legs wobbled. She sat down quickly.

Bill greeted her and she smiled in return before bowing her head in silent prayer. Soon she was caught up in the hearty singing and Scripture reading. Then Pastor Baxter stepped into the pulpit to deliver his message.

"Each one of you is standing in the doorway of time, looking out into the future. Life stretches out before you. Its potential is paramount—for good or for evil. God has given to each one of us a free will. We can choose to invest our lives or squander them. We can use the time we have left or abuse it. The decision is yours."

As Marie listened to the sermon she vowed inwardly to make her life count for God. *Lord, I am open to whatever You have for me to do,* she whispered in her heart.

When the last notes of the closing song had faded away, Bill turned to Marie. "That was a powerful word from the Lord and to think how easily we can be tricked into making wrong choices," he said.

Marie nodded, too deeply moved for words. She guessed Bill was speaking of a personal decision, but he gave no further explanation. Was he referring to her? Marie wondered what she should say to him that would seem natural. She was on the verge of asking about Marilyn, but decided instead to brooch the subject of Burton Greenfield's preliminary hearing scheduled for next Friday.

"The preliminary hearing is a chance for the crown to present its case for the judge to decide whether there is sufficient evidence to go ahead with the trial," William said in response to her inquiry. "Abraham Rosenberg, the prosecuting lawyer, feels there is strong evidence against Burton and the witnesses will back it up. Olivia will be called on as you know, and the Chows. And of course, Beryl and John. Seems Pauletta Fleet flew back to Calgary as soon as she realized Burton didn't follow her so she will be expected to testify. Then Joe Bruce will shed more light on what happened."

"Joe? Have the police located him?"

"They have known where he was for some time. He was not hard to find. All they had to do was to notify the rodeo officials to look out for him because sooner or later he would show up on the circuit."

"Where is he?"

"He has been working on a ranch in the Peace River area. When the police contacted him he told them everything he knew."

"Then he was involved?"

"Let's say he was aware of what was happening. I will be able to tell you more after the hearing. Keep praying about it."

"I will," Marie promised as she turned to go.

As the day of the hearing drew closer Anna became more and more ill at ease. On Friday morning her red-rimmed eyes and puffy eyelids showed evidence of a night of weeping. She did not speak during breakfast except to say that she would be out for lunch. She offered to set lunch for them. Quickly Marie assured her this was not necessary since she could take a bag lunch to school.

"I will be away, too," Olivia said. When she mentioned that she would be driving to Sundre with the owners of the

Double C to witness at the hearing, Anna's face took on a look of horror. Seeing her reaction Marie and Olivia waited until they were back in Olivia's room upstairs before referring to the matter again.

"It seems strange the way Mrs. Charter feels so attached to Burton," Marie said.

"Testifying against him doesn't bother me," Olivia stated, "But I feel almost as if it's a personal thing against Mrs. Charter." Marie had a final word of advice for her friend.

"Oli, despite how you feel about Bill at the present, remember you are on his side in this hearing."

"I won't accuse him of what he has done to you, if that's what you mean," Oli shot back, "But I may do a little sleuthing to find out what is going on in his mind."

"Oh Oli, you are not going to say anything to him about me, are you?"

"Don't worry. You can trust me," Oli said with a laugh as she ran down the stairs.

When the ranchers and Olivia arrived at the courthouse they were seated next to the prosecuting attorney. Rosenberg was a robust individual. His imposing size, matched by a booming voice, was enough to intimidate many a defendant in the courtroom. He had a reputation of using these qualities to his advantage.

"The charges pertaining to the jewellery theft have been dropped," Rosenberg informed them. "There was not enough evidence to incriminate Greenfield on that one."

"Not enough evidence to incriminate him?" Olivia gasped. "I thought..."

"Maybe they know something we don't," William reminded her. "We will have to wait and see."

Even without mention of the stolen jewellery the list of charges against Burton was long: cattle rustling, selling stolen goods, false impersonation, forgery, and kidnapping.

William was the first one called to testify. He told of the number of cattle disappearing from the herd on the Double C Ranch during the previous summer. They had been on a lookout for trucks that might be hauling them out, until on a skiing outing in November they had discovered that the old church building on the lake shore had been used for a slaughterhouse. They had found that a makeshift wharf had been erected nearby, indicating that the meat was taken out by boat. The day after the discovery, the place was destroyed by fire. He told of how Marie had been kidnapped at the airport and left in the house on the ranch which the hired man had vacated only hours before, unbeknown to his employers.

"Olivia Barr."

Rosenberg's voice echoed through the small room. Olivia took the seat and looked around at the faces before her, many of whom she recognized. Friends of either William or Burton, or both.

In answer to the prosecuting attorney's questions she related Burton's attempt to escape to Brazil. In retrospect her impulsive attempt to disguise herself sounded so unprofessional and childish that she was rather embarrassed to have to relate it, even though it did thwart Burton's plans and indirectly led to his arrest.

When Joe Bruce slid into the witness chair his eyes sought and held William's gaze as though pleading for understanding. His former employer hung onto every word as Joe explained how he had been befriended by Burton when he first entered the bank to open an account.

"He even took me out for coffee. He was excited about the fact that I was working for the Double C. I thought he was a special friend of my boss or something. When I talked about the rodeo he said he was interested in horses so I invited him to come see mine. He showed up the next evening. We rode around the ranch. Then we stopped for a drink. We was sitting at the table, drinking, when he tells me he needs a truck to haul some stuff he's bought. Do I have one he can borrow. I'm flattered by all this attention from him, see, and I thinks, what harm will it do so I say, why not? 'I can use the boss's truck any time,' I tells him. So I take the truck home after work the next day. When he comes out I'm ready to take him to the city. But he says, No, he don't need me. I don't like him to take the truck, but it's too late to back out now, I think, so I let him go.

"Then he comes again and again. I know then something is going on, but if I don't co-operate he'll tell Bill I've been loanin' out his truck. So I just keep still.

"When I find out about the operation I gets scared. But he says I can't back out now. I'm already a partner. When Beryl phoned about the fire I knew it was set on purpose so after that I run to get away from it all."

When all the witnesses had given their evidence the judge called the defendant. The atmosphere in the crowded court-room was heavy with suspense as a subdued Burton Green-field stepped into the witness box. He repeated the oath and sat down. His face pale under the florescent light, he returned the steady gaze of the judge without flinching.

"You have heard the charge against you. How do you plead?"

"Not guilty."

Abraham Rosenberg rose to his full height and glared down at Burton. Keeping his eyes diverted from William, Burton fielded the questions fired at him in swift secession by Rosen-berg, his voice so low that William could not catch the words.

"Speak up," the prosecutor barked.

Burton shifted uncomfortably and cleared his throat. Rosenberg repeated his question, his voice resounding through the quiet room.

"Between May first and November tenth did you not sell 3600 pounds of beef to Chow Restaurant in Calgary?"

ECHO VALLEY

William leaned forward, his hands clinched on the table in front of him, while the banker cleared his throat again.

"I did," he answered evenly.

"And did you or did you not pretend to be William Cardinal and on at least some of the occasions use his truck to make the delivery?"

"I did."

"And did you not receive payment totalling $11,210.00 in checks made out to William Cardinal?"

"Yes."

"And did you not endorse each one of those checks and draw out the cash at the Bank of Montreal where you were manager?

"Yes, Sir."

William settled back in his seat, satisfied that the case would be wrapped up in short order. Burton was not playing games any longer. Then suddenly the proceedings took a bizarre twist.

"And you rustled the cattle from the Double C Ranch, did you not?" Rosenberg was asking.

"No, I did not steal cattle," Burton answered evenly.

Under further questioning Burton maintained that he bought the meat ready for delivery.

"Mr. Greenfield, where did you buy the meat?"

A hush fell over the room and eyes roamed from Burton to William and back again.

"I bought the meat off the boat at the wharf. How was I to know..."

"Whose boat?"

"I do not know who owned the boat, or even if it was the same boat that brought the meat each time."

"Who delivered the meat to you?"

The rancher leaned forward, his hands gripping the table in front of him. He strained to hear the answer that did not come.

The attorney repeated the question, but still no reply.

William was obviously puzzled over this change of events. Someone else was involved, that was evident; maybe even the instigator, but who? Who could have slaughtered the cattle in the old church and ferried the meat across the water under cover of darkness?

More and more the net of suspicion was tightening around Joe Bruce and William didn't like it. Could it be that Joe was guilty of more than he had admitted in his testimony? Was it he who had turned the old church building into a slaughterhouse? In his mind William maintained his trusted hired hand was not guilty of more than he had revealed, much less instigated it. And yet...

All the evidence was to the contrary. William's ranch was the only one hit. Joe had already admitted to securing the truck for Burton. Did he also utilize the Cardinal boat to ferry the meat across the lake in the dead of night? And that disappearing act...Joe's link with the banker had been made obvious that night.

"There has got to be an explanation," William moaned through clenched teeth. He could do nothing but wait while the judge called for recess.

"What will happen now?" he asked Rosenberg.

"If Greenfield keeps hedging we will have to call up Bruce again. Unless he can identify the man for us the judge will give Greenfield no choice but to name his accomplice."

When the hearing resumed Joe Bruce once more took the stand. The prosecuting attorney came right to the point.

"Bruce, did you slaughter or in any way aid in the slaughtering of the cattle?"

"No, Sir."

"Do you know who did?"

"I don't know the man."

"Did you ever see him?"

"I seen him once. Me and my boy went down to the lake to go fishin' in the moonlight. We saw someone piling boxes into a boat. We sneak up on him."

"Would you recognize him if you saw him again?"

"Yes, sir."

"Do you see him in this room now?"

Joe's eyes travelled over the faces before him and came to rest on someone in the far corner. Slowly he raised his arm and pointed a finger.

"Him."

There was a rustling sound as people turned to look in the direction Joe was pointing. Olivia swung around just in time to see a dark figure rise from his seat. An audible cry escaped from her lips as with head held low and shoulders drooping he made his escape through the fire exit directly behind him. A stunned silence settled over the room.

42

The Bitter and the Sweet

Marie hoped Olivia would be back from Sundre by the time she arrived home from school. She was anxious to know the outcome of Burton's preliminary hearing. When she entered the house, however, there was no sign of anyone about. She bounded up the stairs and knocked on Olivia's door. There was no response. She walked through the house and found no sign of Anna.

It was unusual to see no supper under way and the breakfast dishes still in the sink. Marie enjoyed a cup of tea with a bran muffin while she scanned the day-old Sundre News lying on the table. Then donning an apron that had been tossed over the back of a chair she set about washing the dishes.

She was sweeping the floor when she heard footsteps on the stairs. She was relieved to see Anna Charter, but at the same time concerned over her appearance. Never before had Marie seen this energetic and immaculate woman with her long hair hanging loose and her face puffy from sleep.

"Oh, Mrs. Charter, I didn't know you were here. You must have been sleeping. Are you sick?"

"No, no. Just tired. I laid down and slept," Anna said groggily. She ran her fingers through her hair. "I'll go wash and comb."

No wonder she fell asleep, Marie thought as she finished sweeping the floor. She probably has not slept for many nights.

Anna soon reappeared as her usual tidy self, but her face still drawn and pale. The shrill ring of the telephone sent her hurrying into the hall to answer it. After a long conversation in a voice hoarse with tension, she came back to the kitchen.

"I'll make supper now," she announced in a tearful tone.

"No, Mrs. Charter, I will make supper. You do not look well. Just tell me what to do." Her landlady sank into the nearest chair without further coaxing.

"Where Olivia?" she asked suddenly.

"Olivia has not come back yet. She phoned that she is eating supper at the ranch before coming home," Marie answered. "Will Mr. Charter be home or will it be just you and me?"

"Why do you ask? You do not know?" Anna's eyes opened wide in bewilderment. Her lips quivered. "Don't you know he can't come home?"

"What is the trouble?" Marie asked gently, taking Mrs. Charter's hands in hers. "Is he sick?"

"Why are you asking? You know why Olivia went to Sundre."

"Listen. I am sorry about Burton being charged. I am sorry we had to get involved, but we could not avoid it."

Anna shook her head, but said no more.

"I see some leftover ham in the fridge. How would you like potato salad and sliced ham? That is one of your favourites, right?"

Anna nodded absently.

With supper out of the way Marie settled her landlady on the chesterfield with a cup of coffee and her knitting. She sat down in the easy chair nearby.

"Marie, I am glad you are here with me." Anna looked at her through moist eyes.

"I'm glad to be here, Anna," Marie replied. "That reminds me, I have never told you how it was that I came to Echo Valley in the first place, have I?"

Anna looked at her expectantly. So Marie began.

"A year ago I was engaged to be married to a man by the name of Marc Forrest. He finished university in January and came out to this area on a temporary job on a ranch. He worked for Bill Cardinal."

"Yes, yes, I remember. The man what got killed. Oh, too bad, Marie. Too bad. Sorry."

"So when I saw in the paper that Echo Valley needed a teacher I decided to come here and see the place Marc enjoyed so much and to meet his friends. I am glad I came. I enjoy teaching. I enjoy living here." Marie waved her hand to indicate the house. "And I have found something else in Echo Valley."

Anna listened attentively as Marie told of accepting Jesus as her Saviour and the change it made on her outlook on life.

"I always thought I was a Christian because I tried to live a good life. Then I came to understand that we cannot go to heaven because of the good we do. 'All have sinned and come short of the glory of God.' Jesus took our punishment and died on the cross. We become Christians by accepting His forgiveness."

Anna Charter sniffled as she wiped away her tears with her hand. She rose to fetch a box of tissue and blew her nose.

"Have you accepted Jesus into your heart?" Marie asked when Anna had settled herself on the chesterfield again. Her response was a shake of the head.

"Would you like me to pray with you now for Jesus to take away your sin and give you a clean heart?"

"Yes, yes, you pray with me." As Marie led in a prayer for forgiveness the elder woman repeated the words after her.

"When we open our hearts to Jesus His Spirit comes to live in us. The Bible says He makes us children of God. He gives us everlasting life. That means when we leave this world we go to live with Him in heaven. Do you believe Jesus has done this for you like you asked Him to?"

Anna nodded.

"Then do you want to thank Him?"

Bowing her head and folding her hands again, the new Christian expressed her thanks to God in a few words. Then with a grateful smile she looked up at Marie who was wiping away her own tears of joy. Marie reached out her hand and Anna grasped it firmly.

At the sound of the front door being pushed open Marie looked up to see a sombre-faced Olivia hesitate on the threshold with William behind her. As they slowly advanced into the room Marie noticed Anna's body stiffen. She clasped her hands tightly as she awaited the news they were bringing.

"Good Evening, Anna," William said, holding out his hand. "I am sorry. I had no idea."

"I didn't want Stewart to do it!" Anna blurted. "I told him, 'No.' I always told him, 'No.'"

"W-what..." Marie's gaze shifted from Mrs. Charter's face to William's, to Olivia's as she tried to make sense of the situation. Olivia's eyes locked with hers and her lips formed the word, "Butcher."

Instantaneously Marie's hands flew to her face that suddenly turned ashen. She sank against the pillows piled behind her in the easy chair and sat motionless while the cogs of her mind spun furiously. Bits and pieces of information suddenly surfaced from somewhere deep in her subconscious. An ugly picture was taking shape.

The deepfreeze full of beef, Stewart coming and going at odd hours, Anna's fear of Marie's involvement with the ranchers, discrediting the Cardinal name...Vaguely Marie remembered hearing that Mr. Charter had been a butcher for the military. Suddenly sick to the stomach she hurried from the room. Olivia followed.

"Oh Marie, I have so much to tell you," Olivia said as soon as they were alone. "You know how we thought Mrs. Charter was a klutz not to recognize what kind of person Burton was. Well, maybe it was just me that thought that. Anyway, it was her husband she was protecting. I was the klutz not to see who Burton's partner was."

"We both were. I still can't imagine it. I thought him such a nice man." As Marie turned to go Olivia caught her sleeve.

"One more thing. Bill and I had a good talk today. I changed my mind about him, too." As they returned to the living room, Olivia hoped Marie understood what she had gleaned from William by her forthright discussion.

William was seated on the chesterfield quietly talking to Anna.

"Bail has been set at $500," Marie heard him say. "I will drive you into Sundre in the morning to see him if you like." The old lady grasped at the chance.

"Yes, I want to go see him. I have the money. But why would you do that for me?"

"For several reasons," Bill answered, "For one, you are not guilty. Two, you need help and I want to be available to help people in need. And the third reason is this: Christ teaches us to forgive and to do good to those who have wronged us."

"You're a Christian," she smiled for the first time then. "I am a Christian, too."

Marie's heart leaped on hearing her landlady acknowledge her decision so recently made and added a few words of explanation of what had just transpired. As she spoke, Bill's gaze darted from one face to the other while Anna nodded in agreement.

"Oh Anna, I am so happy for you." He grasped her hand in both of his. "That is the most important decision you will ever make in your life. Before I go I would like to pray for Stewart." The group stood while he prayed aloud. Then, taking Anna's hand, he said good night, assuring her that he would call for her at nine o'clock in the morning. He thanked Olivia for her assistance in testifying. Then looking at Marie across the room he indicated for her to follow him.

"Marie, I want to talk to you. Alone." William paused. "I know it is late, but will you come for a drive?"

"I don't suppose it will take long. I can come if..." She turned to Mrs. Charter. "Will you be okay? I will be back shortly."

"You go ahead," the woman answered. "I'm going to bed. Tonight I think I'll finally be able to sleep." Marie gave her a hug.

"Go on," Olivia prompted with a wave of her hand and a knowing smile.

Once in the car William gave Marie a brief review of the day's events. Though Marie was eager to know what had happened she knew this was not the reason for this private meeting. Olivia could have told her about the hearing and was probably bursting to do so. What did he really want to say to her?

Reaching the ranch William turned the car along the trail across the pasture toward the lake. There he stopped and got out.

"How about a stroll?" he suggested, opening the door for her. Without a word she stepped from the car and fell in step with him.

"What is it you wanted to talk to me about? Do you have a new idea for the retreat centre?" Marie asked. "Where is Marilyn?"

"Marilyn? Marie, Marilyn is no longer involved in the project." He slipped his arm around her waist.

"She isn't? But I thought..."

"You thought I was personally involved with Marilyn? I am sorry if I gave that impression." They followed the edge of the lake till they came to the pier, while Marie tried to sort out her thoughts

"Marie, there is no one except you."

There is no one except you. Did he really say that? Walking the length of the pier jotting out over the lake, they stopped on the point looking over the water shimmering under the setting sun. William pulled her close.

Before asking her to marry him, he had intended to tell her all the words he had thought that night in the pasture after his experience with Marilyn. He had wanted to tell her how he had felt so responsible for her because of Marc, not realizing the comfort and encouragement she had been to him. He had meant to thank her for the way she had filled a vacuum in Peter's life and all the other wonderful things she had done.

But suddenly that speech no longer mattered. All that could wait. Ever since that night he had known she was the only one with whom he wanted to spend the reminder of his life. He knew he loved her and wanted to care for her. And that was what he told her.

"Oh Bill, I love you, too," Marie said softly, lifting her face to his. He kissed her then. After that they stood for a long time cheek to cheek without saying anything. Eventually they sat on the edge of the pier and watched the last rays of sunlight fade from the sky. They talked then of many things.

"Marie, when you told me about leading Anna to faith in Jesus Christ and then we prayed together for Stewart, it was like a confirmation to me of the ministry you and I will be sharing together in the future."

"What a thrill to explain to her how to be saved! Oh, Bill, that is what I want to do for the rest of my life, to help others come to know Jesus Christ."

"So do I, and by God's grace, that is what we will strive to do—together."

The End

About the Author

Martha Toews Anderson grew up with two brothers and six sisters in their farm home where she was born three miles northeast of the village of Waldheim, Saskatchewan.

She attended elementary and high school in Waldheim. Writing for Saskatchewan Valley News, a weekly newspaper, was Martha's first job, which she continued until she left home to attend Millar Memorial Bible Institute (now Millar College of the Bible) at Pambrun in southern Saskatchewan. Her summers were spent in teaching Vacation Bible Schools for children.

Martha enrolled in a correspondence writing course from Christian Writers Institute, Wheaton, Ill. And began writing news items and devotional columns for various newspapers and general publications.

Martha was a founding member of Alberta Christian Writers Fellowship (now Inscribe Christian Writers Fellowship) and served on its executive. She has attended many writers' conferences and workshops and conducted writing classes. Although the family moved numerous times, Anderson continued to write, taking God's command to Habakkuk as her challenge.

> Write the vision and make it plain on tablets, that
> he may run who reads it (Habakkuk 2:2 NKJV).

Anderson's works include feature articles, devotional columns, news reports, short stories for both adults and children, quizzes, and other fillers. She has been published in church publications, agricultural and trade magazines, and newspapers. She has taught many Bible studies and writing workshops, often writing her own material. Over the years her byline has appeared in print roughly 1,000 times.

Martha married Eilif Anderson, whom she met at college. Two sons and four daughters came to fill their home, bringing much joy. The children are grown and have provided the Andersons with 15 grandchildren and 10 great grandchildren.

Martha and her husband, a retired inventor and manufacturer, now live in a seniors complex in Edmonton.